Knight

"Always hilarious on page one, JJ Knight delivers romantic comedy like no one else. Each book is an irresistible seduction and a tale of connection that pulls you in and leaves you smiling."
—Julia Kent, *New York Times* bestselling author of *Shopping for a Billionaire*

"Every time I finish one of JJ Knight's steamy, hilarious books, I think this is the best one yet—then she writes another one that becomes the best! Slapstick comedy combines with heartfelt romance and some sultry scenes that will have you fanning yourself."
—Blair Babylon, *USA Today* bestselling author of *Rogue*

"JJ Knight is delightfully funny in an incredibly creative way. She will make you laugh so hard you will cry, and then wrench your heart until you shed real tears. Each new book has me wondering, What is she going to come up with next?"
—Olivia Rigal, *USA Today* bestselling author of the One Favor series

"Funny, romantic, sexy, sweet. JJ Knight wrote a real winner!"
—Lynn Raye Harris, *New York Times* bestselling romance author

"Dogs aren't the only ones panting for this saucy romance between a brooding veterinarian and his upbeat receptionist. *The Wedding Confession* is immensely enjoyable and the perfect combo of heat and heart."
—Jennifer Bardsley, author of *Sweet Bliss*

"*The Wedding Confession* is an absolute delight! Ensley and Drew's chemistry is electric from their very wet meet-cute, and it just gets better from there. Another JJ Knight book you won't want to miss."
—Addie Woolridge, Amazon bestselling author of *The Checklist*

"*The Wedding Confession* is a fun and flirty romp, filled with grumpy-sunshine goodness and steamy will-they-won't-they chemistry."
—Kelly Siskind, author of *50 Ways to Win Back Your Lover*

"A laugh-out-loud romantic romp with so much heart."
—Stephanie Jayne, author of *I've Got My Mind Set on Brew*

"Booze brawls and stingrays and smoking-hot tension . . . hilarious from the very first page. A must-read escape for any romance lover."
—Lainey Davis, *USA Today* bestselling author of *Vibration: An Accidental Roommates Romance*

"JJ Knight does it again! *The Wedding Shake-up* is a one-sit read—I was rooting for Gabe and Tillie from their crabby meeting right to their surprise HEA."
—Danika Bloom, *USA Today* bestselling author of *Rhodes to Love: Daring with the Single Dad*

"*The Wedding Shake-up* is the perfect beachy escape with all the fun and magic of a well-mixed drink!"
—Olivia Sinclair, author of *Deal with the Devil*

"*The Wedding Shake-up* is the best rom-com I've read this year! It's the perfect beach read that had me laughing out loud and wishing I could join Gabe and Tillie on the beach (and have one of their drinks)!"
—Krista Lakes, bestselling author of *Saltwater Kisses*

Not Exactly a Small-Town Romance

OTHER TITLES BY JJ KNIGHT

Big Pickle

Hot Pickle

Spicy Pickle

Royal Pickle

Royal Rebel

Royal Escape

Tasty Mango

Tasty Pickle

Tasty Cherry

Juicy Pickle

Second Chance Santa

Single Dad on Top

Single Dad Plus One

The Wedding Confession

The Wedding Shake-up

Not Exactly a Small-Town Romance

JJ KNIGHT

 Montlake

This is a work of fiction. Names, characters, organizations, places, events, and incidents are either products of the author's imagination or are used fictitiously. Otherwise, any resemblance to actual persons, living or dead, is purely coincidental.

Text copyright © 2024 by JJ Knight
All rights reserved.

No part of this book may be reproduced, or stored in a retrieval system, or transmitted in any form or by any means, electronic, mechanical, photocopying, recording, or otherwise, without express written permission of the publisher.

Published by Montlake, Seattle

www.apub.com

Amazon, the Amazon logo, and Montlake are trademarks of Amazon.com, Inc., or its affiliates.

ISBN-13: 9781662523960 (paperback)
ISBN-13: 9781662523953 (digital)

Cover design by Hang Le
Cover images: © Rix Pix Photography, © Andrey_Kuzmin, © NeonShot, © Lovecta, © Manamigraphic / Shutterstock

Printed in the United States of America

For Kurt.
I was small town.
You were California.
And we had one HECK of a meet-cute.
I swear I didn't do it on purpose. (Or did I?)

Chapter 1

Kelsey's Boss and Other Demons

Any minute, somebody is going to fall vinto the pool. They'll make it look like an accident, but it will totally be on purpose.

It's a classic move, a staple of Hollywood movies because it happens so often in real life.

I sip a glass of champagne that costs more than a tank of gas as I stand on a terrace overlooking an impeccably manicured yard filled with Hollywood glitterati. Everywhere you turn is someone you've seen on a big screen, small screen, award show, or interview.

Clear plastic balloons twinkle with lights as they bob at the base of a waterfall. A band plays on a stage across the lawn. It's a perfect California night, the subject of movies and songs. We're on the cusp of summer, the air warm and breezy, with the ocean only a whiff away.

But I wish I were anywhere else.

I'm hoping to hide up here until an acceptable hour to leave. The tension below is thick, evident in the uptight body language, false laughter, and wild gesticulations.

Everybody's working angles, trying to seem more important than they are to secure a nebulous advantage. It's so fake. So stressful. It takes incredible mental energy to make it through every interaction.

But right now, I have a moment of peace. Nobody's trying to put their arm around me, or tell me what they can do for me in the business, or worst of all, walking away when they realize I'm only a lowly casting assistant.

A grating voice makes me jump. "Kelsey? What the hell are you doing up here?"

Dang it. I've been spotted. It's Desdemona Lovechild, the hottest casting director in Hollywood, if she may say so herself. And she does, regularly, followed by a hollow laugh that makes you wonder if she's kidding or being self-deprecating.

But no, she means it.

She's also my boss.

I drain my glass before she can take it away. She's dressed dramatically in a silver lamé shirt with wide sleeves that flap like bird wings when she waves her arms. The color matches her hair.

"Hello, Desdemona."

"Call me Ms. Lovechild here, you know the rules." She says this while faking a brilliant smile as people glance our way, then adds a tinkling laugh as if I've said something funny.

This is the worst. I'd rather be home watching movies in my Care Bear pajamas, but Desdemona insisted I come to do her bidding.

Nobody says no to Desdemona.

Her minions, me included, secretly call her the Demon. It's right there in her name.

She flutters her fingers as if she's conducting a firefly opera, looking past me at anyone who might climb the stairs to approach her divine self. "I need you to go talk to that hot young thing by the champagne fountain."

I turn to look. "The one in the eight-hundred-dollar T-shirt?"

Her voice is laced with irritation. "Oh, you and your silly hobby. But yes, him."

I ignore her dig. Adding up the cost of an outfit is one of my favorite pastimes. I'm quite good at it.

Mr. Pricy Shirt has $400 Diesel jeans and, oddly, $60 Converse. Grand total: $1,260. This is good information. He's a working actor if he can afford those clothes. He's not running to auditions between shifts at In-N-Out.

Not that it's bad to be in that place. Everyone starts somewhere. But it helps to know how to approach him.

Desdemona can't take her eyes off him, which would be creepy, given she's sixty-three and he's barely twenty, but I get it. She's picturing him on-screen.

"Get his name. His agent. His credentials. I want him on my roster by Monday morning. Go!" Her flapping arm flutters her silver sleeve. "Get him before anyone else fills his head with other plans."

I set my empty glass on a tray and hurry away. I hate when she does this at parties. She doesn't see how awkward it is for me to walk up to young, successful actors in a casual setting.

Desdemona insists I try to fit in. I work hard to ensure my thrifted $40 red sheath and vintage $35 silver stilettos *look* $1,500. But because of my blond hair, the dress, and the shoes, my approach to this actor will seem like a come-on. Hollywood party hookups are legendary.

Desdemona, on the other hand, is a cross between Meryl Streep in *The Devil Wears Prada* and Cruella de Vil. She's not in it for the rug burns.

But as I slowly navigate my way around the pool toward Desdemona's new mark, I get it. If she talks to him, and the next role he accepts comes from Arista or Jenny Wolfgang or any of the other casting directors that Desdemona considers her rivals, she looks like a chump.

If I fail, well, blame the lousy assistant for botching the deal.

I know the drill.

Before I can wade through the crowd surrounding the booze, someone bumps my arm. I turn to see Zachery, who also works for Desdemona, holding two fresh glasses of champagne.

My heart leaps a smidge, even though it shouldn't.

"You look like you need this," he says, passing me a plastic flute.

I clutch it like a dog with a favorite toy. "You are a lifesaver."

He smiles with the single dimple that got him decent parts before his career dried up. He could have taken it hard a decade ago, washed up at twenty-six, and disappeared from the industry. But instead, he invested his money wisely and nurtured his network.

Now, like me, he gathers actors for Desdemona.

And at this moment, he's exactly what I need.

I lean in close to him. "The Demon wants me to nab that guy in the Diesel jeans."

"What project?"

I shrug. "She didn't say. She might just be collecting."

Zachery's wearing a simple white button-down (Burberry, $800) and navy pants (Santorelli, $250), and he smells so good. He can layer colognes like a chemist. Sometimes I sit next to him at auditions to get a good sniff. If somebody bottled Zach No. 5, I'd sell my car to buy some.

But work proximity is as far as it goes between us. He'll never be mine. He's your classic Hollywood playboy, and his ability to charm up-and-coming leading ladies into attending premieres is legendary.

And undoubtedly the source of his usefulness to Desdemona.

"You want a wingman?" Zachery asks.

"Totally. We can't have a repeat of Plumeria Drive."

Zachery frowns. "My knuckles have never recovered."

I lift his hand to kiss them. He punched a guy who tried to get up my skirt at a premiere party earlier this year. "My hero."

Too bad he's not "my" anything. But we're like this all the time. Jester, our casting associate who schedules auditions, has dubbed us "the old married couple."

And we are. There would be no way to survive Desdemona without each other.

We both love Jester. Zachery and I sometimes fantasize about hanging our own casting shingle, dumping the Demon, and hiring Jester right out from under her.

But this business is built on threats and promises, and Desdemona is one of the hubs. I sometimes regret the day I applied to be her assistant. I should have gone with someone more easygoing. Most casting directors are.

But here I am. Zachery and I often realize we're stuck in this web, right up close to the spider in the center of it all.

Speaking of which, Desdemona has moved into our sight line, frantically pointing at our mark. He's already speaking to Glen Jacobs, who everyone knows has been tapped to cast a new superhero series. If Jacobs pegs our guy for something, he might get too busy for us.

And Desdemona will be pissed.

I glance at Zachery. "I'll take the mark. You take Jacobs."

"Got it."

I down my tank of gas for courage, and we move in for the kill.

Chapter 2

ZACHERY HATES ON THE GOLDEN CHILD

Kelsey and I squeeze through the crowd, and it takes everything I've got to not glower at every man turning to watch her pass.

Nobody here can hold a candle to her. With blond hair, a siren-red dress, and strappy stilettos, she steals all the attention as she walks.

Not that I'm looking. She's a coworker and a kid. Okay, maybe not a *child* at twenty-five, but young in the industry, having worked for Desdemona for only two years. Sharks tend to circle, and I beat 'em back, even if it means I bloody my knuckles.

We head toward this overblown man-child who undoubtedly thinks he's the greatest thing to hit cinema since Marlon Brando.

But Desdemona wants him, and we generally do what she says.

Between her contact list, Jester's organization, and Kelsey's uncanny ability to spot romantic chemistry between two actors, our team makes movie magic.

In truth, there's no reason for me to associate with Desdemona. I live off the interest of the money I socked away when my career was hot. I don't have to work another day in my life.

But I stay for Kelsey.

Strong Kelsey. Trusting Kelsey. Long-suffering Kelsey.

I'm afraid that without me, the Demon will eat her alive.

And Kelsey loves her job. She's good at it. The industry at large may not realize how many projects were cast from her brilliant pairings, but I do.

So does Desdemona, which is why she keeps her assistant so tightly under her thumb. No one can know that the Demon is out of touch, unable to adjust to younger sensibilities, ignorant of trends. She relies on Kelsey now.

But I don't have the clout to do anything about it. Not an actor out of the game.

So I stay, lingering, watching.

Like tonight.

I walk up to the tall, angular Jacobs. "Been a while," I say, easily pulling the man aside so that Kelsey can approach the actor.

Jacobs lifts his champagne glass in a half-hearted toast. "Zachery Carter. Looking for parts or for dames?"

Yeah, this will be fun. "Neither. Just making conversation. And I'm not sure any lady here enjoys being called that."

Jacobs has no business using the word "dame." He's barely forty. But like so many people in this industry, he has an act. He wears a suit, for one, even though it's balmy this evening.

And a fedora. Nobody else out here wears a hat, other than a woman in a pink sequin bra with a matching beret.

Jacobs scowls at my reprimand and sips his drink.

I've taken the wrong tack. I'm here to keep him off Desdemona's new golden boy. If I piss him off, he'll make a point of stealing the mark.

"What projects are on your desk?" I ask. "I hear you're in demand."

This is the right strategy. Jacobs likes to gloat, and he brings up a limited series everyone wanted to cast but that ended up going to him. As he launches into a spiel about his successes, I look over his shoulder to see how Kelsey is faring.

"I haven't seen you at one of these before," the Golden Child says. "You an actress?"

Kelsey shakes her head, and I'm mesmerized by how the ends of her hair brush her bare shoulders. "Oh, no. I work for Desdemona Lovechild in casting. Have you heard of her?"

He shrugs, and this is far more interesting than these ramblings by Jacobs. How can this kid not know Desdemona? He's green, but he's dressed to impress. Either he's already gotten above-union work or else he comes from money.

Kelsey's probably already put a figure on his outfit. She loves estimating the value of an ensemble. But she'll tease any work history out of him. It's hard for a new actor to break into the industry without our office knowing about it way before the first check is cut.

Casting is a tight community, and we all know each other. If anything other than a shoestring indie film has discovered this kid already, we should know it.

"What have you done?" Kelsey asks.

He gives her a grin that I can totally see on a big screen but haven't yet. *Who is he?*

"Just wrapped my first movie."

He's throwing down his cards right off. Kelsey takes the bait like a good blonde in a red dress, tilting her head as if she could listen to him all night. "What project is that?"

He sips from his glass like it's no big deal when he says, "The sequel to *Darkness Gathers*."

Now I know who he is. Jason Venetian. Plucked by director Harrod Jennings after seeing him in a tire commercial. They totally changed his look. He's unrecognizable as the guy with a midsize radial on his shoulder.

"You have your next one lined up?" she asks.

He slips on a coy expression, and I stifle a groan. That's why it's impossible to talk to actors. Even a simple conversation is practice for their craft. "My agent is considering some projects."

Kelsey plucks a card from her tiny silver bag. "If you want to be up for any of our current casting opportunities, call me or Desdemona."

He looks it over. "You got something in mind?"

Her nonchalant shrug is better acting than half the guild members on the lawn could muster. "Maybe. Give us a call."

But when she heads toward me, I can see that gleam in her eye. She has an idea. And it's bound to be good.

"Where's Jacobs?" she asks me.

I realize I'm alone. "I quit paying attention."

"Easy to do with him." She finishes her glass and steals mine. She does this with coffee, too. I switched to drinking iced espressos with almond milk and a drizzle of caramel, shaken rather than stirred, to match her so she'll keep doing it. "I think I got him for Desdemona."

I glance over her shoulder. Jason watches her, taking in the backside of her dress. I slip my arm around her shoulders, setting the empty glass on a table. He can watch us both walk away. Together.

"I saw that look you had," I tell her.

Her face brightens like it's lit from within. Casting is her happy place.

"Remember the girl from the Rosenberg Netflix show that just wrapped, the one with the horse farm?"

"I haven't seen her pop up anywhere yet."

"Exactly. She would be the perfect pairing with Jason in *Limited Fate*."

"The artsy film? You think he'd do it after the action flick?"

She scrunches her face in the most adorable way as she thinks. "He'll need to establish that he has range. That sequel is going to tank. We have to get him moving in the right direction so he can roll past that stinker."

"You think that's what Desdemona wants Jason for?"

"No idea. But this movie could make him. Really make him. She'll balk at getting that girl. Dang, what was her name?"

"Gayle Sumners."

Kelsey snaps her fingers. "Right. Can't you see it?"

"I can." Kelsey's doing it again. Working her magic. She's on fire when she's putting couples together on-screen. And it doesn't stop with the idea. She'll coach them for the audition and coax out their best performances, especially if we're sending in screen tests.

She's made more than one person redo a self-tape to ensure they put their best effort out there. Heck, she's gone to their roach-infested apartments to record their tests and help them nail a part that can get them their shot. She studies the various directors' aesthetics and is incredibly good at delivering what they want.

She glances around. "Do you think we can sneak out? I want to go look up Gayle's history and find the right headshot. I could present it to Desdemona Monday morning, while she's high on finding Jason."

"We could. But maybe have a little fun first."

"Fun? Here?" She lets out a huffy laugh.

"I have an idea."

I definitely have an ulterior motive as I steer Kelsey toward a shadowy corner of the party.

Chapter 3

Kelsey Seeks Her Fortune

Zachery holds my arm lightly as he leads me away from the crowd to a quieter spot.

This is a good move. We can escape Desdemona without actually leaving. I'd rather work on a laptop, where I can pull up histories and open multiple windows, but my phone will do, as long as she doesn't catch me. Desdemona gets incredibly angry if she spots me staring at my screen at an official function.

We wander away from the tables and end up in a quiet corner, where a bored-looking woman in a flutter of gold scarves sits in front of a fake crystal ball.

"Oh, look," Zachery says. "Should we find out what our futures hold?"

"By an actress?" I whisper, not wanting to insult her to her face. But even so, this is one terrible gig, especially if you're seen by industry influencers. They'll remember.

"I hear she's the real deal." Zachery leads me forward.

I'm not sure about that. Lots of actors take any work they can to keep the dream alive. "Do we have to?"

"It looks like she could use a customer."

He's right. And I'm a sucker for someone who is faltering in public.

I sit in the red-cushioned chair opposite the woman. "Tell me my future."

She adjusts her scarves as she lifts her arms.

"Such a lovely young woman," she says with a gravelly voice. "Someone beautiful enough to be on the screen, but sensible enough to stay out of the fray."

Okay. Score one for her background knowledge.

"I'm Kelsey," I tell her. "What do I need to know?"

"Do you wish to understand your past or reveal your future?" Her hands press into both sides of the glass ball at the center of the table, and it starts to glow.

Nice parlor trick.

"Future, please," I say. "My past is pretty simple." And something I don't talk about at Hollywood parties.

The ball swirls with a concoction of light and fog. This is a nice prop.

She runs her hands over the surface. "Southern girl. Came to California, drawn by the industry."

That's an easy hit. "I never lost the accent."

She nods. "Skilled. Smart. Knows how to play the part but longs for something more meaningful. Something to call her own."

My stomach clenches, but I force a smile. "Isn't that all of us?"

"Indeed." She peers into the ball. It illuminates her face, revealing all the lines around her eyes and mouth. She's older than I first thought. What an illusion!

"You're single," she says.

I hold up my hand. "No ring!"

"But you haven't dated in quite a while. In fact, my fair girl, you have never been in love."

I glance up at Zachery. He stands with his hands behind his back, his white shirt glowing from the ball. He nods at me encouragingly.

"I thought this was about my future."

"It is. You long for love," the woman says. "But your time is running out, as you have always suspected."

I stifle a gasp. My mother died of breast cancer just shy of forty. Will it get me even earlier in life?

"Am I going to . . . die?" My voice catches.

Zachery steps forward. "Hey now."

The woman waves him back. "Not yet. But this life amongst those who pretend to be something they're not is beginning to tarnish your hope. Soon, your faith in love will completely wither."

My throat feels thick. I want to play this off. It's generic advice, like a horoscope or Dear Abby.

But it hits me hard. I *have* been feeling increasingly jaded. I love watching romance on the screen, but I've never been able to feel it myself. Everyone seems after something, like they have some other motive for asking me out. It's never pure like sunshine. It's a fake tan from a bottle.

The woman has my attention.

"What do I have to do?"

She peers into the ball. "You must go on a journey, away from this poisonous life, and find a love you can believe in."

Zachery plunks both hands on the table, rattling the flimsy legs. "What do you mean, a journey away from here?"

I ignore him. "Where should I go?"

The woman sits back. "Return to the land of your birth. Take the long way."

"Back to Alabama?" I haven't visited my father in years. "Why?"

"You are a great lover of romance stories. Think of the ones that move you. That make you feel something. Seek out the honest worker. The small-town community. Remove yourself from the big city, the harsh lights, the jaded." She waves her arm at the party, where sparkling dresses glitter as people move. "And along the way, you will find him."

"The one?"

She leans forward, her face so close to the ball that it's almost white. "The *very* one."

I glance at Zachery to see if he believes her, but he's scowling.

"Are you sure?" I ask.

"Most definitely. But don't delay. You must find your great love before summer's end or it will be too late."

"That's only three months!"

"It's enough."

"What if I don't find him?"

"Your faith will disintegrate to dust."

I hold on tight to the table's edge. "Do you have, like, an exact date? I work better with a deadline."

She laughs, but it's rough, like a cackle. "Before the summer moon turns to autumn."

I lean forward. "Mid-August, then? September 1?"

She holds my gaze. "You will know when your time is up."

My breath comes fast. I try to pull up the rational side of my brain, but she's kicked me into panic mode, thinking about my mom dying so young, and how I've wasted so much time dating unlovable scoundrels.

Zach takes my arm. "We should go." He seems displeased to have brought me here. "Come on, Kelsey."

I stand up. "Thank you."

Her ball goes dark, and she no longer looks old, as if only the strain of premonition aged her.

Zachery leads me away. "I think we need more champagne."

I keep looking at her, astonished at her youthful face. What just happened? Did she hypnotize me?

We thread our way through the tables as I try to shake off the unsettled feeling. Zachery procures more champagne, and I sip it absently. Should I do what she said? Go home this summer? Take the long way?

There's a splash. A woman has fallen in the pool, and two men in outfits worth more than the average mortgage payment of an Alabama farmhouse wade in after her.

She looks up at one with big heart eyes. Yup. She did it on purpose. She orchestrated her own meet-cute.

Is that what the fortune teller meant by learning from the movies I love? Maybe my encounters need a nudge?

I should go back and ask.

And get her name.

I could look up her history. I bet she's done method acting on paranormal activity and that's how she got me so out of sorts. Heck, the way she could use lighting to age herself may mean she's worked in makeup or special effects.

But there's a crowd around the pool watching the woman get pulled from the water. I have to fight my way through them to go back the way I came.

"Are you okay, Kelsey?" Zachery asks, but I ignore him. I want to find out more about this fortune teller. If I can prove she's a fake, then I don't need to listen to a word she said.

But by the time I make it to the corner where the woman was, her table is gone.

Chapter 4

ZACHERY'S SECRET OBSESSION

When I get back to my condo after the party, it's almost four a.m. Kelsey and I tried to make a break for it after the fortune teller incident, but Desdemona found us.

We approached two more actors at her behest, wooing them to Team Demon for a TV pilot we're currently casting. Kelsey's mark was a hard sell, having heard rumors that Desdemona was the Disney equivalent of Ursula—she'd give you a part, but at a price.

The actress hadn't even wanted to send in a headshot, but we convinced her to contact the office next week after our boss leaves for Cannes.

We've been up against this sentiment before, particularly with new actors who seem to think a casting director is a commitment, like an agent or manager.

But no, we're hired by the producers or director and often see the actors only during the casting process, although sometimes we're invited to the first few days of shooting.

Desdemona loves going on set and is well known for her ability to convince an actor it's in his or her best interest to straighten up and fly right, lest they *never work in this town again*.

They fall for it, even though there's a certain cachet to getting targeted by Desdemona. Casting directors like Arista and Jacobs delight in finding work for the Demon's rejects.

I set both my cell phones on the dresser. My business one, the only one Desdemona has access to, is filled with messages. I'll get to them in the morning. Or, I suppose, in a few hours.

The other is personal. It's rare for any of the women I've dated, especially if I met them with business intentions, to move from the official phone to the private one.

But Jester's on there. We sometimes get a beer together.

My mother. My sister. My niece, who somehow has her own phone at age six. A few of my acting school buds, the ones who haven't gotten too big to take calls from washed-up old me.

And Kelsey, of course.

Kelsey.

I almost say her name out loud, but stop myself. I'm failing to stop myself more and more with her lately.

Stop working extra hours to be near her.

Stop making up excuses to do things together.

Truth is, she's the person who knows me best. We text nonstop, any time of day or night. She doesn't seem to have a life outside of Desdemona, and often, neither do I.

We're getting too tight, though, and it worries me.

Which is why I want to push her toward dating again. I'm wrong for her. She needs to find herself someone more suitable, someone who isn't an industry joke who made his name in gross-out comedies and then failed even at those.

My phone buzzes, the private one.

It's Kelsey.

Jason Venetian already texted me.

This one gets me in the gut. They'd looked good together. Kelsey has that fresh-faced appeal that would have been killer for her career if acting were the direction she'd gone in. She could have played twenty-year-olds for two decades like Jennifer Aniston or Reese Witherspoon.

And Jason was way into her. I could see it from his posture, the way his eyes kept taking in that red dress.

But he's an actor. The exact sort of man who is wrong for her.

I quickly tap out a message.

Kelsey Whitaker strikes again.

She sends a fire emoji back at me.

Which brings me back to that red dress. Now that was fire.

I strip off my shirt and pants, trying to decide between showering or sleep.

But Kelsey starts rapid-fire texting me all her ideas for Jason. *Limited Fate* is her priority, but the Demon has to approve pitching them to the director, which takes a bit of a dance to make her think she thought of it.

And, of course, the director gets the final say. In this case, it's Drake Underwood. He's got a lot of clout, but he's old guard, like Desdemona. He'll listen to her. If Kelsey can convince the Demon to accept her choices, it's likely they'll get cast.

Kelsey sends me headshots of several women she thinks will work with Jason, but she's after that Netflix star.

I reply to every text, occasionally having to look up a long abbreviation.

FFSDYKWIM.

On days like this, I really feel the eleven years between us.

She's ribbed me about the women I take out, some professionally, others with a thought to something more. They never pan out.

I'm in this weird place. A little famous once, but not a working actor. A stepping stone, not a ladder. And never a place to land.

The texts start to get further apart, and I think she's falling asleep. I try to picture her in her apartment in East LA. Maybe the red dress is draped over a chair.

Nah, she'd hang it up.

There are probably sirens, even at this hour. I've been to her place. It's noisy, near a major street, with a hospital farther down.

Probably she wears cute things to bed, like shorts with bears on them and a matching tank.

Now I'm moving into a fantasy about her. It's not hard after a night like this one, champagne and laughter and her in that red dress. I let it run for a minute—her, in bed, smiling up at me.

But then around five, the texts start up again.

Kelsey: Watched some old episodes with Gayle. There's no better girl. Desdemona has to put them together for Limited Fate.

Me: Why are you staying up all night over this pairing?

Kelsey: I want it settled before I go.

Me: Go where?

Kelsey: On my journey to find love.

I stare at my phone like it's grown two heads.

This is my fault, completely my fault. I sent her to the fortune teller to give her a little push to try again. She's been miserable and lonely. She thinks she's unworthy of love. I know this. She's told me. She clearly sees me as a big brother, and I endeavor to be that for her.

But I never wanted her to leave LA entirely. She's too good at what she does.

Maybe I can convince her to find her great love here in Southern California.

I start and delete several replies, then give up and put through a call.

Kelsey's voice is scratchy from lack of sleep. "Hey."

"You believe this fortune teller business?" I ask.

"It all made sense to me. I've been trying to find someone here in LA, but I think they're all too big-city for me. So many workaholics worried about their careers, caught up in the race."

"Says the woman who is working at five a.m."

"Oh, you know what I mean. Tell me the last time I had more than three dates with the same man."

"Last June. That tech bro."

"Driving him to LASIK does not count as date four."

"Oh, right. He ghosted you after that."

She sighs. "I think needing a driver was his sole motivation for the first three dates." There's the sound of a mattress creaking, and I imagine she's flopped down on her bed.

"He was an idiot," I tell her.

"You think so?"

"I know so." I wander into my kitchen for a drink. "You can't just leave Desdemona to drive across the US. She won't stand for it."

"That's the thing. She's leaving on Thursday for Cannes, then going on location for that Scotland shoot. That takes care of the rest of May. And you know how much she hates LA in the summer. She'll be gone for two months, easy."

She's right. I've worked with Desdemona for five years, and she takes off most summers, browbeating us from other countries. It's part of why she made us work last night's party so hard. It was her last one of the season.

I peer into the bright light of my fridge. It's filled with perfectly arranged meal preps from my two chefs: one for fitness, one for taste. "Where will you go?"

"The lady said to return to the land of my birth, take it slow, and meet people. I'm going to do it."

"You're going back to Alabama?"

"Yes. A road trip. If I go slow, only driving a few hours a day, I can stretch it out to two weeks. Or more, if I find someone along the way and I stay in his town."

I pluck out a bottle of water and slam the fridge door. I already want to punch this hypothetical Midwest yokel in the jaw. "Will you take off work? Desdemona relies on you when she's gone."

"My laptop works just as well at a hotel as it does in the office. I'll even take that tapestry with me, the one I use in my Zoom calls. I'll hang it behind me for anything using a camera. As long as you and Jester cover for me, she'll never know I'm not in LA."

She's thought this through. And fast. We talked to that fortune teller only, what, six hours ago?

I return to my bedroom. Time for confessions. "Kelsey, I don't think you should believe that woman—"

"Why not? Zach, she was exactly right. My faith is turning to dust. And if it does, will I even be able to cast romantic leads? This could solve everything. I need to get out of LA. Find people more like how I grew up."

"Dairy farmers?" I know all about Kelsey's family. Four brothers and sisters. All with chores. A completely different life.

"No. I don't want that. I left it behind, remember? But something slower than here. More authentic."

"I don't like the idea of you driving all by yourself."

"I'll be fine. I used to toss hay bales on a pitchfork!"

I picture that, only with Kelsey in Daisy Dukes. Damn. I have to shake it off. "You haven't done any of that lately."

"I've driven across the country lots of times. I just won't be slamming through it in three days."

She really intends to do this.

I have to tell her about the fortune teller.

But she goes right on. "I can feel it, Zach. This is the shake-up I need. I'm so grateful that I talked to her. It was weird, sure, but it's like my tarot deck."

"You have a tarot deck?"

"See, you don't know everything about me."

Obviously not. "How is it like a tarot deck?"

"It tells me what I already know deep down but have refused to acknowledge: I'm stuck here. Chained to a dictator boss and surrounded by people with agendas."

"People in Alabama have agendas."

"Not like Hollywood agendas."

Well, that's true.

Kelsey sighs. "I'm going. I want to get Jason and Gayle handled. Then I'm hitting the road for a while."

My confession withers. There's no point. It probably wouldn't matter anyway. "It's nearly dawn."

"It is. Get some sleep, Zach. I'll text you later. If you talk to Desdemona before I do, see if you can warm her up to my idea. Really push what a find Jason was at the party, how brilliant she was to notice him. Then I'll come in behind you with my pairing."

"Anything for you, Kelsey." And I mean it.

"I know! You're the best!" Her voice is almost a squeak, which happens when she's tired. "Later, Zach attack!" She ends the call.

I stare at her image on the phone, a picture I took of her a year ago at a premiere party. She got invited not through Desdemona's efforts but via an actor she'd discovered.

She wears a silver sequin gown that glides along her body like a waterfall. Her blond hair is done Old Hollywood–style, in perfect waves held back on one side with a rhinestone clip.

I stared at her so long that my date walked off in a huff and scarcely talked to me inside the theater.

I took a shot with my phone and made it her contact picture. Because we talk so much, it comes up often.

Kelsey spotted the image once and laughed, remembering the event. She'd brought a guy she barely knew because she was embarrassed to show up alone.

Maybe I should have taken her, but I felt like an old has-been, and she was so bright and young.

And right now, she's happy talking about the trip.

So I'll shut my trap. Keep the secret about this night.

She can't find out that I talked to the fortune teller ahead of time and slipped her money to tell Kelsey it was time for love.

I hoped it might nudge her in a good direction. Get her to go on dates again. She's my favorite person, and I want her to have everything. I know she isn't for me. I'm not sure any woman needs to be saddled with an industry joke for anything more than a waltz down the red carpet and a splashy bit in the tabloids.

But with the fortune teller sending her on a romance road trip, my foolish act is going to drive Kelsey right out of my life.

Chapter 5

Kelsey Mourns the Mug

I can't believe it!

After all my work, Jason's agent turned down our request for him to audition for *Limited Fate*. I delivered a sixteen-point dissertation to Desdemona yesterday to contact him!

Granted, she quit listening after point three, but it was such a good pitch. She agreed that diversifying Jason out of the gate was a good move. Plus, this director would seriously owe her when he saw what she'd delivered.

And then, this morning, the agent wouldn't even give Jason the script.

I text an upset message to Zachery and push my thumbs so hard that the phone flips out of my hands and lands on the ceramic tile floor, cracking ever so slightly in the corner.

Dang it!

Jester glances up from a call that has already gone on for twenty minutes, no doubt Jonathan Brady, an actor who once got a role as a corpse on a cop show in 1988 and still thinks Desdemona will deliver a career-changing part. He calls every Tuesday for an update.

Looking at Jester usually makes me happy. His wardrobe palette can best be described as *Easter egg*.

Today it's purple pants (Hreski, $50) and a yellow shirt (unknown vintage) with a belt that ties it together in all the rainbow pastels. With his full head of snow-white hair and perpetually pink cheeks, he's like a Care Bear. Or maybe a fashion-forward leprechaun. He might scrape the five-foot mark in his heeled boots, but that's pushing it.

We love him.

But right now, nothing can soothe my rage. Not even Jester's beautifully bright outfit.

He mouths, *You okay, babe?* as I shove the cracked phone in my dress pocket.

I shake my head and walk over to the tea bar, the one thing I am fanatical about in the office. I get my coffee from a shop, always, but for work I need my calming teas, my all-natural unbleached sugar, and, most importantly, a clean and dry collection of *Peanuts* mugs.

Today I'm feeling like Lucy, although I should probably take Linus and try to absorb some of his blanket wisdom.

Jester pounds the mute button on the phone. "I forgot to tell you. Charlie Brown bit the dust. I dropped him when I was washing."

And that's the last straw on this devil of a day. I whirl around, pick up my heavy white bag, and tell him, "I'm working from home."

"Baby girl, I'm so sorry. I'll replace good ol' Charlie."

"It's okay. It's just a mug."

But it's not. It's representative of my life's downward spiral.

There's one more workday until Desdemona leaves for Cannes and nothing interesting to fill it with now that Jason has turned us down.

I have to avoid my boss for the moment, since she's ultra annoyed that I suggested a path that embarrassed her.

Besides, I need to plan my route home, pack some things.

Decide who I'm telling I'm headed to Alabama, if anyone.

I wave at Jester. Desdemona is holed up in her office, trying to finagle some other way to "discover" Jason, even though he's already filmed that bad sequel. She really wants him. Probably Jacobs already filled his head with superhero dreams. We were too late.

When I step outside, even the sunny California day fails to brighten my mood.

I park my car a quarter of a mile away at a cheap lot since there's no dedicated space for me here, but our office is only a few blocks off Hollywood Boulevard. Desdemona pays a ridiculous price to be close to it.

This funk calls for The Walk.

If I go a little out of my way, I can stroll along the stars embedded in the sidewalk and soak up the energy of the buskers singing and playing, and the endless array of people in costumes working the tourists for tips.

Today, I need that pick-me-up.

The call of the silver screen brought me to LA. I was practical about what I could accomplish, focusing on behind-the-scenes skills rather than aspiring to be the talent in front of the camera.

I interned for free during the day, mostly as a gofer, and worked nights at a coffee shop known to be a favorite for studio interns and bit players. I listened to gossip and tried to figure out any way to break in.

When Desdemona's former assistant quit, then the new one snapped within a few weeks, I heard all about it.

I sized up what I had gleaned about the young women who hadn't lasted and determined I could manage.

I went on a mission to impress the casting titan with what I knew about the people she worked with. I scoured the receipts for names to drop, connecting it with industry gossip and who was going where.

I used it to fill in the application, liberally tossing in tidbits that I thought would appeal to a casting director like her.

And it worked. I got the job.

I wouldn't have to go home like so many dreamers who ran out of resources and hope. I was determined not to crawl back to Alabama.

Dad still lives on the farm, of course. My oldest brother, Cal, and his wife, Katie, stay there with their kids. Sid and Vanessa come and go, working with Dad when they wind up adrift. The baby, Alana, is in college.

Part of the reason I stuck with Desdemona is that she's never out of work, and therefore, I'm not, either. I won't wind up back in the barn, smearing Bag Balm on cows and mucking stalls. I'll put up with a lot to avoid that fate.

I reach Hollywood Boulevard and start the trek along the shops, dodging tourists and keeping an eye out for paparazzi, a sure sign that someone famous is nearby.

A woman sings "Rolling in the Deep" at the top of her lungs, her upturned hat at her feet. A few yards down, a man rocks out on a set of drums made from buckets, scarcely noticing passersby.

A set of Teenage Mutant Ninja Turtles takes pictures with kids near Bruce Lee's star. I find the juxtaposition of the original martial arts hero and the turtles completely fun and satisfying, like something in the world makes sense.

Unlike Jason Venetian turning down *Limited Fate*.

The street in front of the famous Chinese Theatre is thick with tourists and buskers. I wave off Willy Wonka and Captain Jack, walking until I spot an empty rose-granite star and wonder who might one day be embossed in gold on it. Jason Venetian?

Not if he doesn't listen to me! His agent is a mid-lister, and possibly reeling with interest for his new acquisition. People in this position often make short-term decisions. Not everyone can see the big picture.

This is one thing Desdemona is good at, and why I knew how to make her approach Jason about *Limited Fate*. But casting for that picture will go on as usual without my perfect pairing.

I sure could see the two of them reading the beautiful lines. Love stories like that movie don't come along very often, particularly not with a decent budget attached.

Desdemona will go more traditional with it now. Get one A-lister to sign on, then use that as leverage to lowball someone who will work for less to keep in budget.

The pairing might work, or might be lackluster. It will end up based on lots of factors—availability, relationships, agent clout, and money.

That's Desdemona territory. For me, it's about the intangibles. Posture. Expressions. Charisma. The way they look together, or at least how I imagine it. I can see one person in a commercial and another on a talk show, and still, that whiff of how they'll perform in certain roles comes to me like a movie in my mind. It's a feeling, smoke and magic, but I can see it.

There are pairings I wish I'd made, ones that have worked over and over again.

Drew Barrymore and Adam Sandler. Always fresh. Always funny.

Julia Roberts and George Clooney.

Emma Stone and Ryan Gosling.

So many perfect duos.

I want to make one that iconic.

But apparently it won't be Jason Venetian and Gayle Sumners.

I hear a voice calling my name. At first, I pay no attention, thinking maybe it's my brain trying to make sense of the cacophony of Adele, Taylor Swift, and Dua Lipa coming from buskers trying to outdo each other.

But then I realize it *is* my name. I turn around.

Zachery rushes toward me, holding two coffee cups. I haven't seen him yet today. He met with an actress Desdemona is courting.

He looks amazing in a silvery gray suit (Brunello Cucinelli, $5,000), and my breath catches. His dark hair curls with the humidity and the exertion, making his couture look even more effortless.

But no doubt brokering a deal this morning with Perine Jetée involved an invitation to multiple upcoming events, and no telling what additional *benefits*.

He's a natural-born charmer, and as he arrives with an outstretched coffee made just the way I like it, I wonder if he keeps a database on his phone. Name, birthday, coffee preference, sexual proclivities . . .

Nope, don't think about it.

To be honest, I love his attention. It scratches that itch to be seen, to be pampered, to be, well, *chased after*, without any of the drawbacks of a relationship. Namely, heartbreak. But also, what the fortune teller brought up. The withering of faith. Each relationship failure is another petal off the rose.

"Thank you," I say, accepting the cup and immediately taking a sip. I desperately needed a caffeine boost. And here Zachery is, fixing it.

I don't have to ask how he knew where I was. He's caught up with me en route to my car before. He knows that when I'm in a hurry, I go straight from the office to the parking lot.

And on bad days, I take Hollywood Boulevard.

We really are an old married couple.

If one half of the couple is rich and semifamous and way into courting every female actor who will have him.

He falls into step beside me. "It was a great pairing," he says, not even out of breath from the rush. He takes his workouts as seriously as his women. He's done five miles before most people shut off their alarms for the first time.

"Can't win them all," I say, dodging a mime pretending to pull on a rope.

"So, does this mean you're heading out of town?"

I shake my head. "Desdemona doesn't leave until Thursday. I'm packing, though."

"Do you have a route?"

"Just a rough idea."

Up ahead, three of the Transformers block the sidewalk in their bulky costumes. We pause while a mother takes a photo of her brood with the grouping.

"What's your first stop?" Zachery asks.

"I think I'll go north to I-40 through Barstow since I usually drive south through Palm Springs."

"Because the fortune teller told you to take the long way?"

"I mean, if I'm going to listen to her, I might as well do it right. But going through the Midwest feels like the best choice."

"What if she told you to go on foot?"

I lean in to bump his shoulder. "Don't make fun of me. It's a good move. The stops will be smaller, more intimate, and less touristy."

"More farmers, fewer golfers?"

This makes me laugh. "Maybe."

I can tell from his expression that he doesn't think any of this is a good idea. "Don't worry about me. I'll see my dad, probably feel foolish for listening to a fake fortune teller, and head back to LA inside of two weeks."

"About the fortune teller—"

I squeeze his arm. *Hello, biceps.* "Let's not talk about her. I feel weird following her advice. I'd like to think of it as her being the person who got me out of my rut, and only rational thoughts are setting me on this journey."

He nods. "Okay."

The Transformers finally step away from the tourists, and we walk on.

But as we approach another cache of stars in front of the Hollywood Wax Museum, I slip on a bit of melted ice cream.

Zachery moves swiftly to catch me before I fall. "Careful there."

His gaze meets mine, his body close. We're a Hallmark meet-cute, right here on Hollywood Boulevard. For only the length of an inhale, I imagine this is our big moment, the one where we finally notice each other. Zachery and Kelsey, the ultimate Tinseltown pair.

Then it's over. I glance down at the splat of pink. "Where there are tourists, there are spills."

He sets me up straight. "Can't live with them, can't maintain our tax base without them."

I realize I'm standing on Vivien Leigh's star. I step aside, as if I'm on her grave. Vivien and Clark Gable. Now that was a power pairing if there ever was one.

Could I do that? Create a match that powerful?

Even if I did, Desdemona would be the casting director of record. Zachery still holds my arm, and the heat of his hand feels good on my skin. He fits in so well here, in front of the museum, as if he might be one of its iconic figures come to life.

And me? An Alabama farm girl.

Maybe Vivien's name beneath my feet will give me some good luck, and on this journey I'll find someone as wonderful as Zachery, but available to a normal human like me.

Chapter 6

Zachery's Rom-Com-a-Thon

Kelsey goes home to pack, but I'm in no mood to return to the office.

I do a second workout for the day in my home gym, and open the fridge to grab one of my meal preps, noting that the fight between the chef and the trainer rages on inside.

One stack of boxes reads, "To maintain body composition."

Those are from Armond, the trainer.

Another stack has a rebuttal, one word per box: "To enjoy life like he should."

That's John Luke, the chef.

I chuckle, pulling one box from each stack. John Luke's is significantly heavier than Armond's.

I kick the fridge closed and open them both.

John Luke has prepared lobster fettuccini.

Armond has made grilled chicken on a bed of asparagus.

I shove the chicken back in the fridge.

Today is a pasta day.

I stick the box in the microwave, tapping my foot as I lean on the kitchen island. My condo is immaculate, gleaming, and modern.

Some would say it's not a home, but it's what I know. My family comes from banking money, and their palatial house in Beverly Hills looks exactly like this inside, only with more help.

John Luke is their personal chef, but he makes seven meals a week for me. I hired my own trainer, who consults with a nutritionist and a sports chef they employ for clients. He brings me the other extreme in my diet.

I also have a housekeeper, the sister of the woman who runs my parents' house. She works over there five days a week, and two for me.

I don't need a showy mansion. I generally don't seek attention, and I don't tip off paparazzi to my whereabouts, unless Desdemona requires it to get my date some press.

I'm not famous anymore. Ten years will age you out of getting recognized on the street. I haven't done a talk show or so much as a commercial since my twenties.

When I washed up, I landed on an entirely different shore. No-man's-land. And anonymity is where I'll remain, unless they ever invite me to an anniversary show or reunion piece. That will be short-lived, too.

It doesn't matter.

The microwave dings.

I take the box to the island, not bothering to plate it. Mother would have a fit if she saw me eating out of cardboard like a commoner. But I'm almost twenty years beyond their influence.

Kelsey texts me, and I'm grateful for the diversion.

Kelsey: I'm doing research for my trip. Want to come?

Hell yeah, I do.

Me: Be there in thirty.

Kelsey: Bring pizza. The good one from Mod's.

Me: As you wish.

I can see her smile when she reads it. She's always amused when I quote romantic lines from leading men. She's such a sucker for a good bit of dialogue.

Once, she asked me for something from one of my movies, but given they were mostly ribald comedies, the best I could do was "Lady, I'm here to take your cherry."

She did laugh at that, though.

My whole career was a joke. One big hit comedy. Two mediocre ones. Then a string of increasingly ridiculous low-budget flicks that ultimately petered out into junk that didn't even get distributed.

But the hit keeps me in residuals, and since it has a rather hilarious Thanksgiving scene, it sometimes comes up on lists of movies to watch in November.

It's more than a lot of actors get. I'm not bitter. I played my cards for as long as the people in charge let me.

When I arrive at Kelsey's apartment, pizza box in hand, she has laid a dozen outfits all over her living room.

There are sundresses, denim shorts, tank tops, and flowy skirts. Nothing she would wear to work or a party. Half of these things I've never seen.

"You go shopping?"

She shakes her head. "Alabama stuff. It feels right for a love story, right? No reds, no blacks, nothing flashy. I want to be the girl next door, not the siren."

I like her in siren mode, but I see her point.

"You're going all in."

"No reason not to." She picks up a flowery peach dress with a square neckline. "Is this too much for a barn dance?"

I choke on a laugh. "Barn dance?"

"I'm going across Wyoming, Nebraska, and Kansas in the summer. There better be a barn dance somewhere."

"That's pretty north for an endgame in Alabama."

"It's not the destination; it's the journey." She leans across her ottoman to grab the remote. "I've been looking at all the sweet made-for-TV romances, and they're literally all Midwest. Cornfields. Hayrides. Barn dances."

"I see."

She powers on the television. Her watch list is filled with romantic films.

I set the pizza box on her coffee table. "Is this what we're doing tonight?"

"Yes. I want to list every meet-cute."

"How are movie meet-cutes going to help?"

"That woman who fell in the pool at the party Saturday night—she did it on purpose. She was trying to get that guy to rescue her. It gave me an idea. I'll create a list of viable meet-cutes, then make them happen. You know, trip and fall in the guy's arms. Spill a drink on someone's shirt. We need to watch more and get ideas."

It's probably better if I don't say anything about this wild idea. I head to her kitchen. "I'll grab plates. You cue the first movie."

When I return, she's cleared her sofa of clothes.

I open the pizza box and stack three narrow slices on Kelsey's plate. She likes to eat them in a pile. I have to get our orders cut into twice the usual slices.

"So first up is *A Meadow Wedding*?" I ask.

"Isn't it already dreamy? I can picture the final scene, the breeze blowing the bride's dress, ribbons flying." She sits back with her plate.

And we watch, mostly beginnings and ends. Kelsey has no patience for the sagging middles. She makes a list in a spiral notebook. "Okay, we have eight meet-cutes."

"What's the top one?"

"Trip and fall."

"Classic. Next?"

"Get rescued or saved."

I nod. "Like Pool Girl. And?"

She taps her pencil against her cheek. "Be a runaway."

"Which you are."

She looks up. "Should I create a good runaway story? Brides are the most popular."

"Do you really want to start a lifelong commitment with a lie?"

She frowns. "Okay, fine."

"Next."

"Get caught doing something embarrassing."

"That will be no problem for you," I tell her.

Her leg shoots to the side to knock my foot off her ottoman. "Hush."

"Okay, what are the rest?"

"Get the wrong luggage or food order."

"That's an easy one to pull off."

"Right?" She's got that happy gleam going. "Then bumping together in elevators." She makes a note on her list.

"Might be fewer of those in small towns."

"Oh, right. Hmmm." She frowns and crosses that one out. "Intervening in a confrontation."

We saw one of those. "That seems risky."

"I better be careful who I do that with."

I elbow her. "I thought you used to move hay bales with pitchforks."

"Point taken. And the last one is reaching for the same item in the store."

"That's a good one," I say. "Easy to force, with the bonus that it establishes that you like the same things."

She tilts sideways to lay her head on my shoulder. "See, this is what I love about you. You get me. You're on my side."

"Team Kelsey all the way."

She feels good there, even if we're talking about all the ways she'll meet someone else, surrounded by the clothes she'll wear to impress him.

This is good. It's what I wanted for her when I took the fortune teller aside. She only needed a little shove.

"I should pull a card before I go," she says, jumping up to search her bookshelf.

"Pull a card?"

"Tarot card. The things that tell me what I already know, remember?"

Oh, that. "Sure."

She brings a small box to the table and tugs off the lid. Inside is a stack of cards, larger than playing cards, and each with an illustration in luminous color.

She shuffles the deck in her hand. "I'm going to do a single pull for this one. A message from the universe."

This is overly woo-woo for me, so I sit back against the cushions to watch.

She closes her eyes, shuffling through the cards until she suddenly stops, sets the deck on the table, and cuts it in half.

She takes the top card from the lower half and opens her eyes.

"This is it," she says. "My message from the universe as I plan for my great journey." She flips it over and lets out a gasp.

I lunge forward, imagining the Grim Reaper or some other harbinger of death. "What is it?"

She shows me a card with two people, each holding a yellow goblet. A lion head with wings floats above them. "It's the Two of Cups."

That doesn't seem bad. "What does it mean?" I ask.

"It's the card of commitment, of relationships. It can stand for true love." She clasps it to her chest like a treasured gift. "That means the fortune teller was right. My faith will never wither."

Her happiness at getting that card should have silenced the alarm bells in my head. She's clearly doing what she wants.

But my sense of unease only grows as she tucks the card, face up, at the top of her box and packs it into the suitcase at her feet.

I hope I haven't inadvertently set her up to believe in something that might bring her nothing but disappointment and misery.

Chapter 7

KELSEY ASKS, "WHAT WOULD REESE DO?"

The Thursday morning I take off across the US of A is bright and sunshiny.

It's perfect.

I double-check with Jester to be sure that Desdemona is headed for the airport, then leave LA on I-15 toward Vegas. I'm not going anywhere near there, though. For someone trying to find a small-town romance after leaving a big, jaded city, Las Vegas would be going from the fire into an inferno. I'll pop southeast and drive near the Hoover Dam instead.

I sing to Taylor Swift and Beyoncé until I have to stop to charge my hybrid.

Thankfully, I'm parked when the Demon makes her first call. She's in the executive lounge waiting for her flight to France.

"Kelsey, send Drake Underwood the headshots for Caleb Jonas and Salena Cole."

My body goes still. Not this director! My voice is more tremulous than I like when I ask, "For which project?"

"Don't be ridiculous. The one he hired us for."

She means *Limited Fate*.

"Isn't Caleb outside the age range? The script called for—"

Her voice slices through mine. "I'm not interested in your opinion. Send their agents the script and prep them for self-tapes. Be subtle. Caleb in particular might not appreciate direction."

I'm so choked up about how wrong those two are for that beautiful movie that I can't even answer.

"I expect an update when I land." Desdemona ends the call.

I drop the phone in the passenger seat and scream, "No! No! No!"

A truck driver walking past pauses to watch.

My face flushes. I wave him on.

Unless this is a meet-cute. I didn't put "distressed damsel" on my list, but it fits in with the rescue trope.

He tilts his head as if he's considering checking on me. Tall, fit, dressed in jeans (faded Levi's, probably slightly vintage, $35, and a polo, possibly Walmart, $15).

I'm about to open the door to dramatically sob by my car door when a bit of gold flashes on his hand.

Wedding band.

I hold up my phone and shrug, as if that explains everything.

Seeing me act normal, he nods and continues on to the station.

I smack my head against the back of my seat to resume my professional lament. Caleb Jonas and Salena Cole!

Caleb's strength is in police roles, not the tender young sculptor in *Limited Fate*. It'll be hard for an audience to get past his commanding presence from those movies.

Salena could work as the snappy, jaded graffiti artist from the Bronx, but she'll need a serious accent coach. She's only done small parts with a few lines here and there. She's completely untested in a nuanced role.

But even if both of them can rise to these parts, and I do believe in the flexibility of most actors, there's something about the two of them that doesn't make a romantic mix.

I could put a lot of actors with Caleb who would work better. And many leading men for Salena. But Caleb and Salena . . .

I'm making myself crazy. I have to stop.

Desdemona is the boss.

I might as well take this moment to notify the two of them they need to record a reading. I know *Limited Fate* inside out, and as I wait for my hybrid to charge, I use my phone to scroll through the script to select pieces for each of them.

By the time I'm ready to hit the road again, I've submitted the scenes to both actors' agents and bought myself a fried apple pie to make me feel better.

I'm about to pull out when I get a text from Zachery.

Zach: Jester told me about LF. I'm sorry.

Me: It's a nightmare but it's done.

Zach: Maybe they'll pass.

Me: They'd be dumb to, although it won't be the same movie with them.

Zach: You're not texting and driving, are you?

Me: Just charged the car.

Zach: Good. Check in on your next stop.

Me: Will do.

I decide to go with podcasts instead of music for the next leg, in hopes of keeping my mind off the tragic casting I had to submit.

My phone has obviously been illegally listening to what I've been doing for the last two days, because it pops up a suggestion for a Hallmark movie review show. I click on it and start listening.

Within an hour, I've absorbed two perky hosts' defining characteristics of the genre. They've given me far more information than the meet-cutes Zachery and I studied.

I can't stop and type a list, so I commit it to memory.

One: My future husband will be wearing a flannel shirt.

Two: He will work with his hands. Handyman seems to be the top preference, but he could also be a farmer, a mechanic, or possibly a police officer.

Like Caleb Jonas.

No, no. Don't think about *Limited Fate*.

Unfortunately, according to the statistics on the podcast, the leading lady is supposed to be a baker, and if not, a reporter traveling to the town to do a news story.

I can neither bake nor write articles.

Alternatively, I should be coming home to save the family business or as a celebrity in disgrace.

Neither of those applies, either.

Nobody writes movies starring assistant casting directors. The closest thing to my situation is *The Devil Wears Prada*.

Mine would be *The Demon Casts Chick Flicks*.

Since I won't be baking cupcakes or raising money for a failing farm, I'll have to double down on the meet-cute. There's no other way.

The plan comes to me.

First, stop in the coffee shop of every appropriate town I encounter.

Second, wait for my future husband to walk in.

Third, rush toward him, trip, and spill my coffee.

I'll be careful. Iced coffee only to avoid burns. Angle the splash so I won't ruin anything fancy. In fact, I'll get most of the coffee on myself, and only a dribble on him. That way, if he isn't offering to clean me up, I can offer to clean him up.

Yes! That's a standard opening beat of every romance. The pair gets in close, wiping up the mess.

Proximity is important.

Then their eyes meet.

It will work.

It *always* works.

I tap my phone to bring up Google Maps. I need a small town and a coffee shop. How wild would it be to have a success on the first day? The very idea brings me out of my funk.

I approach my first tiny town a half hour later. I could have easily bypassed it on the freeway, but I changed the route to follow a small highway that bisects the community. Main Street is adorable, with stone storefronts boasting a hardware store, a beauty parlor, and YES, a coffee shop!

It's called Good Brew.

I mean, how perfect.

I park a block away so that my car won't be too close if my new man and I get a chance to walk awhile after the big spill. We'll need time to establish that we want to see each other again.

I check the rearview mirror, fixing a smudge in my eyeliner. More lip gloss. He needs to think about kissing me, even though that's not allowed for a while. I think we need to have an interrupted kiss before we can do the real thing.

Oh, this is exciting!

Will he wear flannel?

Be a little older? My age? Have a beard?

I'm open to anything. They'll all be different from the hot messes I've dated in LA.

I peel myself off the seat, which has adhered itself to my thighs in the car.

As I walk the block, I realize flannel will not be a thing. It's sweltering today, and we're in the middle of the desert, only a couple of hours outside Vegas.

I don't see a soul as I take my time looking over the storefronts. I can picture the scene as it would be filmed by a camera on a dolly on the opposite side of the street.

EXT. A SMALL-TOWN MAIN STREET—DAY

KELSEY, 25, strolls along the sidewalk with innocent interest. The skirt of her pale-blue dress swishes near her knees. She wears sensible shoes with a modest chunky heel and sassy ankle strap. Her blond hair flows to her shoulders, held back with a silver headband.

HERO, 28, exits the barbershop. He spots Kelsey and tips his hat.

I pause. Hmmm. There's nobody on the street. Nobody exiting any of the stores.

Nobody at all, actually.

I arrive at the beauty parlor window adorned with cartoon scissors and a comb. It's mostly empty inside, but two women talking by the hair dryers definitely notice me. They fall silent, their gaze following as I pass by.

Should I acknowledge them? My movie scene falters as their stiff postures and narrowed eyes don't fit my perfect imagining.

I opt to speed up, wondering if there's something wrong with my dress or shoes. Is my hair flying every direction?

When I'm beyond their windows, I turn to see my filmy reflection against the hardware store display. Everything seems all right with my appearance.

Near the door to the hardware shop, a woman about to walk out stops to watch me. My anxiety grows. Maybe I'm not in a Hallmark movie at all, but *Children of the Corn*.

I'm getting horror vibes.

Maybe I should go back to the car.

But doing that would mean passing by all those people a second time, so I gamely head for the door to Good Brew.

Obviously, this is such a tight-knit community that they recognize when a stranger arrives. Probably they're already gossiping about me. Perhaps they'll run me out of town with pitchforks if they pick up on my LA vibes.

I might not blame them.

No, that's my big-city pessimism taking hold.

I reframe. Maybe they are little-old-lady matchmakers, and their curiosity is all about figuring out which single man would be exactly right for me.

Maybe they're planning a meet-cute of their own.

I open the door to the coffee shop.

A young woman in a black apron leans on the counter, looking bored out of her mind. Her gaze flicks up to me from her phone, disinterested.

Only one table is taken. Two elderly men sit at it, both looking frustrated. One says, "Turn up your damn hearing aid. I'm tired of repeating myself."

The other one shouts, "You ain't got a damn thing to say that's worth listening to!"

This is good. Grumpy old men are a staple in a good rom-com. They'll advise the potential guy not to miss his chance, and that if they were forty years younger, they'd give him a run for his money.

That's better.

I don't bother to look at the handwritten chalk menu. "Can I get a tall iced espresso with almond milk and a drizzle of caramel, shaken rather than stirred?"

A midfifties woman walks up behind the younger one. Their resemblance tells me this is a mother-daughter pair. "What do you think this is, Beverly Hills Starbucks?" She turns to the younger woman. "Get her a drip with half a packet of white hot chocolate and dump it over ice."

That sounds disgusting. I open my mouth to protest, but then close it. They seem to be expecting me to go on a rampage. Even the old men have fallen silent.

I think of *Legally Blonde*, when Reese Witherspoon's character, Elle Woods, realizes her handwritten notes with a fuzzy pen don't match the other students'.

What *would* Reese do?

She'd smile. Big. And hold it.

So, I do, even as I get charged seven dollars for a cup of something incredibly undrinkable, served to me with a grimace only Oscar the Grouch could love.

I sit at a small table by the window so I can do double duty of watching the sidewalk and the inside of the shop. The old men pay me no mind, continuing their circular argument about the hearing aids, and never having a damn thing to say.

The young woman resumes her position at the counter.

And a tumbleweed, a literal tumbleweed, blows down the middle of the street.

I let my coffee sit untouched, although at one point I forget the bastardized order and take a horrible, chalky sweet sip.

Ugggh.

And how did they know I was from Beverly Hills, anyway? I'm a farm girl from southern Alabama!

Have I changed that much?

My phone chimes with the tone I set for Zachery's text, an incredibly long sequence called "Minuet."

The sound reverberates in the coffee shop, and even the man who needs to crank his hearing aid turns to stare.

My face flames. "Sorry, so sorry."

I frantically shut it off and switch the phone to silent mode.

Zach: The Demon has left the country.

That's a relief. She won't check in nearly so often, particularly during the festival.

Me: I'm in a town so barren a tumbleweed is the only thing moving.

Zach: Which town?

Me: Bris-something or another.

Zach: Why did you stop?

Me: I found a coffee shop to try my first meet-cute, but they called me out on being Hollywood. Do you think I look Hollywood?

There's a suspiciously long silence.

Dang it.

Zach: You are very glamorous.

Me: I'm wearing cotton!

Zach: Doesn't matter.

Me: Do you think I should dye my hair brown?

Zach: No!

An exclamation mark. That's rare.

But I'm considering it. Jester likes to call me a Beverly Hills unicorn because I'm a natural blonde.

But maybe people here assume it's fake.

That, coupled with the order I made, tipped them off.

Lesson learned.

Since I've obviously blown this gig, I might as well learn a thing or two.

I take my cup to the daughter at the counter, doomscrolling on her phone.

She doesn't look up when I approach, her dark hair falling forward so that it's hard to see her face. But she knows I'm there. "Don't like it?" The question has a laugh in it.

I skip that question. "What would be a normal order for a place like this?"

"Just a coffee."

Surely not. "No macchiato? No almond milk? No drizzle?"

Her voice is deadpan. "Just coffee. Plain or french roast."

I'll have to find a way to work with this. "Am I allowed to get cream?"

She points to a shelf on the side wall. "From over there, yeah."

I turn. There's packets of sugar and sweeteners, and a small silver pitcher with a lid.

"And this is how most small-town coffee shops work around here? Can you even make what I asked for?" The only coffee I ever drank in Alabama was from my dad's burned-bottom metal percolator that sat on the stove. Once I got to LA, fancy coffee became a line item in my meager budget. I got hooked.

She shrugs. "We can make espresso drinks, sure."

"And you wouldn't give me one because . . ."

"Your order was ridiculous." She pretends to flip her hair. "Iced with blah blah milk and drizzles of junk and oh, let me tell you even how to make it because obviously it will suck if I don't."

So, my order wasn't precise; it was insulting. "I see. Thank you."

I've learned.

Just a coffee. Ask for it kindly.

Be simple.

If this is what I'll have to get at every coffee shop all the way to Alabama to avoid looking like a big-city brat, this is going to be a long trip.

Chapter 8

ZACHERY PLAYS BIG BROTHER

Kelsey doesn't write me again after my rather emphatic reaction to her suggested hair-color change.

She's off the deep end. Dressing different. Planning to force a meeting with a strange man.

I'm worried.

I don't have a desk of my own in Desdemona's office, so I sit at Kelsey's, watching Jester attempt to type a letter with one finger. It's excruciating.

Kelsey's desk is neat and organized, all the items laid out at right angles. I shift her mouse an inch to the left to break the pattern, then move it back.

Her space includes a framed photo with her mother, a kitten mug that holds her pens, and a collection of small blown-glass unicorns. It strikes me that I have never asked her where they came from.

I've had miles of confidence my entire life, which led to auditioning for parts, getting them, and while maybe not having a lifelong career, surviving in the business long enough to be well set.

There hasn't been a single woman Desdemona has sent me after, or one I've pursued on my own, who has made me feel this off-center.

There's something about Kelsey that brings it out. It's the combination of her drop-dead looks, her smarts, and her sunny attitude that gets me.

I know how she sees me. She teases me about it. A manwhore. An opportunist. A man angling for press and limelight.

And I've been those things. I'm probably still those things.

But letting sweet, naive, bubbly Kelsey go on this wild-goose chase doesn't sit well with me. Not all alone.

Who knows who she'll run into. And with this fortune teller nonsense in her head, the withering-faith business and end-of-summer deadline, she might not make rational decisions.

I don't have to be a contender. I'm acutely aware of all the reasons that I'm not.

But I can be a protector. A big brother.

I should fill in for those siblings she doesn't see anymore. Talk some sense into her.

"You miss her already, don't ya?" Jester's eyes remain fixed on the keyboard as he asks this, typing at roughly one word per minute. He looks like a flower in a pink shirt with green pants, his head topped with a pale-yellow cap.

"It's fine."

"It's not. There's no foolin' Jester."

"She's out there all alone."

"Kelsey can handle herself."

I grunt in reply.

"What are you doing in the office anyway? You only come in here to fight with Desdemona or flirt with Kelsey."

Flirt? I do not. I'm about to sputter out a vehement denial but Jester waves me off. "Don't bother. There's—"

"No fooling Jester," I finish. This shtick of his is funny only when it's about other people.

"You're going to get frown lines if you keep scowling like that," Jester warns, sticking his tongue out as he concentrates on what must be a particularly difficult piece of typing.

I should get out of here. I don't have any duties, no women to woo on behalf of Desdemona, no files to study to learn what might get them to accept some project that matters to the office.

The chair squeaks as I roll away from Kelsey's desk.

"Will I be seeing you around?" Jester asks.

"Probably." Summers get light without Desdemona directing my actions. Maybe I should take a vacation. Cozumel. Ibiza. Costa Rica. All of the above. It might keep my mind off Kelsey.

"Keep tabs on our girl!" Jester calls as I stride out into the blinding sunshine.

I should take up surfing. Dye my hair blond.

Now I'm rambling in my own head.

I know what I *want to do*.

Catch up with her. Watch for her. Keep her from getting in a scrape.

But that's insulting. She's a grown woman.

I slide into my silver Jag. There are a hundred women I could call. Most of them would jump at an opportunity to dress up and get some photos taken on the strip or at a club, even if they aren't too interested in me.

But instead of doing that, I head for Highway 1.

Driving this stretch of the coast always fills me with awe. The ocean. The beaches. The craggy cliffs. It gives me perspective.

I had the chance, early in my career, to do the New York scene instead. I met a playwright who had gotten a backer and wanted me for his lead. He ended up penning a well-reviewed production that had a multiyear run.

But my father pulled strings to get me an agent and a manager, and I was promised a role in a comedy. All the players involved were Hollywood regulars, so as long as I did a good job and handled myself on the set, I would have connections that would lead me from one project to another.

And it worked, my first character leading to a stronger part that landed me a supporting role, and then my first headliner.

After that, it tanked as fast as it rose.

I shove those thoughts away. They're interfering with the peace of my view.

I park at one of the roadside stops to step out and take it all in. It's midafternoon, and the clouds break the sunlight in long, straight beams.

My shoulders unknot, and I exhale in a slow, even breath.

I could put together a crew. None of my male friends are close, but they're good enough for a guys' trip. I could choose from actors on our roster, the ones still trying to get a solid break.

Add a few of the bit players from back in the day, the ones I keep in contact with. The big shots are unlikely to take a call from me. They stayed in the game.

I lean against the side of the Jag, ready to look at itineraries, when my phone serves up an old photo, a memory from two years ago.

It's Kelsey, looking harried, and none too pleased I'm taking her picture as she packs a pile of folders in a box after a long day of auditions. She was new and unaccustomed to those long days.

We don't do casting marathons anymore, using self-tapes and highlight reels to push our selections.

But that day was a doozy, and I pitched in to help the three of them, plus two temps we hired to help with check-in and flow.

Her hair is half in her face, and she's clearly exhausted. But the glint in her eye as she dares me to take that shot is pure Kelsey. I don't know why I did it. Maybe to tweak her. Maybe I already understood who she would become.

And now she's out in the world, all alone, trying to wrangle her one true love.

I can't leave the country, not even for a day.

In fact, I should be closer.

Much closer.

I pull up her texts from earlier. Didn't she say where she was?

Bris-something or another.

I head to Google Maps to figure out her route. There's Barstow, but that's not very far. She surely got more miles down than that.

Then I spot it. Briston. It's about five hours out, off the interstate on a small highway. Definitely a candidate for tumbleweeds.

That's where she is.

But will she stay put?

No. She surely kept going.

It's three o'clock. She'll stop for the night somewhere. I follow the most likely trajectory of her journey. She'll be close to the Arizona border, and knowing Kelsey, she'll make that a goal.

I can take a more direct path and be only about six hours behind her. While she's sleeping, I can catch up.

There will a problem at some point with my own sleep, but I'll worry about that when the time comes.

Right now, I need to grab some basics and hit the road.

Oh, and let Jester know I'm going without him saying *I told you so.*

Chapter 9

KELSEY LOSES AN EYE

By the time I leave Good Brew, which was anything but, the sun has slanted enough that I can't see into the windows of the other businesses.

I shield my eyes from the glare and drop into the driver's seat of my car, pulling up a map to see where I should go next.

Do I try again? Or call it a day?

I'm in range to make it to Arizona. I didn't book hotels because, for one, this was a very last-minute trip, and two, I wasn't sure when I might end up stopping for a while if something worked.

It definitely isn't going to be in Briston, Nevada.

On the map, just across the border to Arizona, I spot a lodge and a bar not far off the interstate.

Done.

I like the idea of meeting my future husband at a lodge. We could go there for every anniversary.

The tires crunch as I pull away from the crumbling curb and leave the town of bad coffee, feeling optimistic despite the failure. I got the first attempt out of the way, and didn't spoil any real prospects with my missteps.

This is good, right?

Totally good.

I go back to my girl-power playlist and sing along.

As the afternoon wears on, I subsist on snack mix and warm Diet Coke. My hybrid switches to gas, but there's nothing anywhere by way of a charging station on this tiny highway, so I let it go.

When I pull up to the Pitchfork Lodge, I wonder if I've made the right choice. It's rustic and small town, but the aesthetic is heavy on taxidermy. Huge antlers make a rather ominous archway at the entrance, and every window has a stuffed bear in it, looking out, jaws open, arms up.

I sit in my car a full minute trying to gather the gumption to go in.

Come on, Kelsey. It's miles to anywhere else.

I blow out a breath and reach in the back for the smaller overnight bag I prepared so I didn't have to haul a big suitcase around. I need to be nimble in case I happen to trip and fall into someone's arms, or have to hurry to catch up with someone so I can *then* trip and fall.

Or reach for the same magazine in the lobby. Or perhaps a cup at the water station.

So many possibilities.

But as I enter beneath the antler arch, I wonder if I've stumbled into Gaston's lair from *Beauty and the Beast*. Inside, everything is rough-hewn wood. The floor is covered with rugs made of dead animals, and there are so many glass eyes. So many.

There isn't a single woman anywhere, but quite a few men lounge about, all holding big beer steins.

Some are in jeans, real-life distressed, not artificially, mostly Levi's, $55. Others are in camouflage, and definitely not Coût De La Liberté, which clocks in at $1,900. A couple of the men sport full coveralls. I can't put a price on those.

One is cleaning a shotgun, right there in the lobby.

I consider backing out slowly, but really, this is a meet-cute waiting to happen. I don't have to marry them. It's *practice.*

So, I swing my day bag around, planning to have it bump my leg so I can take a cute, controlled tumble right into the middle of them all.

And see who catches me.

But I misjudge the weight of the bag. It knocks me off kilter, and I reach out to grab anything I can to steady myself. My hands wrap around the stiff, creepy fur of a stuffed beaver.

I let go, and the dead critter starts to tumble. I drop my bag to snatch at him, but I'm not quite fast enough, and he topples.

He hits the ground with a crash of his heavy base on the hardwood floor, and one of his glass eyes dislodges and rolls across the lobby.

"Oh, God," I say, scrambling across the wood planks to capture the errant marble, feeling the air on the backs of my thighs. I'm bent over too far for a short skirt and probably flashing the whole room, trying to trap the glass eye with my hands.

I finally nab it, although my knees crack against the floor with a bone-jarring thud. The beaver is still on the ground, right next to my ridiculously Barbie-pink bag.

I would like to die now.

Someone clears their throat. Then several somebodies.

I look up, and no fewer than six men are offering their hands to help me get up. A couple of them jostle each other for position.

Well. Okay.

I take them in. Two have wedding bands. I'll skip those. One fits the bill for Gaston, with shiny black hair and a rock-hard jaw.

But next to him is a boy next door, clean cut and sandy blond with the bluest eyes. His expression is earnest and concerned, while Gaston is bemused.

Boy Next Door, it is.

I take his hand, and the others step back.

Okay. They're gentlemen.

"You all right?" Boy Next Door's voice is like melted butter.

"Yeah," I say. "A little embarrassed. There's nothing like taking a fall in front of an audience." But even as I say it, I'm singing inside. It worked!

The man releases me to set the beaver back on the table. "I told Watson he needed to bolt down the critters. He doesn't listen."

"I have his eye." I hold out the glass ball.

He takes it. "Scottie is losing his touch if his eyes aren't staying put." He pops it into the beaver's empty socket.

"His name is Scottie?"

The man turns. "The beaver? No. He's Ace. Scottie is the taxidermist in town. He did all the work in here, other than the rugs. His wife handles those."

Wow. The couple who skins together, wins together, I guess.

"So, the beaver really does have a name?" I ask.

"For sure. All the critters do. You want a tour?"

A tour of the taxidermy? I glance at the entrance, then the front desk, where an older man watches with what my daddy would call a shit-eating grin.

"I haven't checked in."

"Oh, Watson can wait." He calls out, "Can't ya, Watson?"

The man shrugs.

"See?" He picks up my bag. "We'll set this behind the counter for a minute. I'll give you the grand tour."

I guess I'm staying.

"I'm Kelsey," I say.

"Grant." He holds out an elbow. "Shall I introduce you to the former wildlife of Pitchfork?"

"Sure."

Why not? I slide my hand into the crook of his arm.

INT. PITCHFORK LODGE LOBBY—EVENING

GRANT, 25, good looking, outdoorsy, in jeans (Wrangler, $55) and a mint-green polo (Gap, $20), leads KELSEY, 25, blond, in a blue dress, around the various

*taxidermy of the lodge. They smile at each other. It's a
meet-cute.*

Grant points over the fireplace to a deer head with an enormous
rack. "So that one is Buck the First."

"Buck, really?"

He looks confused. "Male deer are bucks."

"I know—I meant that's sort of on the nose."

Grant tilts his head. "There's something on his nose?"

All right. The bulb might be a little dim.

It's practice, Kelsey. Just practice.

"Never mind. Is there a Buck the Second?"

He whirls us around. "Right over here." We walk to a side wall,
where another deer is centered in a bookshelf, otherwise filled with
leather-bound volumes.

"Buck the Second likes to read?"

"What makes you think he likes to read?"

"He's by the books."

"Oh." Grant takes in the shelves like he's never noticed their contents before.

Whew, boy.

Grant leads us to the back corner with a collection of smaller
animals.

They must be older than the beaver, because their fur seems to be
rubbing off, making them look like they have mange. Or maybe something has been slowly eating them.

Grant gestures to the animals. "Here we have Scrubby the Squirrel,
Rudy the Raccoon, and Freddy the Fox."

"I guess alliteration makes it easier to remember."

Grant's expression collapses into confusion. "You lit what?"

I should stop trying. "I like their names."

His face brightens. "Me too!"

Yeah, I'll be racing out of town in the morning.

I turn to a shelf with a second beaver, much larger than the one I knocked over. "What about him?"

This sends a roar of laughter through the room. We've apparently been the subject of everyone's attention.

"That one's a girl beaver," someone shouts.

"Tell her, G-spot!" says another voice.

"G-spot"? I assume they mean Grant. I really don't want to know the origin of that nickname. At least, I *think* I don't.

He *is* pretty.

"Nah." His cheeks pink up adorably. "We'll skip that one. Let's go look at the bears."

I have a feeling whatever this beaver is named is not going to be very female-friendly. There aren't any women here.

I don't feel uncomfortable right now, though, so I head for the front windows, my arm still tucked in Grant's elbow.

"Who is this?" I ask when we arrive at the bear I first saw from the parking lot.

"Horndog." His face gets pinker.

I pretend not to get it and point to the one on the other side of the front doors. "And that one?"

"Dick." He's gone beet red.

"I see." I turn us away. "Thank you for that very educational tour. I should check in." I release him. "Perhaps I'll see you later?"

"Yeah, sure. We'll be down here."

I wonder where they're refilling their beer. "Is there a restaurant?"

"There's a bar through those swinging doors. They have burgers and chicken wings."

Of course they do. "Great. That sounds good."

"You want to have dinner, like, with me, maybe? No big deal, just down here?"

The room goes quiet. The man at the front desk pretends to sort through a drawer of plastic key cards.

I hesitate. Do I want to have a burger and beer with G-spot under the watchful gaze of Horndog and Dick?

It's what I'm here for.

"Sure," I say. "Is seven good?"

"Yeah," he says. "See you at seven."

He wanders back over to the circle of chairs by the fireplace. Several men reach out to give him high fives.

"G-spot's gettin' lucky tonight," one of them says.

They're not even trying to be subtle.

"Can I book a room?" I ask Watson, assuming that's actually his name. They seem to like their nicknames here at the Pitchfork Lodge.

"Sure. How many nights?"

"Just the one."

At that, the men burst out laughing. "Better make it a good one, G-spot. She's a runner."

I pass Watson my credit card, and he scans a key. "Second floor. Elevator's busted. Stairs are behind this wall." He aims his thumb behind him. "Right beyond Dick."

Awesome. "Thanks." I take my key and reach behind the desk to grab my pink bag. I'm glad that I didn't roll in the larger luggage. It would have been a beast to get up the stairs. I avert my eyes from Dick the Bear as I pass by.

Once I'm in my room, fake-wood paneled and decorated with paintings of ducks, I flop back on the bed.

It might not be smooth or easy following a fortune teller's directions across the country to find true love, but I'm doing it.

Chapter 10

ZACHERY PACKS THE SOAPS

As I race back to my condo, my foot on the gas pedal has no interest in speed limits.

I never should have gone out so far on the seaboard. I'll have to make up even more time now.

I text Kelsey at a stoplight to see if I can get any concrete information.

> So where is your next stop?

I'm not surprised when I get all the way back to my condo without a reply. She's likely driving, and even if she isn't, the signal is notoriously bad in the desert.

When I make it inside, I consider my closet. I can dress fancy or plain. Casual or to impress.

Unable to choose a direction, I start cramming random outfits into suitcases. In the middle of my efforts, my housekeeper, Carmen, arrives.

"Mr. Carter, let me. You're going on a trip?"

She pushes me aside to fold the clothes properly.

"Maybe." I step back into the closet and pull shoes. Ferragamo, Gucci, Hermès, Dior.

Carmen takes them from me. "Don't forget your toiletries."

Right. I pick up a small case and throw everything in. Colognes. Hair products. My formulated soaps. They rattle around in there, so I stuff a towel on top.

Carmen has left my organized suitcases by the bedroom door. It's a lot, like I'm headed overseas. I should cut back.

But catching up to Kelsey feels urgent.

I try calling Jester to let him know I'll also be out of town, but I keep getting voicemail. Obviously one of our actors is keeping him on the line. The office is roughly on the way, so I decide to make a quick stop.

When I get there, Jester has the office phone to his ear, his cell phone in speaker mode on the desk, and he's trying to mend a Charlie Brown mug with superglue. Obviously, he finished whatever he was typing earlier.

He looks up. "I'm on mute on both conversations."

I push down my urgency to leave. I'm going to need him to cover should Desdemona call. "It turned into a two-phone kind of day?"

"It sure did. The big film festivals get everyone in their feelings."

I walk up to the pieces of the mug. "Does Kelsey know Charlie bit the dust?"

Jester's default smile inverts to a frown. "She ran out of here when I told her. I haven't seen her since I broke it, and now she's gone on this journey to the center of the earth." He lets out a long sigh. "What if she never makes it back? What if some rootin' tootin' Wyoming ranch boy steals her heart?"

He's taking this hard, his ruddy cheeks pinker than usual. The low squawking sound from his cell phone sounds a lot like the teacher in the *Peanuts* shows.

"I'll look online for a replacement mug," I tell him.

"I already did," he says. "The set is discontinued."

Kelsey loved this one. "Find something similar and buy it. If Desdemona balks, I'll cover it."

Jester sets down the mug pieces. "You'll do anything for that girl."

It's true. "I'm going after her."

Jester leaps from his chair. "Finally! Love will prevail! Do you have roses? Champagne? She likes—"

"Perrier-Jouët Belle Époque Brut."

Jester claps. "Of course you know."

"But no, I'm not doing any of that. I just want to keep her safe. She's not thinking clearly." When Jester raises an eyebrow, I add, "You know she's not for me."

Jester sits back down. "If you say so." He fiddles with the piece of the mug that contains the whorl of Charlie Brown's hair.

"I don't want anyone taking advantage of her. So, if Desdemona calls—"

"I know. I'll cover. But I don't expect to hear a peep until after Cannes."

I stand at the door. "Do all of us finish each other's sentences here?"

The cell phone goes quiet, and Jester punches the mute button and says, "I agree with you, honey." Then mutes it again. "Not Desdemona. She doesn't care enough."

He's got that right. "I'll be in touch," I tell him. "Hold down the fort."

Jester salutes me, then clicks a button on the office line. "I told you it would come to this." The voice continues its monotonous drone.

I hop in my Jag and take off for whatever's next.

I'm sitting in traffic on the interstate when Kelsey finally writes me back.

Kelsey: I stopped at the Pitchfork Lodge in Arizona. Had a meet-cute!

My stomach drops. Already.

The cars aren't moving, so I write her back.

Me: A good prospect?

Kelsey. God, no. But good practice.

I unknot a little.

I pull up the map and search for Pitchfork. With traffic, it will take seven hours to get to this lodge. That will be eleven p.m. Not too bad.

Now for the next problem.

Do I tell her I'm coming or not?

My phone buzzes with a call from her. I tuck an earbud in my ear to minimize the traffic noise. Even so, she instantly knows.

"You're in your car?"

"Stuck in traffic."

"Going someplace fun? Do you have a Desdemona date tonight?"

"No." Time to deflect. "I just left Jester. He was on two phone calls."

"He does that. Mostly the actors want to hear their own voices."

Funny how often Kelsey forgets I used to be one of them.

"Tell me about your meet-cute."

Traffic moves forward, but I listen as Kelsey fills me in about a fallen beaver, a taxidermy tour, and the six-to-one ratio of men to her.

"I'm having dinner with Grant. I think he's the least scary of them."

Grant. So, it's already happening.

"Someplace close to the lodge?" I open the map again.

"There's a bar with burgers right here."

My chest tightens. "Your date is at the hotel. Is he staying there, too?" That's close proximity to beds.

"You know, I'm not sure he is. I get the impression that these locals hang out here."

Traffic starts to loosen as we hit the suburbs. "You sure this guy is all right?"

"No, but I have a plan to extricate myself if I need to."

"Tell it to me."

"I went over the fire escape map, and it looks like there's a hallway between the bar and the public bathrooms, and on the other end is a back staircase that I can use to return to my room."

"So, you can say you need to visit the bathroom and then just escape."

"Exactly."

"He doesn't know which room you're in?"

"No, and I don't plan to tell him."

I suppress my sigh of relief. "Tell me what you're going to wear."

I follow Kelsey's happy chatter about her dress and her ideas for hair and makeup all the way to the desert. By the time our reception gets spotty, she's off to have dinner.

And I'm well on my way to reaching her.

Chapter 11

Kelsey and It's All Poison Here

When I descend the stairs to the lodge's lobby, different men lounge below.

The camo men are gone. Their replacements are dressed a little nicer, as if they're all about to go on Thursday-night dates.

Gaston is still there, though, and he sits on the biggest chair, a high-back with leather cushions lined with metal nailheads. Like a throne.

He whistles long and low as I reach the bottom, elbowing a new man, this one in khakis, possibly from Target, $29.99, and a white button-down with no distinguishing features.

"That's the one I was telling you about," he says. "G-spot is buying her dinner."

Khaki Pants examines everything from my strappy sandals (Gianvito Rossi, $900 retail but $75 at a reseller), past the peach cotton dress ($45, Alabama Kohl's, circa 2019) to my curly updo. His intensity sends a tendril of unease through me. It's like he's sizing me up for himself.

Even so, I gamely keep walking. "Have you seen Grant around?"

"He's in the bar," Gaston says. "If he doesn't work out, we're right here." He and Khaki Pants share a laugh.

Gross. When I push through the swinging doors, Grant sits at the long oak bar on the back wall.

"Kelsey!" He stands and holds out a hand.

It's the wrong angle to shake, more like when Aladdin reaches for Jasmine as he leads her onto his magic carpet. I accept the gesture, allowing him to close his fingers around mine as we walk to an empty table near the foosball.

There are two other couples sitting nearby, and I'm relieved to see women. So, they do exist around here.

Grant pulls my chair out, and I can't remember the last time I saw anybody do that, much less do it for me.

"Thank you," I tell him as he scoots me in.

He sits beside me and lifts a laminated card standing between the napkin dispenser and a bottle of ketchup that looks like it might have been continuously refilled for the better part of a decade.

He holds the sole menu between us. "I've tried everything other than the fried mushrooms."

"What's the best choice?"

"Plain burger. The wings will set you on fire."

"Thanks for the warning."

He grins at me. "Wouldn't want to take that pretty mouth out of commission."

Oh, boy. I ignore the comment and look at the burger options. Bacon. Double bacon. Double bacon with chili.

Plain burger it is.

"You want a beer?" Grant asks.

A beer. I haven't had one of those in years. They probably don't have Perrier-Jouët Belle Époque Brut.

Not that I'd ask for that if they did. That's a Hollywood order for someone like Zachery. "Sure."

"I'm a Bud man, but I get it if you want something lighter."

Lighter than Budweiser? Now he's annoyed me. "I can handle my beer."

He grins. "Whatever you say, little lady."

I channel my inner peace not to get up and leave right then.

It's practice. I'm getting the bad pancakes out of the way, heating the grill just right for the perfect one.

A woman in all black other than a green apron pushes through a door in the back wall. She's got a beehive like it's 1966 even though she can't be over forty.

She looks me over. "Huh, G-spot, you weren't lying. You do have a date."

"I told you," Grant says.

I have no idea what this exchange might mean about Grant's romantic history, but I say, "I'm Kelsey."

"Becca," the woman says, pulling a pen out of her hair. "What's your poison, and trust me, it's all poison here."

"I'll have a Bud," Grant says.

I glance at the taps on the wall behind the bar. "Guinness Stout."

"Stout," Becca says. "You got yourself a real corker, Grant." She writes the beers on her pad. "You want food or are you just drinking?"

"It's a proper date," Grant says. "I'm getting a double-bacon chili burger. No onions." He grins at me like he's thought of everything.

"And for the lady?"

"A plain burger," I tell her.

"You mean nothing at all, like a kid? Patty and bread?"

"Veggies are fine."

"Like lettuce, tomato, onion?"

"Sure."

"No onion," Grant says.

"Extra onion," I counter.

Becca looks between us. "All righty. Fries with that?"

"A double," Grant says.

"I'll steal some of his," I say.

"Good on ya." Becca takes off.

I think Grant is going to bring up the onion order, but he looks around the room, drumming his fingers on the table.

I haven't had a date that felt like this since coming to California, but it's familiar. This is exactly what high school in Alabama was like. Awkward. Unsure. The flashback is intense.

"So, Grant, do you work?"

He turns the tray of sugar packets around in circles. "Yeah. I repair lawn mowers."

Interesting. "Is it a family business, or did you start that on your own?"

"My dad works at a garage, but I wanted to branch out."

"Nice. How many mowers do you repair in a week?"

"Depends on the season. Summer's started, so it's kinda intense. Lots of people pulled out their mowers, and they wouldn't start, or needed their blades sharpened."

"Is it only you, or do you have some help?"

"I have a boy this time of year, usually someone from the ag class at the high school. I keep him on through summer."

"I guess business gets slow in the winter."

"Naw. I send out flyers, reminding people not to wait. It stays pretty steady."

Huh. A real entrepreneur. "Do you like it?"

"Yeah. I'm saving up for a house. Should be able to get one when I'm ready. When I have a wife to help pick it out." His face goes red, and I remember how easily he's embarrassed. It's one of his charms.

"That sounds lovely."

Becca comes back with the beer.

Grant frowns. "Mine looks like piss water compared to yours."

The stout is heavy and black.

I lift mine and tap his glass. "To piss water."

He doesn't laugh at that but takes a sip anyway. I'm starting to understand how he thinks. He needs to be the man. He wants me to be the delicate flower.

Nope. Not gonna happen.

I take the lead on conversation from then on out, asking him about movies and TV shows, getting the expected answers involving block-busters and action flicks.

Grant probably won't ever be catching *Limited Fate*. He hasn't asked me what I do. Or anything about me, actually.

Becca brings the burgers, and I marvel at the height and breadth of Grant's double-bacon chili burger.

Mine is thick with onions, and I opt to slide the bulk of them out from the bun.

This makes Grant grin. "I thought so."

Yeah, I'll probably be using that back stair escape.

He demolishes his burger and double fries like nothing I've ever seen. I frequently pause in amazement as he shovels enough food in a single bite to choke a bear.

Mine is serviceable, and I nibble my way through about a third of it. I don't steal any fries. The way Grant is going at it, I might end up minus a finger.

Conversation stalls while he eats. Once Becca has taken the baskets away, the date seems to have run its course. Grant looks around, eyes trained on a basketball game on a TV in the corner.

If he'd parry even half the questions that I offered to him back at me, he'd have another hour.

"You want a second beer?" he asks, even though I've made it only halfway through my pint.

"I'm okay for now." I chide myself on the *for now*, as that suggests I want this date to keep going. I'm already dreaming of my Care Bear pajamas, a black-and-white movie on the lodge's antiquated cable net-work, and maybe a rundown of the high points with Zachery.

But Grant rallies. "Let's play pool." He tilts his head at the table at the far end of the bar.

My quiet night dissolves into a faraway dream.

I contemplate saying no. Getting this over with.

But right then, Gaston and his khaki-pants friend come in to refill their steins. They bang on the bar and laugh until Becca wanders in from the kitchen.

"You big brutes, shut your damn mouths," she says, snatching up their mugs and turning to the taps.

This makes them laugh louder. Gaston spots us at our table and nudges his friend. "Looks like G-spot hasn't blown it yet."

Looking at the two of them, I figure I might have the catch of Pitchfork. "Sure," I tell Grant. "Let's play a game."

His face lights up, which tells me he's probably a decent player. That's fine. I've done it enough to avoid total embarrassment no matter his skill level.

Grant racks the balls and selects a cue for me. "Ladies first."

I break the triangle apart, and a striped ball lands. "I guess I'm stripes," I tell him.

My second shot fails to sink anything, so he takes over.

While he examines the table, I side-glance at the bar. Gaston and his co-conspirator are watching. Their attention makes me think of vipers holding out for the right opportunity to strike.

Everyone seems to like poking fun at Grant. I wonder why that is, but nothing about our date has been intimate enough for me to ask a question that personal.

Grant knocks in a blue solid, then an orange. He's got good game. When he finally misses, Gaston calls out, "G-spot can't handle his balls." But the insult falls flat.

I watch the other people in the room to see how they react. They seem to be pretending we don't exist. Becca has made herself scarce.

This is the behavior of people who are either sick of Gaston, or a little wary of him.

But I've had it with his commentary.

"Get over here and beat him for me, then," I tell Gaston.

Khaki Pants elbows Gaston. "Go do it."

But Gaston frowns. "Nah. It's his date."

Grant leans on his cue stick. "It's all right, Kelsey."

"No, I want to see him play. See if he can use his stick at all or if it's as ineffective as I think it will be."

That does it. The couples turn to look. Probably, like my ill-ordered espresso at Good Brew, I've outed myself as "not from around here." It doesn't matter. I've met plenty of Gastons in Hollywood, and I know exactly how to tweak their egos.

Gaston sets his beer stein on the counter. "I guess I've been called out." He leaves the bar to select a cue stick from the rack.

"I guess I'm the third wheel," Gaston says, cutting his eyes at me. "Sure didn't expect the lady to ask me to join. Maybe she likes it better with two at a time."

Everyone in the room goes still, like Gaston has drawn a pistol in a dusty one-horse town.

I should walk away. I really should. Gaston is bad news.

But bullies are the worst. And I'm all the way back in my Alabama days, watching boys like Gaston try to make themselves feel big by picking on the kinder, gentler kids.

Screw that.

"I'm stripes, in case your memory is as weak as your game," I say.

"Now this is fun," Khaki Pants says.

"Shut up," Gaston snarls.

And I start to wonder. Maybe he's not very good at pool.

Gaston takes his time rubbing a cube of chalk over the end of the stick. He waits, then Grant reminds him, "It's your turn."

Gaston frowns in concentration. He leans over the table at all the wrong angles. His grip is poor. He doesn't have control of the stick.

He spends a ridiculous amount of time lining up an attempt that is doomed. And then, when he finally takes the shot, he doesn't even get a clean crack at the cue ball, skidding it sideways.

I bite my lip.

"Take another," Grant says. "You probably need more chalk."

Interesting. Grant is trying to bolster this jerk.

Gaston rubs the stick against the chalk again before lining up another try. This time, he cleanly strikes the cue.

But it doesn't hit another thing other than the side rail, a real feat given that only three balls have come off the table.

The game is mercifully short, with Grant cleaning up the entire rest of the solids as well as the eight ball without giving Gaston another turn.

Gaston shrugs as he tosses his stick on the table. "Everyone knows Grant is a pool shark."

I poke Gaston's chest. "Then next time, don't be a jerk. Show some damn respect."

"You have no idea what you've stepped into," Gaston says. "Waltzing in here with your California attitude."

"I'm from Alabama!" I argue, once again annoyed that someone has pegged me so easily.

"You might have started out there," Gaston says, "but you're Cali through and through."

"Did Watson tell you where I was from?" I ask, but Gaston has already headed to the bar. He collects his stein and motions for his friend to come with him.

Dang it.

I turn to Grant. "Do you think I'm more LA than Alabama?"

He shrugs. "I've never been good at figuring those things out." He fiddles with the stick. "You want to play another game?"

I do not. I need to think. But first, I want to learn from this mistake.

"What made so many guys come over to me when I chased after the beaver's eye?"

Grant slowly reracks the balls. "You seemed like you needed help."

"From six people?"

He painstakingly pulls one ball at a time from the pockets.

"Grant!"

"Might have been those pink panties you flashed everybody."

My hands fly to my skirt, even though everything is perfectly in place at the moment. I glance around to see if anyone else is listening, but Becca has disappeared again, and the two couples have left.

"What do my panties have to do with anything?" I hiss.

"Seems like you wanted someone looking."

"What!"

"You obviously made yourself trip and fall. You wanted us to look. It wasn't hard to figure out. Seemed like an easy roll in the hay to everyone in the room."

Oh, geez. Oh, geez. This meet-cute idea has backfired spectacularly.

I head back to our table and snatch up my clutch. "Thank you so much for dinner, Grant. It's been a real experience."

He doesn't come after me. "Okay, Kelsey."

I race past the bathrooms and up the back stairs. I don't pause until I'm in my room and flung across my bed with my laptop. I need to write an email and pour these feelings out.

This failure is more crushing than the coffee shop.

For a woman who likes to think of herself as smart and well grounded, I sure have been acting like the ditzy blonde who's the butt of the joke.

Chapter 12

ZACHERY MEETS THE BEAVER

I make it to the Pitchfork Lodge shortly before midnight. The LA traffic ran me later than I liked, but I'm feeling awake and borderline agitated as I enter beneath the antler arch Kelsey told me about before she left for her date.

I didn't hear much from her afterward. I had to text her three times to get any response. She only said it didn't go well, but she was in her room and safe.

I'm familiar with this pattern. It's the one where some asshole has sunk her pride, made her feel small. She goes silent, even with me.

I'll kill him.

The lobby is deserted other than all the dead creatures staring at me from shiny glass eyes. I spot the beaver she talked about.

This place is something, that's for sure.

I ring the bell, and a bleary-eyed man steps out from a room behind the desk. "Can I help you?"

"I need a room."

"We're all booked."

I glance out the window, mostly blocked by a huge taxidermy bear. The parking lot is half-empty. "Really?"

"We got a whole hunting party here. Came five to a truck. Lent my last room to a young lady a few hours ago."

I sigh. Maybe I can get hold of Kelsey and see her for a minute before I try to find some other place. It's not likely she's asleep at this hour. I know her habits pretty well.

"Thanks," I tell the man and step away from the counter.

I sit on a wooden bench. What should I say to her? She doesn't know I'm coming. She might not want me here.

Me: You need a pick-me-up?

I wait.

Nothing.

Me: I'm about to start making out with a beaver.

It takes a minute, but she texts back.

Kelsey: What?

Me: Rumor has it that she has a loose eye.

Kelsey: Are you seriously here?

Me: I'm downstairs.

Kelsey: Did you get a room?

Me: They're all booked. Hunters everywhere.

Kelsey: One was cleaning a shotgun in the lobby earlier.

Me: This does not surprise me.

Kelsey: Come up! I'm in 203.

I hesitate. This is what I was angling for, but I wonder if it's a good idea. Kelsey and I have spent a lot of time together over the years, but never alone in a hotel room when I don't have anywhere else to go. At least not yet.

But it seems I'm committed.

Me: On my way.

I stand, and the man behind the counter looks up.

"I'm headed up to my friend's room."

He shrugs and disappears through the door.

I dislike that I'm carrying one of my suitcases into her room, and for a moment, I consider taking it back to my car.

But this is Kelsey. I'll simply explain.

I'm not clear how to get upstairs right away. I spot an elevator, but after a moment of waiting, I ascertain that it's not functioning.

I follow the exit signs and finally spot a set of stairs. I take them two at a time.

When I get to Kelsey's room, she's peering out into the hall. "I thought you were lost!"

"The elevator appears to be out of order."

"Oh, yeah, Watson said that."

"Watson?"

"The man at the front desk."

"You already know everybody here?"

She waves me inside the room. "I made quite an entrance."

I follow her inside. I haven't stayed in a room this small since a high school trip. There's a bed beneath an oversize painting of a mallard family, mass-produced and as hideous as anything I could have imagined in a place like this.

But I'm not here for the art.

I tuck my suitcase discreetly in a corner and drop onto a threadbare chair next to the bedside table.

Kelsey sits on the bed, a gray sweater thrown over a pair of pink pajamas. When she turns to me, I spot a cartoon bear on the shirt.

I knew it.

But a quip about her sleepwear dies on my lips when I see her expression, her lip practically quivering. She's falling apart.

I move to sit beside her. "Tell me everything."

She holds off for a good ten seconds, fussing with her fuzzy socks, also printed with bears.

Then it all comes in a rush. "I shouldn't have faked a meet-cute. I tripped, apparently flashed the room, and they all thought I wanted one of them to stuff me like taxidermy!"

Wait, what? "Stuff you?"

"Zach! I mean with their dicks!"

Oh. "And how do you know this?"

"They told me." Her face crumples. "At d-dinner." She shivers.

Damn it. I draw her against me.

She tucks her face into my neck. She's warm and soft and sighs against my skin.

"Kelsey, they're small-town yahoos who have no right talking to a woman at all, much less like that."

"But I did fake the fall. I thought I was making a meet-cute."

"That doesn't matter."

I'm so angry these assholes upset her that I want to bash a whole lot of hillbilly faces in.

Of course, we're in the desert, not the hills, but even so, it was crass and lowbrow.

She shakes a little, and I think she might be crying, but then she pulls away in a fit of giggles. "Are you thinking about punching somebody?"

"No."

She lifts my arm, where my hand is in a tight fist. "So, what's this then?"

I shake my fingers loose. "Nothing."

She laughs again. "I love you, Zachery Carter."

My brain stutters on her words, wanting to interpret them another way, a real way. But I know better. This is Kelsey being demonstrative, full of hyperbole.

I make a typical remark for me. "You and half the women in America. Get in line."

This gets another giggle.

She scoots back on the bed to sit cross-legged. "So, why are you here?"

Right, that.

"I was in the neighborhood."

"Zach!"

I rehearsed several answers to this in the car. It might take every ounce of my acting training to convince Kelsey, though.

"Jester and I discussed your trip this morning and got concerned about you. I volunteered as tribute."

Her gaze takes in every point of my face as if assessing it for authenticity. "You and Jester, huh?"

"He was trying to repair your Charlie Brown mug."

"Right." She sighs. "This week did not have an auspicious beginning."

"But you pulled the Two of Cups."

This gets a genuine smile out of her. "You remember!"

This is exactly the distraction we need. "Let's pull another one. A message from the universe about what's next after those blowhards."

"That's a great idea!" She rolls over to reach into a pink duffel bag, flashing a long, bare leg. I force myself to look away. It's when Kelsey is at her most vulnerable that I find it most difficult to resist her.

She extracts a different box from before. It's a metal tin and has drawings of colorful bears on it.

"What's this?"

"My Gummy Bear Tarot. It's more lighthearted than the other one." She pulls the deck out of the tin. "I think you should pull the card."

"Will it be accurate then? I might be a nonbeliever." My eyes follow the quick movements of her hands as she rearranges the deck.

"The magic works. Even if you do an online pull." She stops shuffling and spreads the deck across the bed in a fan. "Because the magic is in you. It's like dreams. They mean whatever you think they mean. It's your subconscious you're tapping. It doesn't have to be mystical. It's more about our feelings."

"Okay." I consider the cards. One is sticking out slightly above the others, so I take it.

"Flip it over," she says.

Two gummy bears look like they might be in the Garden of Eden. Above them is a godlike bear on a cloud. The words "The Lovers" are printed at the bottom.

"That's on the nose," I say.

Kelsey tilts her head, taking in the image. "Yeah, it's weird. I've never pulled the Two of Cups or the Lovers before, and here I've gotten them both regarding this trip." She winks at me. "Almost makes you believe it's actually magic."

I don't like it. More nonsense to mess with Kelsey's very solid common sense. And it's my fault—again. First with the fortune teller, and this time encouraging her to use her deck.

But I stuff all this down. My negativity won't help in this moment. "Does it mean what it sounds like?"

"Not always." She takes the card from me. "It can mean soulmate, or a powerful bond. It isn't always about a lover in the usual sense."

Soulmate. Now that's a word. Has she ever had one? Have I? Is it even a thing?

I'm not a believer in that, either. I can't be, not in my line of work.

Kelsey leaves the Lovers card on top and puts the deck back into its tin.

"How many decks did you bring?" I ask.

"Uh. A few." She drops the tin into her bag. "What was your plan?"

There's a note in her voice I'm not sure about, like maybe I ought to think about leaving.

I shift away from her. "I wanted to check on you."

"Six hours of driving? When we could talk on the phone?" She returns to her cross-legged position, and I work to keep my gaze off the miles of skin between her socks and her shorts.

"I haven't gotten a good set of bloody knuckles in a while."

She tugs her sweater around her middle more tightly, like she's cold, or shy, or maybe uncomfortable. I probably should leave.

"I'm okay, you know. I'm not a damsel in distress."

I was worried she would draw that conclusion. "I never thought you were. But maybe you could use a wingman?"

She considers this, plucking a loose string on the worn bedspread. "Maybe."

"I'll totally stay out of the way. I'm just the bodyguard."

"Like Kevin Costner to Whitney Houston?" she asks.

If only.

"I was thinking more Secret Service to the First Lady."

She squints an eye. "You don't have the right look."

I hold a finger to my ear like I'm listening to instructions. "I have the perimeter secure."

She laughs and knocks my hand down. "Okay, I tell you what. You can stay for a little while. But if I get my sea legs, I might need you to step aside. I'm from a small town, so I know how the guys often think. They might not be secure enough in who they are to have a handsome, famous man like you nearby."

"Handsome, eh?"

She shoves me, and I pretend it's hard enough that I fall off the bed to land on the floor. I peer over the edge of the mattress. "You think I'm handsome."

"Every woman in the world thinks you're handsome. Now get back up here and do my bidding, bodyguard. You work for me."

I return to the corner of the bed. "I can be inconspicuous."

She lifts a single eyebrow, a look that kills me. "Right. You are about as inconspicuous as a Hemsworth."

"Comparing me to a Hemsworth. You really do love me."

She shoves me again. "You know I do."

I shouldn't have taken us back to this sort of talk. It's physically painful. But I play it off. "Now that we've established the parameters of our relationship for this trip, I should find my own hotel. This one is full."

"You can stay here."

Now it's my turn to lift an eyebrow. "There's only one bed."

She laughs. "And that's how you know we're living in a rom-com. Meet-cute. Villains. A taxidermy beaver. And only one bed. Are you going to sleep on the floor?"

"For you, I would sleep on the floor."

"Have you ever slept on a floor?"

Never. But I humor her. "I might have fallen there a time or two in my misspent youth."

"I'm sure we can handle the only-one-bed situation without any trouble."

But as she gets up to pull back the covers and form a barrier down the middle with the extra pillows, I'm not so sure.

Not in the least.

Chapter 13

Kelsey's Trouble with Tinkles

When Zachery heads into the bathroom to change for the night, I wonder how this is going to work.

He has no idea how intimidating he is. If those Pitchfork men pegged me as Hollywood despite my efforts, they'll spot Zach instantly. And that's even if they *don't* recognize him from his movies.

Those wild comedies were probably right up the alley of guys like Gaston.

Is this going to work?

I do like that he's here. He's someone I can bounce ideas off. He would have helped in the beaver situation. And I wouldn't have been near as anxious heading into that bar to meet Grant.

Gaston wouldn't have gotten his digs in.

Yes, everything about how tonight went would have been better with Zachery around.

The door to the bathroom sticks a little, and Zachery jostles it before it pops open.

He wears a luxury white undershirt (Derek Rose, $170) and gray shorts (Moncler, $600), and dang, even his sleepwear costs more than the contents of my overnight bag.

"I like your pillow barrier," he says. "Sort of like the Walls of Jericho from *It Happened One Night*."

"Exactly like that." We keep bringing up love stories. It's putting ideas in my head. But watching Zachery slide beneath the sheets on his side of this not-quite-queen-size bed is making my body tingle.

We've done a lot of things together. Movies. Dinners. Late-night talking.

But never with a bed in the room.

And now we'll both be in it.

I put the pillow barrier up because of my nighttime habits. I'm a cuddler. And if there's nothing separating us, I'll be all up in his business by morning.

To be honest, I'm not sure the pillows will be enough.

I pad into the bathroom, acutely aware that Zach recently dried his hands on this towel. That the toothbrush inside some fancy blue-light case was in his mouth.

Wait, is that a sanitizing case?

I glance at what else is out. Caswell-Massey soap. Philip B. shampoo. Geez. That man is high maintenance.

But I like it. It means when I'm with him we have good service, excellent champagne, and the best of everything. And it's not like he can't adjust. He's doing it right now.

I'm sure a hotel like this is utterly below his standards, but he won't complain.

He's amazing, actually.

And he came after me.

I wash all my makeup off and brush my teeth. I need to pee, but the walls are so thin, he'll be able to hear.

I can't handle it.

Can I hold it all night?

Did he pee? I didn't hear it.

Maybe the walls are thicker than I think.

But when I start to pull down my shorts, I stop. I can't risk it.

I step toward the door, but then my need to pee magnifies times ten. Okay, fine.

This time, the panties hit the floor, but despite my bladder practically screaming, nothing comes out when I sit down.

Oh, geez. Come on.

I turn on the water full blast.

Nothing.

How can I make this quieter?

I string toilet paper across the lid so it will slow the flow and lower the splash sounds.

And finally, I go.

Ahhhh.

It works, the toilet paper tarp slowly disintegrating and plopping into the water.

Oh, no. That sound is worse!

He's going to think I did number two!

I flush and wash my hands, wishing I had never agreed to let him stay. This is the worst!

I wait as long as possible, then wonder if he'll think something is wrong with me, and open the door so fast I bang it on my toe.

Zach jumps to his feet. "You okay?"

I wave him off. "Just clumsy."

He sits back down, and the combination of his closeness, the intimacy of sharing a room, his casual bed clothes, and a small knowing smile makes my heart do a strange little flip.

That's weird. I haven't had that happen since Joseph Keen smiled at me in ninth grade. Of course, I smiled back like a big fool before realizing the catch of North High was actually aiming his megawatt attention at the cheerleader behind me.

But this one is for me, and it's a powerful look.

"Hey," he says.

"Hey."

Crawling into the bed next to him, even with the pillow wall, is way sexier than I expect. My heart hammers as I slide beneath the sheet. I'm wearing the gray sweater because otherwise, in this thin sleep shirt, my headlights are *shining*.

But it's not lost on me that I'm beneath the same sheet that is covering *him*.

"Are you a cover stealer?" he asks.

"The worst."

He clutches the sheets with both hands. "I'll sleep with one eye open, then."

"It won't help. I'm a ninja when it comes to midnight bedding thievery."

His laugh is low and rumbly and reverberates through my body. I feel it in my chest, my belly, my toes.

This is a lot.

"Good night, Zachery," I say. I snuggle down on my side, facing our pillow wall. I can just see his face above it.

"Good night, Kelsey." He reaches over to the lamp and flips it off.

For a few minutes, he stays on his phone, the light illuminating his face.

He's beautiful. He has no bad side. His jaw is sharp, his dimple visible even when his face is at rest.

It's shocking, really, that his career dwindled like it did. But it happens most of the time. A sustained lifelong place on the A-list is a real rarity, even though those graying actors with decades of movie credits are the most visible.

It's easy to forget the leading players of ten years ago when they've fallen out of the limelight.

I've watched Zachery's movies. He was miscast in all of them, a career doomed by a bad match of his strengths to the trajectory he found himself on.

It happens a lot. The only real way to combat getting pigeonholed early in your career is to diversify as soon as possible. But Hollywood, like a lot of industries, is comfortable with its known quantities.

If the directors you've worked with are comedic, the actors in your circle are comic, and the hits under your name all fall in the same category, that's where you'll keep getting work. Those will be the scripts that come your way. And it's your name that will come to the casting directors' minds when the same type of story needs a lineup.

It's a self-perpetuating cycle.

And it was all wrong for Zachery. When the scripts got mediocre, and his talent wasn't aligned with them, no movie magic was made. So he got dropped for the next pretty face.

His phone fades out as he sets it on the nightstand.

I listen to his breath, feeling every shift of his body on the stiff mattress.

The last thing that goes through my mind before I fall asleep is that I like sharing a bed with him.

Even if the Walls of Jericho come between us.

Chapter 14

ZACHERY GETS STEALTH CUDDLED

Sleep should have been elusive. Hard bed. Scratchy sheets. Thuds and door slams and late-night laughter.

But Kelsey's deep, even breathing was the perfect white noise. For a while, I propped myself up on my elbow, watching her slumber in the moonlight seeping through the threadbare curtains.

Then I slept.

I wake when I try to shift to a new position, but can't. Something weighs down my legs.

The light from the window is no longer blue, but orange-gold. Dawn.

And Kelsey's body is partially thrown over mine. The pillow barrier is behind her, and the two of us lie on one side of it.

She scaled the Walls of Jericho in her sleep.

I lie on my back, pinned by her leg and hip. Her head is tucked against my neck.

How long have we slept like this?

It takes self-control not to wrap my arm around her and draw her closer. I'm afraid to move or to touch her anyplace new, lest she wake and withdraw in embarrassment.

I breathe slowly and evenly, taking her in. Her leg is tan and toned, not that she's exercised a day in her life. It's the heels. She wears them always, despite the lengthy walk from the office to her car, and how she loves to spontaneously dance or twirl around a lamppost. She likes living life like it's a musical.

This trip is no different, even though the genre has changed. Is she really going to find her great love using rom-com story beats?

She sure seems determined to try.

A lock of wheat-blond hair tickles my arm. I try to ignore it and hang on to this moment as long as possible.

But eventually my muscle twitches involuntarily, and Kelsey startles awake.

She lifts her head, disoriented, then looks up at me and groans.

And not in a good way.

"You all right?" I ask her.

"I stealth cuddled you. It's my thing."

"It's all right. It's a cute thing."

She pulls away and rolls back over the pillow wall. "That had to be so awkward."

I sit up and make a show of stretching with clear nonchalance. "I'm used to women being unable to resist my animal magnetism."

The pillow smacks the side of my head before I even see it coming.

"Hey!" I snatch the pillow from her and wallop her midsection. "I'm a brutal survivalist when it comes to pillow fights."

She dives beneath the bedspread. "I surrender!"

I drop the pillow in its place against the headboard. Our silliness has created an ache in my chest. I don't get mornings like this. Not as a kid. My parents would have fired a nanny who let us carry on with pillows.

And it certainly would never have happened with the upwardly mobile women trying to leave a perfect impression after spending the night. I've caught more than one of them refreshing their makeup in the wee hours, presumably so I would think they *woke up that way*.

And here's Kelsey, emerging from the covers with her hair a wild mess, her cheeks pink, the remnants of a crease from my shirt imprinted on her forehead.

And she's perfect.

I wouldn't change a thing.

"Do you accept my surrender?" she asks.

"I do."

She grins. Her gray sweater is askew, revealing the tiny sleep top, pink with Care Bears dancing across the front.

And it's thin. There's nothing hidden, not the shape of her, not the fullness, and definitely not the taut nipples.

I look away before she catches me noticing.

Then I strategically shift a pillow over my hips.

Down, boy. Those are not for you.

"Do you have a plan for today?" I ask.

She pushes her hair out of her face and thankfully hugs a pillow to her chest. "No. I specifically set out to choose each day based on how the previous one went. There might come a time where I stay put awhile."

Right. When she finds her great love.

"And today?"

"I'm getting the heck out of this godforsaken place." She reaches for her phone. "Let me see what's next."

"I'll take a shower while you do that."

She nods. "I aim to only drive a few hours. I have all summer to find him."

All summer.

I contemplate this as I head to the bathroom. Can I hang out with Kelsey for three whole months? It's unlikely. Not just for me, but for her, too. Auditions will come up. Jester will need us.

The Demon might set up something in person with a contact of hers, and we'll have to scramble to get back.

All the more reason for me to travel with her. I'm acutely aware that Kelsey's salary isn't adequate for living in LA, even in the neighborhood she found. She won't be able to fly back on a whim.

But I can.

She's going to need me. Not just for safety or emotional bolstering, like last night. But to keep her job.

In the shower, I try to focus on the practicalities of the situation. Hotels. Two cars. Charging stations for her.

But my thoughts creep back to this morning. Kelsey in the golden light of dawn, snuggled up against me, her breath feathering across my skin.

Thankfully, I don't need to hide how my body is reacting in here, so I cut loose for a moment with the thoughts and let them run their course until I'm gasping, my arm propped against the shower wall.

These feelings aren't going away anytime soon.

Chapter 15

KELSEY'S HEART SKIPS TOO MANY BEATS

By the time Zachery comes out of the shower, looking absolutely perfect in a navy fitted T-shirt (Luca Faloni, $150) and khaki shorts (Ralph Lauren, $500), I have a plan.

"There's a pickle festival happening this evening in a small town near Durango, Colorado," I tell him.

He shakes his head as he carefully folds his nightclothes into his bag. "Pickle festival?"

"Yes! Isn't that hilarious?"

He tucks his red boxers into a special pocket of the bag, and I try not to imagine them on him. Red? It's like the Zach equivalent of lingerie.

"Pickles sound more like a hookup than a husband."

"I'll admit the word and the object are hookup adjacent, but still, it sounds like fun. And doesn't it make a great how-we-met story?"

He pauses in zipping up his suitcase. "To the grandkids? 'I met your father at a celebration of phallic food'?"

I reach for a pillow to throw at him, but then remember our earlier incident and think better of it. "Pickles don't have to be dirty."

"Keep saying it. It gets dirtier every time."

There's no stopping me at that one. The pillow sails over the bed and smacks him in the head.

He catches it neatly, and before I can make any kind of move, he's got me pinned back on the bed, the pillow between our chests. "I've warned you about my pillow game."

He's close, and this time, on top of me. I can barely breathe, but it has nothing to do with the pressure of his body.

It's just him.

My heart hammers, and I can't think of anything clever to say to play off how intense this feels.

But he has no such problem. He leaps up. "Got you again. And here you are, practically half my age."

I stand as well, sputtering at the very suggestion. "Eleven years, Zachery Montgomery Carter! That's all! Or are you saying I act eighteen?"

He shrugs. "Maybe I'm saying I act fifty."

Right. But this argument isn't new. He likes to act all big brother on me.

Even if that moment on the bed wasn't brotherly in the least.

He finishes zipping his bag. He's all packed. I haven't showered.

"We have the rest of the day to kill," I say. "I do not want to do it here in Pitchfork."

"Is there anything in this area you want to see?"

"How far is the Grand Canyon?"

He unlocks his phone. "Let me look." After a moment, he says, "A couple of hours."

"I've always wanted to see it. I'm not ready to leave yet, though. Did you want to drive on ahead?" I ask.

"And stand on the precipice alone? No, thanks." He plunks down in the chair. "I have some calls to make. And I should probably be with you when you go downstairs."

He's right. The Pitchfork club could be assembled below.

"All right. I'll be quick."

He waves his hand. "Don't rush. I have a lot of calls."

As I lock myself in the bathroom, I wonder if any or all of those conversations are with women Desdemona sent him after. How much of it does he want to do?

Is he a scoundrel?

I can't imagine. Not Zach. He's so flirty and sexy. He's impossible to resist.

I'm sure most of them are eager to fall into his bed. Zachery Carter never misses the mark. That's why he's Desdemona's leading man.

It even works on me. Boy, does it.

His toiletry bag sits on the counter, and I take a moment to sniff his soap. It's so good. I suppress a groan. So good.

In the shower, I run through the rather meager list of men I can call relationships. Joseph in high school. Daryl at LSU. Since coming to California, I've struck out hard on my dates. Many didn't even last long enough to hit second base.

Not that a California baseball field is the same. In my experience, men at Hollywood parties tend to go from "hello" to "home run" in a single pitch.

Or at least, they try.

I remember the guy on Plumeria Drive a month ago, when Zachery bloodied his knuckles. The guy was an actor going by Brad, even though we suggested something else for a stage name. He thought he could do for Brad what Chris Pratt, Chris Hemsworth, and Chris Evans have done for Chris.

He was not that handsome *or* talented.

But he did try to get up my skirt.

Desdemona sent me after him to find out if Arista was getting him to read for a thriller she was casting.

I'd known we were in the danger zone when he steered me into an unoccupied cabana at the far end of the pool from the party.

Hollywood hasn't cornered the market on people who think they can get away with anything. Most industries where there is a power dynamic this big, where people can make or break someone's dream, have their players who misbehave. But in Beverly Hills, the tabloids and the glamour and the stardom up the ante like nowhere else.

It's something I would fix, if I had the power. But the lowest rungs on the ladder never have any, particularly when somebody else thinks they already wield it. Brad was one of those.

Normally I can handle myself, but Brad was wily. He got me pinned against a wall, and I wasn't able to pop his knee. That's my signature move when a guy gets too handsy.

It's hilarious watching their leg collapse from such a simple move. It's also easy to play off as an accident. I'm always all, "Oh, my! What happened?"

But it hadn't worked on Brad. I couldn't get into position.

Zachery must have been watching us wander away, because only seconds into the situation, Brad was jerked away from me, and his chin was in the air from Zach's well-placed uppercut.

Zach probably would have gone unscathed, except Brad decided to come after him, so it took a second shot to discourage him, and this one broke open the skin on four of Zach's knuckles.

We left Brad on his butt in the cabana and went to rinse the blood off Zachery's hand. I assured him I was all right. And I was. Brad wasn't the first to get me in a tough position, and he probably won't be the last, not as long as I work for Desdemona. I'm in the den of vipers, especially for those new to the game, who assume casting couches still exist, and beautiful women will do anything for a part.

They have a rude awakening when they learn most casting is done via phone footage collected by people like me and Jester, and the big decisions are made without any bit players in the room.

Even so, maybe I should take a self-defense class. Some of those moves would come in handy.

But it was better that Zach did the punching, and he said as much. He could handle the negative press, should it come about, and generally it wouldn't. Lowlifes like Brad wouldn't want anyone to know some other man had bested him. A story about the incident would come with the risk that Brad would look like a chump in the tabloids.

Zachery is excellent at tabloids. They love calling him a playboy and an indisputable bachelor. But always a gentleman. And always a catch.

Just not one to keep.

No, the irresistible Zachery Carter is not for me.

I go through all my prep, in case it's in the cards that today is the meet-cute to rule them all. I won't be looking until we get to the pickle festival, but naturally, love is always unexpected, at least in the good scripts.

Shower, shave, moisturize. I take my time afterward doing makeup that looks natural, but is anything but.

I squeeze my damp hair to make soft waves rather than blowing it straight. And I choose pale blue shorts and a flowered top. Very girl next door.

And no heels. Flat sandals only. It almost feels weird, my feet on the ground. But it'll be good. Nobody wears heels to a national landmark.

That would peg me as high maintenance, as Hollywood. I might need to buy more flats.

When I step out, Zachery is no longer on the phone, and simply waits by the window. He smiles when he sees me. "Now don't you look like a fresh-faced southern girl?"

I turn in a circle. "Nobody would call me California like this, right?"

"You've nailed the small-town look."

"Thank you." I tuck my toiletries into my overnight bag. "Now escort me downstairs, and don't let any of these Pitchfork numbskulls so much as talk to me."

He grins and opens the door to let me pass. "I'm just a boy, holding the door for a girl, asking her to let me beat up a few numbskulls."

I try to ignore the ridiculous number of times my heart skips a beat.

Chapter 16

Zachery's Ken Fragility

There's nobody downstairs but Watson yawning behind the front desk, so only the beaver bids us farewell. Kelsey gets in her car, taking a moment to repack her overnight bag with new clothes.

It's a good system, and I consider copying it, only I don't have a smallish bag. Maybe I'll pick one up somewhere.

Kelsey calls me as we hit the highway, so we can talk as we drive. The conversation makes the road trip feel like we're together despite our separate cars. I consider hiring a driver to pick up my car so we *can* be together.

But then I remember that her endgame is a flannel-wearing husband and not me.

I should preserve my ability to bail.

Even though this scenario was the whole reason behind why I paid off the fortune teller, the way it's played out so far has been more difficult than I expected.

Of course, I didn't anticipate doing this on the road, much less sleeping in the same bed and having pillow fights. It's been only twenty-four hours since she started this jaunt, and we've made wild leaps in our relationship. She better find someone I approve of, or this whole situation is going to flame out.

"Hey, Zachery." Her voice is bubbly over the road noise.

"Yeah?"

"Remember that singing war from *Pitch Perfect*?"

"You're not going to suggest we sing, are you?" I'm not worried about this. I had fourteen years of vocal training. For nothing, since I did craptastic comedies, but Mom made sure I exploited what she considered the talent she passed to me.

"No, no, I was thinking I play a song, then you have to play the next song in the story."

"You have a lot more faith in my song recall than I do." I'm hopeless at knowing the top forty of any decade, other than the early 2000s, when I was in high school and obsessed with burning CD mixes for girls, mostly Foo Fighters and Radiohead, right until I got my first iPod.

Kelsey laughs. "Au contraire, I'm about to go straight into your wheelhouse."

"You are?"

"We're going to do this epic battle solely with songs from *musicals*."

She's making a big mistake. My mother performed on Broadway right up until she got pregnant with me. Show tunes were literally the soundtrack of my childhood. "You're aware that I'm going to kick your ass, right?"

"I've been hanging out with Jester. My knowledge has grown."

"What do you know beyond *Phantom of the Opera* and *Cats*?"

"Plenty. I'll even let you start."

I shake my head. She's about ten car lengths ahead of me on this tiny highway through the pine trees of Arizona. She waves, her head turned toward the rearview mirror as though she might be looking at me.

I think for a moment about what to play first. I should avoid any romantic themes, particularly after our rather intimate morning. But I can't make it too hard for her to follow up.

I have it. "We begin our tale with a little town in trouble, but not for the reasons they think."

"Ooooh," Kelsey says.

I have to stay hands-free, so there's no surprising her. "Siri," I say, "Play 'Ya Got Trouble' from *The Music Man*."

"I love it!" Kelsey shouts.

We both sing along for a while, but then she goes quiet, I'm assuming so she can think about her follow-up.

Finally, she says, "And the young men in the town need a total makeover! Siri, play 'I'll Make a Man Out of You' from *Mulan*."

She went Disney on me.

Well played.

Her fake-baritone singing along with Donny Osmond is hilarious, and I feel my cheeks starting to get weary from smiling already.

How to follow that one up?

But then I have it.

This time, I mute myself before verbally cuing up the song.

As Mulan comes to its dramatic conclusion, I unmute to say, "But the women need no changing!" Then I punch play on my song.

When it starts, Kelsey lets out a squeal. "I know that's right!"

She doesn't know every word, but she sings the best parts from the *West Side Story* tune: "I feel PRETTY!"

When it's done, there's a pause, like she's trying to figure out her next move.

"Do you bow to my magnificent prowess?" I ask.

But then her next song begins, and I feel my throat tighten.

Her voice is in narrator mode. "But the pretty woman all fall for the manly men, as long as they're not from Pitchfork, Arizona." It's followed by the opening notes of "Hopelessly Devoted to You" from *Grease*.

She knows every word to this one.

With an ache I scarcely recognize, I long to follow up with "You're the One That I Want."

But I can't do that.

So I bring the tone back around, and the minute Olivia Newton-John has sung the last note, I immediately punch up "I'm Just Ken" from the *Barbie* movie. "And the men aren't worthy," I say.

But this doesn't have the effect I thought it would. We're not even a minute into Ken's lament when Kelsey's blinker turns on, and she pulls into a scenic overlook.

I slow down and pull in beside her.

"Are you okay?" I ask on the phone, but she kills the call and gets out of her car.

I stop the music. *What's going on?*

The heat outside is oppressive, but the wind gusts make it manageable.

Kelsey walks past the brushy clearing to stand at the edge of the canyon, looking over the massive geological wonder, her arms crossed tightly over her stomach.

"Kelsey?"

She doesn't turn to me. "Is that what you think of yourself?"

For a second, I don't know what she means. Then I realize, it's the song.

"'I'm Just Ken'? No."

She steals a glance at me, then turns back to the sweeping vista. Birds circle over an outcropping. We're not on the desert side, but among the brushy trees that gradually slope down into the canyon. There's no sign of human life anywhere. Nobody even drives by.

I stand beside her, trying to read her expression. Her gaze remains firmly on the view, but I'm not sure she sees it. The line of her mouth is tight. Her blond hair flies behind her like a veil.

"Kelsey?"

"Why did you play that song after mine?" Her tone is firm, like Desdemona's when she wants an answer.

"I don't know. I thought it was funny."

She turns to me at that. "Funny? The woman longs for a man. Then you play . . . that?"

Now I'm starting to wonder if she saw something in my choice that I didn't. "What did you make of it?"

Her gaze locks on my face. "You don't see any resemblance?"

"I'm not Ken."

"The longing? The wanting to be more than you are? To getting stuck in a role you never asked for?"

Okay, I see it now.

"I'm okay, Kelsey. I know who I am."

"I'm not sure you do. You're magnificent." She gestures toward me. "You can do anything you want."

It's not true, and she knows it. "I could make a list of all the doors that are closed to me."

"When was the last time you tried to open one?"

Does she mean audition? I'm way beyond casting calls. Too proud, anyway. And I don't need the money. "I stayed in Hollywood."

"At a casting agency!"

"Desdemona is at the top of her game." Or she was, when I first came on board.

"Your talent is so incredible. Do you know how many perfect pairs I could make with you?"

She's thought about this? "It doesn't matter. I'm typecast, and the type of movie I did is too offensive now. And there are real comics to play the legit roles in comedies."

She sighs. "Actors do eventually age into a new type of role."

She doesn't have to remind me of how long it's been. "Only the really good ones. Look, I did everything right. I didn't piss anyone off. I didn't throw any tantrums. I invested my money. I walk as many red carpets as any working actor."

"But you're not happy."

How does she do that? See through me?

But I admit nothing. "I'm happy enough." I'm ready to talk about something else, anything else. "What do you think about this hole in the ground?"

She stares at me a beat longer, but eventually turns back to the landscape. "Is this it? The Grand Canyon?"

"We're on the northwest side, but yes. Not the most popular spot, but it gives you an idea of the scope."

"The biggest hole in the world. Or is it? I don't even know."

"There's a bigger one in Tibet."

"Tibet," she whispers.

"Do you want to see that one? I'll take you."

She laughs at that. "You'd take me to Tibet?"

"Sure."

She walks forward, uncomfortably close to the edge. This tiny over-look doesn't have a guardrail or stone wall like the more popular spots. It's brush and rock that simply falls away.

Then she sits, her legs dangling over the abyss. "It's beautiful. Vast. And not empty at all."

I sit next to her. "What did you expect?"

"I don't know. I guess for it to be desert down there. But there's everything." She gestures into the chasm. "Trees. Water."

"Most pictures you see are the South Rim. It's more desert. That's where the touristy areas are."

"I like this. There are birds." The wind rushes through the piney trees, stirring up dust. "Isn't that a line from one of the love songs from *The Music Man*?"

I can almost hear the words. "Yeah. It's called 'Till There Was You.'"

She leans her head on my shoulder, and finally, I relax, too. Kelsey has always been rather impulsive and prone to outbursts.

Sometimes she hits a little too close to home.

And other times, she trips herself up.

Like when I found her on Hollywood Boulevard a few days ago.

She'd stumbled right into my arms.

Like a meet-cute.

Except this is not something we're supposed to have. This trip is not for us.

I resist the urge to put an arm around her, or draw her close.

I'm a prop. Something to lean on.

Just like Ken.

Chapter 17

Kelsey Gets the Surrey with the Fringe on Top

I don't know why Zachery refuses to let his marble walls down. Maybe it's a rich-people thing.

He's so kind, so courteous, so gallant.

And yet, he won't talk about anything that matters.

We take in the glory of the Grand Canyon and pose for a selfie to show . . . I dunno, Jester, I guess. Zachery can't exactly post it to his star-studded Instagram.

Zachery snaps it on my phone, but I touch mine to his to transfer the file like I do all our shared profiles when we're working.

Then we get in our separate cars and keep going to our next stop, the small town of Dillville, Colorado. This time, there is no live conversation, and no music challenge.

It's a lot less fun.

I refuse to regret pushing him. Something about Zachery is broken, but I can't quite get to the heart of it.

His parents used the "busy rich" style of parenting, often leaving him with nannies or staff while they jet set around the country.

But he does have fond memories with his mother, which is why he knows so many show tunes. I wanted to tap into that, but apparently something in our musical conversation triggered him.

It's about three hours of quiet until we pull up to the town in the throes of preparing for its Dillfest.

While I showered earlier, Zachery booked a bed-and-breakfast right on Main Street so we could walk to all the festivities. I didn't think we would be able to get something so last minute, but apparently, it's more of a local event than one that draws outsiders.

We had something similar in the small town closest to our dairy. It was called the Root 'n' Toot, and as far as I know, they still hold it. Vendors sell roasted corn, deep-fried candy bars, and homemade jams. There are crafts for kids and a balloon-twisting clown and always a beer trailer.

They make the principal of the high school sit in a dunk tank so the kids can pay a dollar to pitch a ball at the mechanism that will drop him into the pool.

The principal during my years was so unpopular that we made more money than usual. In fact, we got to upgrade prom from a recorded soundtrack chosen by the home ec teacher to an actual DJ from two towns over.

The only drawback was he played too many songs that weren't radio edits, and the same principal who paid for him with his students' disdain pulled the plug. The last third of prom was relegated to the local country and western station piped through the intercom.

With that history, I know what I'm getting into as I slow down to let two teen boys cross the road from a small grocer to a park, where I presume Dillfest will be happening.

The bed-and-breakfast is ahead, pale blue with two stories and a white lattice trim.

A small sign hand-painted with the words VISITORS GO HERE guides me along a concrete drive to the back side. A matching sign says

PARK HERE against the outer wall of an old carriage house, meticulously restored to match the blue Victorian.

A woman leads two horses tethered to a beautifully preserved cart with a double row of seats and a canopy with fringe along the edge.

She's dressed in a long pale-green skirt with a green-and-white-striped shirt, the sleeves puffed out at the top and buttons tight along her forearm. A green hat with a tall white plume sits beside her on the seat as she guides the cart out of the carriage house.

When she spots us, she pulls the horses up short and waves.

I roll down my window. "Hello! Wow! Look at that!"

"Isn't it marvelous?" she calls. "Park right here. I'll be down in a minute!"

I pull in by the blue wall. Zachery is not far behind me, and I watch the woman as she takes in his silver Jaguar, and then her eyebrows lift as she spots Zachery exiting the driver's side.

Yeah, he's pretty. And famous enough to light up a town like Dillville. I don't know why I overreacted to his Ken song. I'm an idiot. This man has life on lock. He's pulling up in a sexy car in front of a gorgeous woman who might actually start singing "I Cain't Say No."

No matter. I'm here to find my own meet-cute. And the recipient of my attention might be across the road, bringing a heavy sledgehammer down on a platform that will ring a bell for his superior strength. The giant teddy bear he wins will get handed to me.

So there.

I hop out of the car and move to the back seat to snag my overnight bag. I already packed my bear-winning, man-attracting yellow sundress, with cute white tennis shoes and a matching bow for my hair.

He'll nickname me Sunshine, and we'll walk arm in arm through the fair, sharing cotton candy.

I can feel it.

By the time I make it to Zachery, Miss Green Stripes has hopped down to talk to him, her cheeks flushed like she pinched them.

"You must be Kelly," she says. "It's not often we get Hollywood at our doorstep! Come inside."

She can't even get my name right. And Hollywood! I've been trying to fit in with the small towns like I used to.

I realize that Zachery is a liability. I can't walk around with him if I want to shed my big-city glitz.

Why did I bring him on this trip?

I sling my bag over my shoulder. "It's Kelsey."

"Oh, my gosh. Of course. Kelsey. I'm Livia. I took over this bed-and-breakfast from my grandmother. I come from a long line of Dillville residents."

Yeah, and I come from a long line of dairy farmers. "Do cucumbers even grow here?" I ask as she leads us inside the back of the house.

She laughs, and it's like the tinkling of a bell.

I laugh like a horse.

"Of course! That's how Dillville got its name. Now, in the higher elevations, it's not as easy. But Dillville has a warmer climate, being so south and west."

Zachery cuts his eyes at me as if to say, "Of course, Kelsey," and I want to go hide in my room for a while. Maybe I *am* acting eighteen to his thirty-six. I feel like it.

Livia leads us up a curving staircase. "Your two rooms are on this end. There's an adjoining bathroom between you."

So, we share a bathroom. I know we did it last night as well. Shared a bed, even.

But today, I'm over it. I want to get out there and find someone, anyone, who will make me feel like I've made some progress.

She hands each of us a physical key, the ordinary kind like I have for my apartment. "For your rooms. Sorry they aren't antique anymore. They kept getting stolen. Now please, excuse me. I have to get the cart over to the park. Please feel free to walk around and help yourself to any drinks and snacks in the main fridge in the kitchen. It will be a little hectic with Dillfest, but I'm sure you are here for that, so I know you'll understand."

She mainly says all this to Zachery.

"Will we see you there?" he asks.

She blushes again at the question, and I catch him glancing at her left hand.

No ring.

"I'll be giving rides around the park. I'm more than happy to include a ride around the grounds of the festival for you as part of your stay, Mr. Carter." Her eyes glitter as she waits for a response.

"Zach, please."

"Oh! Yes, Zach, then." Now even her neck is pink, what you can see above the high collar of the lacy blouse.

"It sounds delightful." Zach lifts her hand and kisses the back of it.

Ugggh. It's one thing to see Zach working an actor at Desdemona's request, but this is another thing entirely. He's on his own time. I turn to open my door.

"Oh, and you, too, Kelsey!" Livia croons, as if realizing she ought to be nice to me, since I'm clearly Zach's underling, or niece or ward or something.

"Sure, thanks!" I don't turn back, but go through my door and shut it.

There is another burst of giggles from old-timey Livia, and I flop on the bed. I'll fetch my bigger suitcase in a minute, when the two of them aren't flirting in the hall.

The room is gorgeous, with wood insets and classic paintings and everything in shades of pale peach and cream. A window overlooks the street and the festival beyond it, mostly a line of tent-topped booths.

I listen as Zach walks around his room, the floors creaking.

I roll over to determine which door is the closet and which is the bathroom.

I can't tell from the layout.

Then one of the doors pops open, and Zachery's head appears. "Boo."

Dang it. I can't help but smile.

"Hey."

He sits on the end of the bed. "You all right?"

"Sure." I push myself to seating, staying well away from him.

"Nervous about possibly meeting your future husband? It's too hot for flannel, sadly. Will you recognize him without his signature look?"

I'm tempted to throw a pillow at him, but the room has a fair amount of china that might end up in the line of fire. "Of course."

"Will he be blond like you?" His grin is infectious. "Or brown-haired like me?"

"It feels like you're about to break out into song."

"What would be the perfect one?" He starts the first line of "Till There Was You."

Dang it. The man can sing. I can't help but feel my heart squeeze. "You old-soul romantic."

He leaps to his feet. "How do you solve a problem like Miss Kelsey?"

"Hey now!" And I'm up, too.

He launches us into a lively dance around the room as he starts the next song, insisting he's going to take me out on a "Surrey with the Fringe on Top."

And I let him lead me across the wood floor. I wonder why he never sang in anything, although of course, musicals are rare, and he got stuck in gross-out comedies. As the song continues, I realize I was jealous. Jealous of a woman in a green dress on a carriage.

And here Zach is, fixing it.

Maybe the other women get the flirts and the photos and the press and, probably, the sex.

But I get the best of Zachery Montgomery Carter. The pizza and movies. The coffee rushed down Hollywood Boulevard.

And the show tunes as I'm led into a dance in a Victorian mansion in Dillville, Colorado.

Chapter 18

Zachery Hates on a Meet-Cute

I shouldn't do that.

Sing to her. Dance with her.

I keep those parts of myself tamped down. Breaking them out feels wrong for someone who is a notorious rake. I generally aim to woo women just enough to keep them on my arm, but not so much that they mistake my attention for real feelings.

Those I keep to myself.

And yet, as I change into jeans and a short-sleeved button-down for the festival, I realize that behaving that way comes naturally with Kelsey.

I'm not trying to convince her to enjoy her time with me. We just do.

I don't have to overcompensate for my lack of recent IMDb entries. I can simply be Zachery Carter, employee to Desdemona Lovechild. Just like her.

It's easy.

But the next part won't be. Unlike the first time she forced a meet-cute at the beaver lodge, I'll be nearby to witness this one.

And I'll have to let her succeed.

If he's worthy of her.

No, that's not going to happen. Nobody is worthy.

But at least I can protect her from the bad ones. The creeps, the stalkers, the assholes, the entitled.

Ninety percent, I figure.

I have no doubt I fall into that category most of the time. But not with Kelsey.

I am at my best with her.

The bathroom door pops open. "Oh!" she says, her eyes wide. "I suppose we should be careful about this, since I end up right in your room."

I picture her tangled up with some Dillville buffoon, and me innocently walking in. I flash with an instant of rage.

"We better pretend the other door doesn't exist," I tell her, mostly as a warning to myself.

"Right." She comes into my room to sit on a chair and watch me fold clothes. "So how do we want to play this?"

"The festival?"

"It can't look like we're together or else I can't meet-cute with someone else."

"I could be your brother."

Her face scrunches in the cute Kelsey way. "I guess it's all about body language. But if I see a prospect, we should part ways."

"Acceptable. I'll make myself scarce."

"And don't be too obviously, well, you know, *you*." She snatches a ball cap out of my open suitcase. "Wear your celebrity disguise. Livia recognized you straight off. If we get a crowd of fawning women, I'll have to ditch you."

"Right." It's rare I get recognized these days, but once it happens, there's no way to return to anonymity. Even people who don't know who you are get caught up in the rush of meeting someone who might have been famous at one point. I tug the Lakers hat low on my brow.

She frowns. "Do you have any other hats? You're telegraphing we're from California."

"I do." I shuck the Lakers hat and pull out a nondescript black one. "Better?"

"Definitely. Sunglasses?"

She wants me to go full celebrity incognito. It's fine. My main pair are in the car, but I have a spare. I dig around the side wall of the bag until I find the case.

I slip them on. "Now am I good?"

She nods. "With the change of clothes, maybe Livia won't out you instantly."

"If we see her, you can scoot away so she doesn't immediately make the connection."

Kelsey elbows me. "And I'm conveniently out of the picture so you can make *your* connection."

I want to point out that this would defeat the purpose of her moving aside, but I let it go. Kelsey logic is not to be corrected. In the end, she's always right.

But she's wrong about me wanting to make a connection with Livia. Dallying with anyone in this small town is wrong on about sixty-five levels. The most important of which is, I can't be distracted if Kelsey needs me.

It's why I'm here.

I hold out my elbow, and Kelsey takes it. She's wearing the yellow dress and tennis shoes and looks like purest sunshine. The bow in her hair is an innocent touch.

Dillville is going to eat her up.

It's my job to make sure nobody eats her alive.

We head down the stairs together. The front door automatically locks behind us, so we cross the street and enter the festival grounds. As we approach, she lets go of me to start our brotherly charade.

Booths are set up, mostly temporary pavilions you can pick up at a sporting goods store. A few have added rustic details, like a rough-hewn wood table or wrapping the metal poles with fabric.

It's green as far as the eye can see, with plenty of pickles. There are cartoon ones, inflatables, and others constructed from papier-mâché. Most of the workers at the booths are dressed head to toe in green and white, and some wear period costumes, like Livia.

The festival surrounds the playscape at the center of the park, with the line of booths backed by trees. It moves on to the baseball field adjacent to the park, and the concession stand seems to be the source of power for a temporary stage with a green awning.

A barbershop quartet is in the process of testing the sound. They all wear round flat-topped hats with striped shirts. Green, of course.

"This is absolutely delightful," Kelsey says, her hands clasped together. She looks like Sandy from *Grease* with her big bow pulling back her bright hair. And all that yellow. Even the white shoes. I wonder if she did it on purpose.

But I don't ask.

"It looks early to scout a future husband." There's precious little in terms of a crowd yet. Most of the people are setting up to work.

"He could be serving."

"Hard to take a stroll with him, then."

She frowns. "True. But I'll keep my options open."

"What flavor of meet-cute are you after?"

"I don't think I want to trip and fall again." Her cheeks pink up.

"What does that leave? There's no elevator. We decided the confrontation one was risky."

She studies her surroundings. "There was picking up the wrong order. That would be easy here if he's in line to get something. I could order right behind him, and then pick up his instead of mine."

"That sounds adorable." I hate it already.

"There's also getting rescued." She points at the midway games, throwing darts at balloons, knocking over pins, and other feats of skill that are likely rigged.

"Are you going to put yourself in the line of the squirt gun?" One of the games is a race where you move your horse by squirting water into a target.

"No, just by losing and being sad about it. See if someone will step right up and win for me."

"That one seems unlikely."

She clasps both hands together next to her cheek and flutters her eyelashes.

"That's good," I admit.

"See?" She drops the act.

"We've watched entirely too many romantic movies."

She laughs. "We have."

We walk the festival for a good hour, eating sandwiches on pickle bread—I wanted to call it "dill dough," but Kelsey read my mind and warned me that I better not dare start gossip. We drink sweetened pickle juice and try pickle fudge.

But nobody seems quite right. Too young. Too old. Too married.

I'm pleased, actually.

Then both of us see him at the same time. Kelsey halts walking.

He's buying a paper bag of pickle popcorn from a vendor. His sandy hair falls near his eye. He has a decent build and dresses well enough in jeans and a collared shirt.

And no ring. He has a younger girl with him who is clearly his sister. She takes the popcorn from him and runs off. He laughs and shakes his head.

"He loves his baby sister," Kelsey says, her voice all breathy.

He buys a second bag of popcorn, all smiles with the elderly lady packing it. She blushes as she gives it to him.

So, the women like him.

Damn it.

The bag is spilling over with popcorn, a few kernels falling to the grass.

"I've got it," Kelsey says. "You're an actor. Follow my lead."

Ooookay.

She takes off across the grass, gesturing with her hands. "Zach, don't run off with your girlfriend before I find Dad—OOF!"

She runs smack into Popcorn Boy, knocking a huge amount of the contents of his bag onto the grass.

"Oh, no!" She turns to him. "I'm so sorry! I spilled your popcorn!" She looks up at him with pleading eyes, begging for forgiveness, and I swear to God she missed her calling on the screen.

But I follow her lead. "Way to go, sis. I'm late. I'll find you in a bit." And I take off, going only so far as a few booths before pausing and pretending to answer my phone.

"It's okay," Popcorn Boy says. "There was more than I expected in there anyway."

"Can I buy you some more? I feel terrible."

Watching her doe eyes makes me melt. Popcorn Boy is riveted. He better be.

"It's fine." He tilts his head. "Did your brother ditch you?"

"Yeah. It's fine. We're on a family trip. I'm not from here."

"Oh? Where are you from?"

"Alabama, originally. You grow up here?"

Damn, that girl can manage a segue.

"Not quite here. Durango. But it's close."

"So you're visiting, too?"

He grins at her, and I have to force myself to unclench my jaw.

"I am. My family is here as well. I guess our two crews had the same idea."

"I guess so." She looks at the popcorn. "I had the pickle fudge. Not my thing. How's the popcorn?"

"I haven't tried it. You want to?" He holds out the half-empty bag.

She huffs. "I wasn't born yesterday. This could be terrible. We'll take the plunge at the same time." Her eyes sparkle as she looks at him. That's not faking. She likes him so far.

I can't watch.

I walk farther down, where they're still in my field of vision but I can't hear their every word.

This job sucks.

Chapter 19

KELSEY'S DREAM IN FOUR-PART HARMONY

I notice Zachery giving me space as the hot young man from Durango and I simultaneously try the dill-flavored popcorn.

"Oh!" I cover my mouth with my hand. "It's really salty!"

He crunches his. "Mine's not. Maybe they're inconsistent with the flavoring." He holds the packet. "Try again?"

My mouth is flooded with salt and dill. I sputter and cough. "No, I think I need something to drink!"

"There's a soda fountain a little way down."

And just like that, we're walking side by side through the fair.

"I'm Simon," he says. "I think the popcorn is a bust." He chucks the bag into a bin as we pass.

"I'm Kelsey. And you couldn't have known I was going to get a salt assault." My mouth is starting to calm down.

He laughs. "Salt assault. Are all the women from Alabama as clever as you?"

I preen at the compliment, swishing my skirt as I walk. This is going way better than Pitchfork Lodge.

EXT. PICKLE FESTIVAL—DAY

KELSEY, 25, in a sunny yellow dress complete with bow, walks along a row of food booths with her new beau, SIMON, 25.

They are clearly hitting it off, laughing at the sights as they plan the rest of their evening together.

They arrive at a green-and-white malt shop tent where THREE WORKERS, all in fake mustaches, work a soda machine and several blenders.

It's happening!

Simon points to the hand-lettered sign over the counter. "They have milkshakes, Italian ices, and root beer floats."

"Ooooh. I want one of everything."

He laughs. "Anything the lady desires."

We order a chocolate milkshake, a raspberry Italian ice, and a root beer float, each with two straws. Small round tables with stools are scattered in the grass near the tent, so we choose one.

"Which first?" Simon asks. "Are you strategic and make sure you go from least sweet to more, or weakest flavor to strongest?"

I pull all three tall paper cups near me and arrange them so my straws are together. "I like to live dangerously." I sip from all three at once.

If flavor could be a cacophony, this would be it. I pull back. "Whoa. That was a lot!"

"Now I have to try it." He gathers his three straws. His face contorts as he takes in a drink. "No, no, no."

"I guess we're even then," I tell him. "Your salt assault and my too-sweet treat."

"So we are."

Our eyes meet over the cups. A gentle breeze lifts the edges of his sandy hair. His eyes are hazel.

Dang. This works. The whole thing works! Meet-cute. Banter. Classic romantic date with an old-fashioned feel.

I feel a tug, like this is how adult dating is supposed to be. Not the awkward teen melodrama. Or the look-at-me-I'm-important Hollywood version.

It's nice.

"Where are you staying?" Simon asks.

"Here in Dillville." Simon seems like a dream, but I know better than to point out that my B and B is across the street.

"We drove down for the evening."

"Is Durango far?"

"Just over an hour. Practically nothing in Colorado time."

I almost quip that this might get you five miles in LA traffic, but remember I'm not from California on this trip. Small town all the way.

Zachery walks along the line of booths, still at a good distance. I recognize his stance, his energy, even in his hat and shades. A young woman leans over her counter, holding up a ball for him to knock over pins. She's into him.

I suppress my flash of annoyance and focus on Simon. "I grew up on a dairy farm that was miles from anything. I understand Colorado time."

"I bet you do."

We settle on me drinking the milkshake, and Simon tackling the root beer float. The Italian ice is good, but doesn't fit. I'm amused that he indulged me.

"Was the popcorn the worst thing you've had here?" Simon asks.

"So far. But there's a booth with chocolate-covered pickles that might give that popcorn a run for its money."

He scrunches his nose in the cutest way possible. "I think I might skip that one."

"Same."

We sip our drinks, watching the people go by.

"You ever make up stories about strangers to pass the time?" he asks.

"Do I?" I can't believe he's asked this. "All the time!"

He leans in. "What about that elderly woman there? She looks fit to be tied with the man buying pickle lemonade from her."

I glance at the stand. "Oh, I bet they were in love in high school."

"But he ended up dating her older sister," Simon adds.

"And when they broke up, she thought she would finally get her chance."

"But he up and married a girl from another town!"

We both erupt into laughter.

"You're good," I tell him. And I mean it.

"So are you."

We grin foolishly at each other. I sip my milkshake and realize when it makes a slurping sound that I'm done.

"The quartet is about to sing," he says. "You want to go listen?"

"You bet I do!" We drop our cups into the trash and head toward the stage. We pass Zachery at his booth, but he doesn't turn to look at us.

Simon waits until we've passed to say, "Looks like someone is trying to tempt your brother away from his girlfriend."

"Figures." I decide not to elaborate, as I don't want to perpetuate the story that he's my brother. This is going to bite me in the butt later.

I did not think this through. Zachery's words from our rom-com watch party come back to haunt me: *You really want to start a lifelong commitment on a lie?*

I have to fix this. "Hey, by the way, Zach and I call each other sis and bro, but we're not technically brother and sister. He watches out for me, you know, like a brother."

"Okay. That's cool."

My relief is intense. I've fixed my mistake. I won't do anything like that again.

And maybe, if this goes well, I won't have to.

We arrive at the stage. A smattering of people sit on the risers to wait. We take a spot at the end of a row.

"Folks, we'll get started in a moment," one of the men says, clearly the baritone based on his voice.

Simon props a foot on the bench in front of us, and I realize I haven't assessed his outfit. It didn't even occur to me.

This is good. Maybe I'm already starting to shed my LA ways.

But the back of my head does the calculation. *Old Navy shirt, $25. Levi's 501 jeans, $55. Vans, $60.* He's going to spend more on food and drinks today than he did his clothes.

Stop it, Kelsey. Just stop. Be Alabama. Not California. Your dress was $25 at a Target in Birmingham circa 2018.

You can take the girl out of Hollywood, but it's sure hard to take the Hollywood out of the girl.

Even so, I'm determined.

The shortest man of the four, somewhere in his midfifties, steps up. Instead of talking, he sings the words, "Are you ready?" His voice is higher than I expected as he holds out the last syllable.

More people come forward to sit down.

The second man arrives and adds his lower voice to the first. "Are you ready?"

Then the third walks to his mike, his sound even lower. "Are you ready?"

The last man is heavyset, his green vest stretching over a mint-striped shirt. His voice is incredibly low, and when he adds his deep "Are you ready?" the crowd starts to cheer.

They launch straight into a quick-tempo rendition of "Let Me Call You Sweetheart."

Simon looks over at me with a huge smile, and we join in as the audience starts to sway in their seats. The voices resonate deep in my chest.

I feel happy.

It's about time.

Chapter 20

ZACHERY'S SORDID PICTURE PAST

As the sun starts to go down over Dillville's damn Dillfest, I pull off my sunglasses. It looks ridiculous to keep wearing them, and besides, Kelsey is well handled.

In LA, getting recognized is no big deal. The paparazzi aren't that interested in me unless I'm gussied up at a premiere with some rising star on my arm. Even if they spot me out alone, they only bother to take a couple of perfunctory photos that aren't used anywhere, just stored in case I die unexpectedly or get embroiled in a scandal.

Here in Dillville, I go about my business for another good half hour before anyone does a double take. As I'm considering buying a beer, a man breaks out his phone, not to take a picture, not yet anyway, but to pull up my name on Google. I see him doing it.

No one else pays me any mind as I stride to the far end of the booths in hopes that he doesn't make the connection. I end up back at the stage, currently empty, although quite a few people linger on the risers to wait on the next act.

Kelsey and her *fella* were here earlier, and I made sure she was all right. So far, no red flags. They were having a toe-tapping good time.

Then I hear my name. "Zachery? Zachery Carter?"

I pull out my phone, pretending to be absorbed in something and not listening.

But it's not the random guy looking me up. It's Livia from the bed-and-breakfast. She hurries forward, the plume bobbing on her hat, holding her long skirt up to keep it out of the way.

She's a picture in her vintage outfit, that's for sure. She sits next to me. "You okay?"

I don't get a chance to answer. A man leans down between us. "Livia, did you call this man Zachery Carter? Like Zachery Carter from that comedy?" He snaps his fingers, trying to recall the title.

I don't help him.

"No relation," I say, but Livia bumps my arm.

"Of course it's him, Sam. He's staying at my bed-and-breakfast."

"You don't say." His eyes flash with recognition. "*Beer Junket Bingo*! I loved that movie. You were so great in it. That part where you farted in that old lady's face when she got a bingo on G-23! Classic." He erupts into laughter.

Several other people surround us. "I have a G-23 T-shirt somewhere," another man says. "My wife bought it for me to wear to bingo. Some of us still laugh when they call G-23."

Great. My worst comic moments are coming back to haunt me. I personally burned all my G-23 memorabilia, but it sold hard and fast ten years ago. The studio made a fortune in merch. And so did I. This elderly gentleman's wife helped buy my house.

Livia leans in. "I haven't seen it." She seems to understand that I really don't like reminiscing about the less savory moments of my old career.

But the men are on a roll. "Remember when ol' Zach here pisses in the fountain in the town square, and the mayor's wife ends up getting a picture of his schlong and hangs it in her bedroom to look at when she—"

I stand up. "Excuse me, gentlemen. I was going to escort Livia to the games. You may recall I was rubbish at pitching a ball."

One of the men slaps his knee. "That's right! You had to throw the opening pitch in that other movie—what was it? And it only went halfway, and the whole crowd tried to keep the cheer going as it slowly rolled across the field."

The original man wipes his eyes. "I think of that every time my son Homer tries to pitch in his Little League."

Yeah, this is a laugh a minute. I hold out my arm to Livia. "Shall we?"

She is perfectly willing to go. "Yes, let's."

We leave the men behind.

"Does that happen a lot?" Livia asks.

"Being the butt of old men's jokes?"

"No, getting recognized as famous."

I shrug. "Not as much as it used to."

We turn down the main row of booths. I scan for Kelsey, but I don't spot her bit of sunshine anywhere.

"Where is your cart and horse?" I ask.

"They were done for the day. They're getting a well-deserved rest." She gestures vaguely in the direction of her house.

"Good for them."

"I apologize that I'm not up to date on your career. Have you done anything recently?"

"No, I retired years ago." I sometimes say something more amusingly self-deprecating, like, "Nobody seems to need their fountain filled," but I'm not up for it tonight.

And where is Kelsey?

"That must be nice," Livia says. "How do you spend your time these days?"

"I work in casting. We help up-and-coming actors get their footing." I look between every tent as we pass. Still nothing.

"That's lovely. They must be so grateful to have someone of your stature assisting their career."

If only.

We walk far enough that we approach the street that borders the park, Livia's bed-and-breakfast sitting grandly on the other side.

"Are you wanting to head back to the house?" she asks.

"Oh, no. I was looking for Kelsey."

"Oh." Her voice drops. "Are you two . . ."

"No, no," I say quickly, in case Popcorn Boy is local and I might start gossip. "We work together."

"Are you auditioning people on the road?" Her voice catches with excitement, as if she might be on the verge of getting discovered herself.

"Something like that. We're casting a new movie."

"Well, I did a fair amount of theater in high school."

And here we go.

We reach the street, and I'm not sure where to look. "The last time I spotted her, she was at the stage, but we just left there and walked the entire length of the festival."

"I haven't seen her." She lets go of my arm. "Do you need to find her?"

Dang it. "I think I do. I'll catch up with you later?"

Her smile returns. "I'll make some coffee. Come downstairs if you want some."

I hear the invitation in her voice. "Thank you, Livia."

I turn on my heel, pulling out my phone. I swiftly text Kelsey.

Are you still at the fair?

I walk the full length of the booths another time, phone in my hand, willing her to respond.

A hundred images go through my mind. Kelsey, in the throes of a passionate embrace behind the cotton candy tent. Kelsey, already running off to some white chapel in the boonies, ready to prove the fortune teller wrong.

The fortune teller I paid.

Damn it.

Or worse, Kelsey getting abducted by some popcorn psychopath.

I can't take it a minute more, so I do something I know I shouldn't. I put through a call.

I think it's going to roll to voicemail, but then I hear Kelsey's shaky voice. My entire body goes on red alert.

"Hey, Zach. You need me for something?" The trembling makes me shake with rage.

"Yeah, it's time to go. Where are you?"

"I, uh, okay." There's a muffled sound. "I'm going to have to go."

I hear that motherfucker's voice, saying something like, "You sure?"

But I also hear something else. Singing. They're near the stage.

I'm relieved she's close enough that I can get to her. I break out into a run toward the baseball field.

"Maybe a while longer?" she says, and that sounds enough like a cry for help that I push into a full-on sprint.

I pass the risers near the stage, hearing the faint delay of what is live and what is passing through the phone. "Are you on the field?"

"Close," she says.

I halt on the far side of the concession stand. The field is black, the metal stands empty.

Then I see the smallest glint of light.

Her cell phone.

They're underneath the farthest set of bleachers. I spot the shadows and a hint of her yellow dress in the dark.

If he's laid a hand on her, I will kill him.

The shortest distance isn't around the field but across it. I don't know where the entrance is, probably by each dugout, but I'm in a hurry. I quickly scale the fence and drop into the dirt of the field.

I race across it, scale the fence again, and in seconds I'm underneath the bleachers and pulling Kelsey behind me.

"What the fuck is going on here?" I demand.

"Nothing," Popcorn Asshat says. "She just started crying."

"Come on, Kelsey," I say.

"Hey," he says. "I'm trying to help."

Hardly. My voice is a roar. "You've done enough."

"Dude, she told me you're not her brother." He takes a step toward me, and I don't have anything else to say. I come in swinging, and my fist hits his chin with a satisfying crunch.

He stumbles back. "What the hell, you piece of shit!"

I'm ready to hit him again, but Kelsey takes my arm. "Let's go."

She folds into me, and I pick her up. I don't have to go the fast way now, so I simply carry her through the packed parking lot.

We dart between cars until we reach the street.

"I can walk," she says. "Let me walk."

I set her down, glancing behind to make sure nobody followed us. There are only a few families lugging tired kids out of the fair.

We're quiet until we reach the bed-and-breakfast.

"You want to talk about it?" I ask her.

"I will. Let's go to your room."

But I swear, as we go hand in hand up the stairs, that if he's done even one-fifth of what I think he has, I will kill him.

Chapter 21

KELSEY ROUNDS THE BASES

I sit on the end of Zachery's blue bed, surrounded by pretty wallpaper and lace, like the setting of an old-fashioned story. *Pride and Prejudice*, maybe. Or *The Age of Innocence*.

It fits the trope. Me, trying to find my Hallmark husband. So did the popcorn meet-cute. The barbershop quartet. We got milkshakes, for Pete's sake.

Then I went off script.

Zachery paces the room like a caged lion, and I know I need to correct his misperception about what went down with Simon.

"I'm okay, Zach."

He stops walking to look at me. "What happened?"

And there it is.

"Do I have to talk about it?" My voice is a mouse squeak.

He frowns at that and sits next to me. "Of course not. I just need to know if I should assemble an angry mob."

"It does seem like a tar-and-feather kind of town."

His body relaxes, his spine less of a tension rod. "Did he hurt you? Did something happen?"

I shake my head. "No. I mean, we made out a little." I press my hand to my chest to steady my breath. I have to say it. My next words tumble out in a rush. "I might have lost my panties in the grass beneath the bleachers."

Zach stands straight up, like he's been jerked by a string. "Your what?"

I stand up next to him. "I know. I blew it. Nobody drops their underwear within two hours of a meet-cute. Not even Anastasia Steele."

"Anastasia?"

"*Fifty Shades.* Look, I know that was too fast. I got caught up in the moment. I did it all wrong."

"You? Or him?" Zachery goes still right in the middle of pushing his hair off his forehead.

I put on my best pleading look. "Can we forget about Simon? That deal is done, between you punching him and me . . . I don't know."

Zachery sighs and resumes his place at my side. "Will you tell me what's wrong?"

"Okay." I kick off my shoes and unclip the bow from my hair. Might as well get comfortable as I confess my crimes against love stories everywhere.

Zach follows suit, leaving his two-toned loafers on the floor.

We lie sideways on the bed, facing each other, both propped up on our elbows like we're best girlfriends at a sleepover.

"We did lots of normal date things. Got milkshakes, listened to the band, played some of the games." I hold out my wrist, which is encircled with a green plastic bracelet. "He won this at the ring toss."

Zach grunts.

"We were holding hands, and it was nice, you know? Then he kissed me by the train the kids were riding."

Zach's lips twitch, and he seems angry still, but I keep going.

"I made a joke about how we were around the little kids, and he asked if I wanted to go someplace quieter. I said I did."

I snap my fingers. "That's where I went wrong. Right there. I should have said no. Stuck to the script. Nobody loses their panties on the first date when it's true love."

"I'm not sure it was true—"

I'm not listening. "I did the wrong bases!" I can see it. "Normally there are first, second, and third in dating. The kiss. The boobs. You know! But in Hallmark movies, the bases are different."

"Kelsey, are you all right?"

I can't break my train of thought. "I think first base is probably the wiping-flour-off-the-cheek moment. You know, the touch that's forced by circumstance, then becomes a spark."

"Like when you held his hand." Zachery's voice has a growl to it.

"No, that was on purpose. More like if I had brushed popcorn kernels off his shirt. Dang, I should have done that."

"What's second base?"

"The almost-kiss. Where you're leaning in, but someone comes in or the phone rings or a horn blares."

"Right."

"And third base is when you actually kiss. But that's nearly at the end. When you've already decided this person is the one."

"So then straight to the home run?"

"No. You fade to black."

"You were definitely in blackness."

I sigh. I was. I used Hollywood bases. Meet. Hook up. Ghost. I resist the urge to get up and pace. We're still facing each other on the bed. "So, we walked around the baseball field in the dark. We kissed. We got caught up in the moment."

Zachery's face is a mask, pure relaxed nothingness. I have no idea what he's thinking of me.

"The panties came off, but then it happened." I can't say anything else. This is Zach. He's a friend, but he's also a man. And, gosh. I can't do it.

But Zach's eyes have narrowed. He's tense again. He thinks something terrible went down. "*What* happened?"

When I don't answer, his tone is tight. "Tell me before I find him and bash his face in properly."

"He didn't do anything wrong," I say quickly. "It's like my girl parts locked up or something. Batten the hatches! Bring down the gates! Vacuum seal!" I cringe at that last one. My mouth gets ahead of my brain sometimes.

Now Zach's eyebrows have drawn together. "So, you didn't end up doing anything?"

"No! It was like, I'm ready, let's do this thing. But my body was like—heck no!" I gasp. "Wait. What if this is what the fortune teller knew! I was drying up! Losing my . . . oh, whatever!" I collapse face down on the bed. This is too much.

Too embarrassing.

This whole idea was dumb.

His warm hand lies firmly on my back. "I don't think any of that is true. You had a negative encounter last night in Pitchfork, and you were simply bracing yourself for another one."

I have no answer for that.

He moves my hair to one side, off my neck. "You'll be all right, Kelsey."

I shift my face so I can talk again. "Do you think this trip was a dumb idea?"

His expressionless mask goes back on.

"You do. God!" I turn my face back to the bedspread so I don't have to see him.

"Kelsey, hey." His fingers find my chin and turn my face to him. "I don't think anything you do is dumb. It's part of the process for you."

"What do you mean?"

"You've been struggling with the men you've had access to. They weren't right for you. You needed to get out there, try something else. This is a new scene. It's probably still the wrong scene, but you're trying."

"But what if I'm not going to get any better? What if I meet a great guy, and my vagina is a steel trap?"

I see him working very hard not to laugh.

"Your vagina is not a steel trap."

"I think it is!"

"It worked before."

"Not in years!" Oh, I didn't mean to admit that.

His eyebrow lifts. "Years?"

Might as well put it out there. "Not since I started working for Desdemona. Life got too intense. I only met these jerks, all full of evil ambition."

His hand returns to my back, applying smooth, even pressure. "It will work for the right person."

"But what if it doesn't?"

"It will."

"I don't know that." But maybe I do. Because everything is feeling warm and happy since Zachery put his hands on me. "Hold up."

"What now?" Zachery asks.

I turn back on my face. "Do that thing with my hair again."

He laughs lightly, but he moves all the loose strands off my neck. My whole body shivers.

I turn my face. "Is that a good sign?"

"Sure."

"Do more."

"Like . . . what?"

"Just the back thing."

His hand applies gentle pressure.

I melt into the bed. It's all perfect. All good.

Maybe Zach is right. Maybe it was about Simon being the wrong guy. Grant being wrong.

But I need to know. After tonight's disaster, if something goes wrong again, I'll fall apart. I need a burner boyfriend. Someone to test this out on. Someone who doesn't make me turn into a Venus flytrap.

Like Zachery.

Obviously, I like him fine.

He's a player. He understands transactional encounters. He does them all the time.

That's it.

I can start again tomorrow with the proper rom-com bases.

But today, I can make sure I'm really ready by using Hollywood time.

And who better than one of the best Romeos in LA?

I sit up and face him. "Zachery Montgomery Carter, will you have sex with me?"

Chapter 22

ZACHERY UNLOCKS THE JELLY JAR

My brain goes offline for a second.

Did I hear what I think I heard?

My hands are still warm from touching her, which was physically painful, given the intensity of emotions I've gone through since we stepped foot in that damn festival.

She sits in front of me in a pool of gold dress, her loose hair in wild disarray.

Kelsey. My best friend. My beautiful, sweet partner in work crime.

Her gaze doesn't falter. She's waiting on an answer to a question I can barely comprehend. All the possibilities lay in front of me like a chessboard of Kelseys, my fantasies about her on the same plane as this one reality.

"Just once," she says, as if rebutting the arguments in my head. "No strings. Like your Desdemona dates. You do have sex with them at least sometimes, right?"

I nod absently, the chessboard overloaded with images of other women, ghosts of my sexual past.

"I don't deserve you," I manage to get out.

This breaks her gaze. "Of course you do. I know you like to drift, but think of me as one of your red-carpet girls, and we'll never speak of it again."

She takes my hand, and it's startlingly warm, as if my body has gone arctic.

"We'll be okay, Zach. It might not work. And if it doesn't, I'll pack up and go find a therapist. Figure things out. But when you touched me, I felt different. I think it will work. Just let me see. Maybe I'm like a jelly jar that's been closed too long. You know how the sugar makes a seal? And it's impossible to open it unless you warm it up under a hot tap?"

"Jelly jar?" My comprehension is miles behind her words.

"I'm a jelly jar and you're the hot water." She scoots closer. "We're two consenting adults. Let's do this."

I'm all wrong for her. A joke. A has-been.

But when I look in her eyes, I know damn well I'm not going to turn her down. This is her leaping-off point. Tomorrow, she'll search in earnest for what she's looking for.

But this is tonight.

She turns around and lifts the length of her hair. "Unzip me."

When I don't reach for her dress, she looks over her shoulder. "Are you saying no? You won't do this? I'm not a virgin, Zach. It's just an act. I'm trying to figure this out with someone I trust."

She's right. She trusts me. I trust her. Otherwise, she'll be afraid. She'll try with someone who could hurt her. Or maybe she'll stop trying at all. This might be what I've been seeing all this time. Her failure to try.

It's what led me to pay that fortune teller.

This is apparently another step in my original plan.

She needs me to play the rake, the playboy, the seducer.

And I will. It's my best role, because it's who I am.

I am not for her, not long-term.

But I can be this.

I reach for the zipper.

A long, lean back is revealed in slow inches. I've seen precious little of this part of her.

As the dress separates, I take in the pale expanse of her skin, the smooth transition from neck to shoulders. The gentle ridges of her spine.

I reach out to touch them, my fingers bumping down until they reach the hook of her bra. Displeased with the interruption of my path, I quickly release it and continue the journey down.

The zipper ends below her waist, but there's nothing else there.

That's right. She left her panties beneath the bleachers at the festival. My anger flares at how that boy mishandled someone so exquisite.

Kelsey is perfect.

She sighs as my hands continue moving across her back, like I did before, but now on her naked skin. I forget her question. I don't think about the wisdom of this choice, or the spotty logic of her request.

I don't know how far I'll take it or if it'll even make sense.

In this moment, there's only her skin, warm and unbroken, and new.

I scoot closer, sliding the dress off her shoulders, so I can see all of her back. The fabric falls to her waist, and I continue my exploration.

My thumbs press into the creases on either side of her spine, eliciting a groan of pleasure from Kelsey.

The sound hits my gut, spreading heat through me.

We haven't done anything yet. We can stop here. A friendly back rub between friends.

And yet, I don't stop. I move closer, increasing my pressure, my hands massaging the tension from her muscles.

I shift her hair to one side, and the tempting skin of her neck is right there, soft and warm. I press my lips to it.

Her breath catches. I make a line of kisses along her bare shoulder. I want to touch all of her.

There's a point of no return, and I'm about to streak by it.

My hands continue their journey around the sides of her waist and to the front. I slip beneath her arms and flatten my palms across her belly.

Another checkpoint. Another gate.

I lean close to her ear. "How are you feeling?"

"Good," she breathes. "Very good."

Her voice is silken, and her words speak straight to my groin. I know what to say. I'm deep in my role.

"I'm going to hold your naked breasts in my hands. Is that what you want?"

"Yes."

I take my time, sliding up her ribs, feeling her catch her breath and hold it in anticipation. Then she's in my hands, heavy and warm.

Her head falls back on my shoulder. I can see her, exposed to me, those beautiful parts of her that have been off limits.

Now mine.

I'm doing this, to her.

She has said just one time, so I will not rush. I take in every detail, the blush across her chest. The deep swell as I press this softness high. The tight, deep-pink nipples.

I run my thumbs across them, and she sucks in another breath. Her hands hold on to the rumpled folds of her dress, bunched up on her lap.

I take my time, molding her to my palms. She rocks against me in a slow, undulating motion that sends fire licking through me.

The next gate appears, where I want to go next. "I'm going to take this dress off you," I say. "Is that what you want?"

"Yes."

I let go of her breasts and tug the dress and bra down her arms. I lift her off the bed and turn her around to stand between my knees.

The dress falls in a whisper. With no panties, she has nothing left.

She watches me look at her, bare feet on the rug, all skin before me.

"You're a vision," I tell her, and the pink across her chest flushes deeper. I reach for her hand. "Sit on my lap." My tone is firm. No one denies me at this stage. They don't want to.

And Kelsey does exactly as I say, fitting her knees on either side of my thighs, which spreads her wide. I drag her closer.

"I'm going to kiss you," I tell her. "I'll start with your mouth, then move down your body. I have no intention of stopping anywhere. My tongue will go inside you until you orgasm. Is that what you want?"

She squirms lightly on my lap. "Yes."

I cup her chin. Her gaze drops to my lips. She's waiting.

I've never kissed Kelsey. I never thought I would.

But tonight, I'll do that and much more.

I have a naked Kelsey on my lap, and I'm going to have her however I like.

It's glorious and painful. This will have to be enough. Kelsey has a plan. I won't keep her from it. She is not for me.

But tonight, she is *all* for me.

Chapter 23

Kelsey Goes Under

I'm completely lost in Zachery, and he's about to kiss me.

I've never felt like this. The desire cuts so deep that I feel infinite, like there's a chasm only he can fill.

I presumed that he would be masterful. That's why he was the perfect person to ask. Experienced. Careful. Considerate.

I wasn't prepared for the demands. The instructions. His expectation that I'll comply.

But I will. Oh, yes, I will.

He takes ages to kiss me. His chocolate eyes are on me, meeting my gaze, focusing on my lips as he runs a thumb over them.

They part for him without a request. I have a feeling the rest of me will, too.

My skin tingles everywhere. The tops of my ears, which he brushed when he pushed back my hair. My breasts, which he handled so delicately only a moment ago. My mouth, where he continues his exploration.

My thighs, which are bare against his khaki pants.

I'm spread wide over his lap, and the cool air hits parts of me that ache for what we're about to do. It seems impossible that nothing worked a short time ago.

He keeps looking at me like I'm a perfect gift, his finger on my collarbone. He brushes against my skin with the back of his hand, letting his knuckles bump across a nipple.

"Exquisite," he says.

I'm so ready to be kissed, to be devoured.

But he's in no hurry. He shifts my hair completely behind my shoulders so nothing can be hidden from his hungry gaze.

Then, and only then, does his hand cup the back of my head, and at last, he draws my face to him.

His lips are gentle, only the softest brush. I shiver, overwhelmed by the light touch and the need for more.

But he doesn't allow me to press in. He holds me where he wants me, the feathery kiss achingly slow. I tingle from my eyebrows to my ankles.

It goes on and on before he finally pulls me closer. My bare chest meets his cool, smooth shirt. His lips claim my mouth with pressure and heat. His tongue finds mine, and I feel like I'm falling into him.

I'm not the chasm. It's him, an abyss where I can lose myself, let go. I can fall and fall.

His face is smooth, and I lift my hand to his cheek. He must have shaved before we went to the fair. The scent of his layered colognes envelops me. There is nothing else but his face, his mouth, his tongue, the smooth shirt, and his hand on my neck.

Then I really am falling. He turns us, laying me back on the cool blue bedspread. It smells of fabric softener, a spring breeze.

The scent of him and the bedding commingle and I feel high, like I'm on a cloud. I want to rush forward, for him to be inside me, but I also want to hover, suspended in this sharp anticipation.

My hair spreads across the pillow. Zachery kneels over me, his mouth still on mine. But his hands move, back to a breast, encircling it as though his fingers were designed to cup it just like this.

Then his hand moves down, his thumb making its way to the hollow at the side of my waist.

I shiver again.

He breaks the kiss, moving down my jaw to my neck.

Then lower, his other hand reverently holding a breast in place for his mouth to take in.

My back arches. I'm utterly lost in him, in this moment. There is nothing else. No comparing this feeling to Simon beneath the bleachers. Or any other time that came before.

He takes his time. His exploration is thorough. Liquid heat pools between my thighs, anxious for him to reach it.

His hair tickles my belly as he makes his way down. It's achingly slow, and I resist the urge to grab his head and shove him there.

He reaches my belly button and lightly nips the skin below it. There would have been a hairline there, but I got rid of it all this morning in the hotel.

That feels like a lifetime ago.

"Spread your legs," he demands, and I instantly comply, forcing my knees wide.

It's intoxicating, seeing his dark head down low, his brown eyes gazing up at me.

He locks his attention on my face as his tongue makes its first long, leisurely lick.

My head kicks back, my eyes closed. Tremors dart through me, making my legs shake and my belly quiver.

But Zachery is only getting started. He grasps both thighs and spreads me more, diving more deeply inside.

I lose all sense of space and time, riding the waves of pleasure. My body can't stop responding, tightening, letting go, like small orgasms leading to something bigger.

"Zachery!" I cry when he adds fingers to his tongue.

And then a wave hits me like the ocean slamming into my back. I'm taken under, the world muffled, like I've fallen into the chasm I first sensed when we began.

My body is pure light, and the jagged bolts of energy take over. Everything in me pulses with the joy of it. Tears leak from my eyes.

It feels unending, the emotion, the pleasure, the intensity.

Then slowly, I recognize the feel of his hair again. Then the pressure of his head against my thigh. Then his breath, now on my skin, and his fingers, slowly and carefully withdrawing from my body.

And I cry, dark, jagged gulps of sorrow. What was that? Is this what an orgasm is supposed to be like?

I've never felt anything like that before.

Zachery slides into place beside me, cradling my head against his chest. I hold on to him like he's the only refuge in the storm.

I don't know why I'm crying, but something has cracked inside me. Love. Lust. Pain. Beauty. It's all jumbled.

"Fix it," I gasp against his cheek. "Be inside me. I want you in me."

He nods, and I help him out of his shirt and unfasten the pants he still wears.

I look with wonder at his body, the sculpted abs and hard-planed stomach.

He's stiffly at attention, and I hold him in both hands, filled with awe at this part of him that has never been a concern in all the years we've been friends.

And, oh, how I want it.

I swear I won't regret it.

Chapter 24

Zachery Glimpses the Infinite

There is a voice, a small one, but present nonetheless, that says this is a bad idea.

Kelsey busies herself with the condom, unrolling it down me with a slowness that is pure torture. I sit on the edge of the bed, watching her hands move along my length.

She's a goddess, her makeup smudged, her hair pure chaos. I can't stop staring at her, the miles of golden skin, her perfect pink nipples. She's shaved bare, and I'm obsessed. I want to live there.

I shouldn't even visit.

When I hesitate, she doesn't wait, but throws a leg over me, and in moments, I'm inside her.

The heat of her envelops me, and I forget whatever bothered me before. She's mine. This gorgeous vixen-creature is mine.

She circles her arms around my neck, shifting up and down, setting a languid pace that makes my blood pound in my veins.

Hell no. I'm done with slow. I grasp her hips and work with her as she moves, thrusting into her like a man possessed.

Her breathing comes fast, in sharp, ragged puffs against my cheek. Mine isn't any calmer.

I want more control of her and stand up, pressing her against the flower-papered wall, her legs wrapped around my waist.

And I plunder her, slamming our bodies together like a boat crashing through waves. She hangs on, her cries in my ear. When she says my name, "Zachery, Zachery, Zachery," some deep, forbidden part of me wants to respond with something tender, but I shove it aside.

This is fucking. A one-off with a gem. A perfect jewel.

My Kelsey.

I reach between us to work her, not softly this time, but with frenzied need.

She whimpers against my shoulder, her tone desperate and pleading. "Again, yes, Zachery."

I whirl us around and press her back onto the bed while I remain standing. I drag her body to mine, forcing her to take in every inch, her legs straight up to my shoulders.

I nip the inside of her calf as I work her again. Her head rolls back and forth on the bed, her entire neck and chest blossoming pink.

When I feel her body convulse against me, I unleash. The tightening of her muscles draws every ounce of pleasure out of me.

I revel in the sight of her, eyes closed, one arm crossed over her forehead.

I feel alive with her, whole, complete. I'm pleased in a way I never experience with the random women who cross my path, no matter how much they purr or preen afterward.

I never go this hard, try this much. I hold back, not sharing the full extent of what I want to do or how I want them.

But not with Kelsey. I wanted everything perfect. Cataclysmic.

She should see what she's capable of.

I can't even believe she'd doubt herself. She's more alive than any woman I've known.

She opens her eyes. Her thoughts must have gone a similar path as mine, because she says with a shaky laugh, "I guess I'm okay, then."

I withdraw to discard the condom, then wrap her in my arms. "You're perfect." I know I should follow her lead, shrug this off, mark it complete, successful, a point proven.

But I can't. I hold her, her head pressed to my neck, hair spilling over my arm.

She lets me, for a little while. Our skin melts together, nothing coming between us for the first time. The last time. The only time.

Something cracks in me, but I ignore it. I've felt it before, when my mother learned I had taken the gross-out comedy movie deal and closed her door, never coming back through it with quite the same smile for her prodigy son.

I felt it again when my sister left home for college with a parting remark about my new career: "If you were going to steal Mom from me all these years, you could have done something with it other than dick jokes."

And later, when the romantic lead from my third movie became a lot more, and I thought we were going to beat the Hollywood-relationship curse, but then she moved on to another actor, a "serious contender," and I learned about it from a tabloid.

I'm deep into my head, which is dangerous. I don't go here. Kelsey is making it happen. She's given me a glimpse into the infinite. A friendship fully blown into a life promise. A perfect match.

And yet, she's already pulling away.

"I should go," she says. "You really do come through in a pinch, Zachery. That was . . . wow." She picks up her dress and her bra and her shoes, holding them in front of her. "Thank you."

Then she's gone, through the bathroom door to her own room.

I want to go after her, tell her no, don't find some flannel-wearing handyman from Smallville. Don't trip into his arms or take his bagel order or accidentally-on-purpose switch bags.

But she's Kelsey, and I'm Zach.

She's a dream girl from Alabama, looking for authentic love.

And I'm a washed-up Hollywood playboy who never got a girl to stick for more than a month.

She got what she wanted. The experienced charmer who could make her toes curl, prove that Simple Simon was only a momentary problem.

I hear her bumping around her room, rolling her suitcase.

I close my eyes and see her clearly still, the flush on her skin, her hair spread.

It's going to take a very long time to get that image out of my mind.

Chapter 25

KELSEY CHANGES THE SO-CALLED SHEETS

I had to escape. It was too much.

Zachery. His touch. His earnest expression.

Give that man a Golden Globe.

This is how he does it. How he woos all those hopefuls Desdemona sends his way.

He's good. Too good.

For a full five minutes, I can only sit on the end of the bed, my clothes in my lap. I can't quite comprehend what just happened.

I was so glib about it, asking him for sex. It was supposed to be transactional, a favor, a test.

Not what I got.

A full-body reset. A mind erasure.

I'm shocked that the women he's given this treatment to haven't become stalkers. I'm tempted. Zachery Carter is a drug.

I already want more.

If I hadn't left as abruptly as I did, I would have never pulled myself away.

The house is full of creaks and groans. It sounds like someone might be coming up the stairs. There are no footsteps, but one of the sounds keeps getting closer.

Surely we haven't stayed at a haunted bed-and-breakfast.

I race to open my bag and put on my pajamas with the gray sweater over them.

Then I hear a gentle *tap tap tap.*

The knock is light. It's not on my door.

It's on Zachery's.

Why would someone come to his door?

There's rustling. The *ting* of his belt. He's trying to dress.

Then the crunchy noises of the door sticking before popping open.

His quiet "Hey."

"Did you want to come down?"

It's Livia, the owner.

I press my ear to the door.

I can't hear what Zach says, if anything.

Livia says, "Sounds good."

What sounds good?

Is Zach going to go for two?

Was I an unexpected appetizer before the main course?

I don't want to know.

I slink to the far corner of the room and open the window. Warmth flows in, as well as the sounds of the festival across the street. An amplified voice cuts through the noise: "And for our last song of the evening to close out this year's Dillfest, we have 'Goodnight, Sweetheart, Goodnight.'"

The quartet is back. The song is melancholy, and I sit on the sill, not caring that I'm wrecking Livia's air-conditioning bill.

If Zachery leaves his room, I don't know it. I'm not going to listen, not going to try to figure it out.

I hum along to the song, trying to channel my inner peace. What happened with Zachery has to be exactly what I asked for. A test. An act. A one-off.

I think of a scene in the fifth comedy he did, after the hit one. Zach plays the best man to his friend, who is getting married. In a ridiculous scene, they're out for the bachelor party and Zach is about to have sex with his second woman of the night, a dark-haired beauty in a red-sequin dress who keeps having nip slips, which makes the groom bite his hand.

The friend asks Zach if he's going to dip into this one right after the other, and Zach holds up a condom packet. "It's like changing the sheets!"

And so, life will imitate art, perhaps.

I shudder.

The song comes to an end. The remaining crowd drifts toward the parking lot. The booths shut down, and carts appear in front of them, tired vendors loading up their wares.

I sit up when I spot the pale head of Simon with the young girl I saw him with initially, as well as an older couple. He looks so normal, walking with the same lanky stride he had with me.

Like nothing ever happened.

I withdraw to the side of the window, afraid he might notice me somehow.

The family gets to the street and wanders along the line of cars parked in every direction. He never glances this way. He doesn't know where I am, or even who I am, really. By now, I'm already a girl he shouldn't have messed with, one who got his face punched.

How can I judge Zach for going to Livia when I was with Simon under the bleachers just hours ago?

This night has been too much. I close the window and lie across the bed.

Tomorrow will be the next part of the journey. I'm not deterred. I'm relearning how to fit in and look less Hollywood. Simon didn't make any connection, taking me at my word about Alabama.

I've confirmed that meet-cutes can and do work.

And Zach showed me that I'm fine. With the right person and circumstances, everything works as it should.

I pull out my phone to decide what's next. I can stay in Colorado, or I can move on to the next state.

If I continue my northern trajectory, it will take me straight to Wyoming.

I've read a lot of romances set in Wyoming. There are sweeping vistas and plenty of cowboys. I zoom to the bottom corner of the state, near Cheyenne.

Then, like a sign straight from the meet-cute playbook, a marker pops up for a local business, almost in the middle of nowhere.

Hanover's Christmas Tree Farm in Glass, Wyoming.

A Christmas tree farm!

A 4.8-star rating. Known for its beautiful trees, which you can chop down yourself or get full service, even delivery.

An alert says, "Half Christmas at the Tree Farm! Don't miss our summer events!"

I quickly click on it. The main events are next weekend, which is early since it's still May, but who cares! It's like they're doing it now just for me. There's a square dance, hayrides, and a pie-eating contest.

That sounds perfect. I couldn't have picked anything more on-theme.

I hunt around for a place to stay. There's not a lot. The motel nearby looks like the one out of *Psycho*. It's cheap, though.

I should consult with Zachery about it.

Tonight? No, I should wait until morning. He might be tied up tonight.

Changing the sheets.

Despite all my internal insistence that I'm fine, something in me is desperate to know if he's in his room or if he took Livia up on what sounded like an offer.

I pad across the floor and ease open the door to my side of the bathroom. The space is still dark, although I can smell Zachery in here in the traces of his expensive soap.

I press my ear to the opposite door. If I hear anything untoward, I'm backing away.

But there's nothing.

I tap on the door. "Zachery? Are you there?"

Nothing.

I turn the handle, not sure I want to look inside.

But I do.

The bed is mussed from our activities earlier. Heat rises to my cheeks when I see the wall he held me against. A curl of desire unfurls in my belly just revisiting this place.

But I wash cold when I realize the room is empty.

Zach is gone.

He left with Livia.

I feel sick and stumble back to the bathroom.

No. I can't think this way.

Jealousy was not part of the deal. Or possessiveness.

I asked a charming rake to do what he does best.

Then he did.

I splash cool water on my face and head back to my room.

I'll write out my feelings and be done.

Then there will be no more thinking about this. Only moving forward.

In the morning, maybe I'll even suggest that Zachery head back.

Except that would be admitting that something has changed between us when I promised it wouldn't.

And I certainly didn't prove that I was fine without him. The whole Simon incident showed exactly how much he's needed.

I have to toughen up. Close that door. Change my own sheets.

I pull out my laptop to clear my head and draft an email I'll never send.

The only way now is to head toward the man I was meant to find, whoever he is.

I sure hope he shows up soon.

Chapter 26

ZACHERY AND THE RED RIVER

Kelsey seems subdued as we load our cars the next morning. She texted around eight that she was headed to a small Wyoming town north of Cheyenne and dropped a pin at a motel she'd found.

It looked atrocious. I quickly searched up a house to rent and found several. I booked one and sent her the link.

She said she would stay at her place, and I could stay in mine.

I get it. The aftereffects of our night have hit me, too.

I spent a good chunk of the evening drinking brandy-laced coffee with Livia. She told a lot of stories about Dillville, and I subtly steered us away from any of her hints about having a dalliance. She didn't push.

It was good. It kept me from brooding about Kelsey or, worse, sneaking into her bed.

When I got back to my room, I checked on her, sleeping soundly in the old-fashioned four-poster bed. She was beautiful and ethereal, surrounded by floral sheets and lace.

I will never forget our night.

There is no open phone call or shared song list on this leg of the journey. She drives ahead of me, and all I see of her is the vague bulge of her loose bun over the headrest. Mostly, I follow her taillights and wonder if we made a grave mistake last night.

We get off the interstate when she pulls into a large truck stop with charging stations. There's a diner, and I park nearby and walk up to her with trepidation as she hooks up her hybrid.

Normally my interactions with women the day after are easy. I set the tone, making clear that I'll let the woman know if another opportunity arises to get her some press, as if everything that transpired was always about her career.

Then I don't call her again unless that scenario comes to fruition, which, honestly, is rare. Desdemona doesn't give them much opportunity to prove themselves. Her list is deep with stalled-out hopefuls.

But with Kelsey, I'm in uncharted territory. We work together. I'm here to help her out of the low period she's been in.

And speaking of periods, she's having one. Right through her cute white shorts. There was no hint of it last night.

She's having trouble with the lock of the charging-port door, bent over, peering at it.

"Hey, Kels," I say.

She bangs the door and it pops open. "There," she says, plugging in the cord. "Now we wait."

"Hey."

I think she might be ignoring me, but then she turns. "Hey."

I fumble for words. "I think something is happening." I shift my gaze to her shorts.

For a moment, her mouth opens like she's shocked I would say that. I realize she thinks I'm propositioning her again.

"No, no, I mean, there's something on your . . ."

She looks down, but I think from her angle, she can't see it.

"What?"

"Bleeding?" I manage.

She bends farther over, and this time, she sees it. "Damn it!" She turns in a circle a moment, then practically leaps into her back seat. She surfaces with the gray sweater she's been wearing to bed and a pair of denim shorts.

"Oh, underwear. And the cup." She isn't speaking to me, but herself. I take several steps back, and she turns around to dig some more.

When she emerges the second time, she ties the gray sweater around her waist. "I guess I'm going in." She's not embarrassed, which makes me glad. It's a normal thing.

"You okay?"

"I'm fine. Just unexpected. It's fine. I should have known. Ugggh." She hurries toward the diner in long, power-walking strides.

I rush to keep up. "I'll see you in the diner in a minute? I'll get us a table."

She stops short, seems to think about it, and turns. "Of course. Yes. Get a table. Thank you."

"Your usual coffee?"

She shakes her head. "Drip coffee with room for cream."

"Oh?" This is new.

"I'm trying to be less high maintenance." Then she's off again.

The waitress inside the diner points me to an empty booth. I order two plain coffees in solidarity.

When Kelsey returns, she slides into the seat with a long sigh. "It's already been a day."

I push her mug toward her. "I'm not sure this is going to help. I'm happy to drive as far as I need to go to get an iced espresso with almond milk and a drizzle of caramel, shaken rather than stirred."

She dumps a tiny prepackaged slash of cream and a packet of sugar into her coffee and stirs. When she takes a sip, she grimaces. "Maybe I can be Hollywood on the road and small town when I have an audience."

While she checks email, I find a Starbucks a few miles away and order a DoorDash to bring it to the diner. She can at least have good coffee on the drive.

We order pancakes and talk about where Desdemona's headed after Cannes, the filming of a snappy mystery set in London. We're not going to be there, but she will.

"I'm worried poor Devonta is going to crack if the Demon gets too harsh with her," Kelsey says. "It's only her second project."

I'm incredibly relieved that we're able to talk business like always. "I'll see who's on the crew. Maybe we can find someone to watch out for her."

Kelsey rims the edge of her pancake with syrup. She doesn't like to pour it on top. "Everybody is scared of the Demon."

"You're not."

Kelsey shrugs. "Neither are you."

"That's how we've managed to stay employed."

"I've seen the books," Kelsey says between bites of pancake. "She doesn't pay you enough to be worth your time."

"It's the intangibles I'm after."

Kelsey aims her fork at me. "You mean the women."

It's like last night never happened. I'm not sure whether to be relieved or disappointed.

"It's the connections," I say. "I get to stay in the fray."

She stabs the last bite of her pancake and swirls it through the remaining syrup. "Do you think you'll get an agent again? Go for parts?"

She's asked this before. "No. If I was going to work on-screen again, I'd call in the favor with Desdemona."

Kelsey sets down her fork. "You think she'd do it?"

"I could make her. But I don't."

"Because people would say you didn't earn it."

I shrug. "People will say what they want to no matter what."

"That's true." She sips her coffee, then grimaces again. "It's worse cold."

I spot a car with a DoorDash sticker pull up. Right on time. A young, lean man steps out, coffee cup in hand, and looks around. I wave at him through the window.

Kelsey spots him. "Did you order yourself good coffee?" She smacks my arm with her napkin.

The man enters. "Coffee for Kelsey?"

"Right here," I tell him.

He sets the cup in front of her and takes off.

The waitress sidles up. "I don't blame you, but seriously?"

I shrug. She'll forget her annoyance when she sees her tip.

Kelsey hangs on to the cup like it's her infant child, both hands wrapped around it, pressed to her cheek. "You love me, Zachery Carter."

I probably do, but I simply say, "I prefer not to be murdered by a menstruating woman."

She lets out a low shriek. "You are the worst!"

I laugh. "I know."

She sips the drink and groans, a sound that hits me straight in the groin. "You know what you never see in rom-coms?"

"What?"

"Menstruation. Nobody gets their period in those movies."

I grunt. "It's too realistic."

"Great. Another thing I'm getting wrong on this trip."

Was last night the other thing she got wrong? I don't want to know. "Come on. We've got to hit the road."

"To the motel?" she asks.

"To the house."

Her eyes narrow. "I'm staying in the motel."

I drop cash on the paper ticket as we slide out of the booth. "I'll get you Starbucks again in the morning if you stay in the house."

"Damn it. You know my weaknesses."

I drape my arm around her shoulders, determined to keep our light banter the way it's always been. "Every single one."

"But still no."

And when she calls me the moment we're back on the highway, challenging me to black-and-white-movie trivia as we drive, I know I've done the right thing in keeping things light after what happened in Dillville.

The world of Zach and Kelsey has been put back in its rightful place.

Somebody needs to tell that to my heart.

Chapter 27

Kelsey Meets the Wrong Cute

I hate when Zachery's right.

My car chugs for a second as I pull up to the Crater Inn, almost as if it doesn't want to approach the sad, sagging building that stretches along the back side of a cracked asphalt lot.

The sign over the glass doors near the front reads Off!, and I can see Zachery snort-laughing in his Jaguar as he parks beside me.

I slam my door as he rolls down his window.

"It's supposed to say Office!"

Somewhere along the way, the rest of the word went black.

"When you said Crater Inn," he says, his face bright with laughter, "I didn't think you meant Crater*ing*."

"Very funny."

"Come on. Stay at the house. The manager is already there to meet us." He turns his phone to me. "Just look at him."

I lean in. The man has curly black hair, a jaw that could rock a movie poster—and is that . . . I take the phone for a closer look.

"Yes, he's in a flannel shirt," Zachery says.

"Is he single?"

"Only one way to find out." Zachery waggles his eyebrows, and I'm in awe that he can be so casual about sending me off to find some other man after last night.

He's a true professional.

"What's his name?"

"Jack."

God. A short, strong name. It could be my own *Virgin River*. Based on the scenery around here, it works.

"Okay, I'm in. Text me the address." I pass him his phone.

By the time I've hopped back in the car, Zachery has sent a Google pin with the location of the house.

We've driven all day, but since hitting Wyoming, I've fallen in love with the countryside. There are miles of sweeping fields, rolling hills, and so much unspoiled land. We've driven through plains, pine forests, and mountains. It has everything.

It's nothing like LA, of course, but it's not like the dairy farm in Alabama, either. I roll down my window and take in the air.

Heaven, that's what it is.

Signs that we're nearing a small town spring up. I've begun to recognize them. A smattering of houses, loose at first, but then getting closer together.

A bar appears, usually, off on its own, as if a hundred years ago when the town formed, it wanted the drinking done well away from the church.

A water tower rises up, a silver cylinder breaking the line of trees and the view of the buttes.

Then the brick buildings begin, crumbling but stalwart, leading to the center of town.

Before we get to actual streets, Zachery signals to turn left.

We bump along a less fortified road until it forks. We pass a lone house, then another a quarter mile later. Then we reach a dirt driveway. I follow the Jaguar almost to the tree line, where a gorgeous two-story redbrick house stands before the wall of great pines.

It's colonial, with tall white columns on either side of the door holding up a balcony with white rails. When we pull up onto a concrete pad next to the white garage doors, the front door opens.

And there's Jack, standing on the long porch in jeans and a pale-blue short-sleeve shirt. His black hair stands out starkly against the white entryway.

He's a picture, that's for sure.

My meet-cute options are limited here. No elevator. No food order to mix up. I'm feeling skittish about trip and fall.

But then I have it. I snatch my rolling suitcase and get it ready to bump up the stairs.

Zachery moves to help me, but I wave him away.

Up a step. Second step.

"I can help," Jack says, coming down from the top.

Zachery tries to intercept me. "Kelsey, you don't want to—"

"Shhh," I hiss. "Back off!"

I have no idea what Zachery is trying to do here, but right as Jack arrives to help with the suitcase, I kick the latch so that my clothes spill down the steps. Here we go.

"Oh, no!" I cry.

Jack grins. "Don't worry, little lady, I'll help."

We kneel together in front of my exploded suitcase. We both reach for the same pair of shorts and our fingers brush against each other.

It's working!

Then I realize it's my white shorts from earlier, the red stains gone brown.

I snatch them away and shove them beneath the pile. More clothes cascade down the steps, all my pretty panties like a pastel rainbow.

God. This scene would never make the cut.

"Kelsey." Zachery's tone has a warning in it.

"What?" Maybe he's trying to thwart my meet-cute after all. Does he care?

But when I look up, he's standing behind Jack, holding up his left hand and pointing at his ring finger.

I immediately drop my gaze to Jack's hand.

Blast it all, there's a wedding ring.

I start shoving my clothes into the suitcase as fast as I can. "Thanks," I tell Mr. Married. "I've got it now."

But he's a gentleman, and he carries the bulging bag the rest of the way up the stairs.

"Sure is nice to meet you two," he says. "This house has been in my family for five generations."

He leads us into a massive front room with a charming fireplace and a white staircase wrapped in . . . Christmas holly? Ribbons? With silver bells?

Jack notices me gawking. "Oh, yeah, there's a big summer Christmas event at the tree farm coming up in a week. We'll be using the house." He rubs his neck. "That's why we only had this week open."

"Wait," I say. "Are you a Hanover from the Hanover Tree Farm?"

He grins. "Sure am."

Zachery frowns. "So, we won't have the option to extend our stay due to the Christmas events?"

"It could be all right," Jack says. "Depending on how things go, and if you don't mind people being downstairs one of the mornings while you're here. We don't book it since most people don't want a bunch of strangers tromping through."

"The event will be here?" I ask.

"They'll be all over town, but we host the Christmas tea here, both in the normal season and now for this." He rubs the back of his neck. "Although I guess it'll be iced tea this time around. I'll have to check with Mom."

"I'm sure it'll be fine for us to be here for the tea, don't you think, Kelsey?" Zachery asks. "You wanted to meet the locals and do the festival. You'll be right in the middle of it here."

"Sure," I say. "And there's other events, right?"

"Absolutely," Jack says. "The hayride is going to be a lot more pleasant in summer than when it's ten below."

"I bet." I look up the miles of stairs, wishing I hadn't brought the big suitcase in after all.

"I'll get your bag," Jack says. "You have the run of the house, other than the storage areas."

I follow him up the stairs, mourning that the picturesque butt rising ahead of me is already taken.

But if Jack is indicative of what I can find in Glass, Wyoming, I'm right where I ought to be.

Chapter 28

Zachery Witnesses the Real Deal

Kelsey has those meet-cutes down. A knock into popcorn. An exploding suitcase.

Eventually one of them is going to stick.

Jack filled us in on the places to eat nearby. I take Kelsey to one of them, a homespun café with checkered tablecloths and only four items on the menu.

We assess the other customers, almost entirely couples over fifty.

"Where's the young people?" Kelsey whispers. "The families with kids? The hot young Jack look-alikes?"

I shrug. "They must go somewhere else."

We stop into a supermarket and a sporting goods store to see who else we might find, but young single men are noticeably absent.

"There needs to be a sign-up sheet in the center of town," Kelsey says. "City girls in search of small-town husbands."

I chuckle. "Wouldn't that be something."

But with no luck on our first day, we retire to our rooms. We're farther apart this time, with no bathroom connecting us. I lie in bed, thinking about how close Kelsey is, and yet how impossibly far.

I'm not sure how much more of this I can take.

I wake the next morning to a sound I can't quite identify. It's regular, spaced apart by about twenty seconds. *Whack, thud, scrape. Whack, thud, scrape.*

The side window tells me nothing, only an empty yard to the tree line.

I move to the back window. There it is again. *Whack, thud, scrape.*

I shift the curtains. Behind the house, a young man who resembles Jack, but isn't Jack, cuts firewood on the stump of a tree.

He lifts the axe, then *whack*, it comes down, and *thud*, the fat log separates and falls. He adjusts the new piece with a *scrape* across the stump and does it again.

He's the right age for Kelsey, late twenties, strong and self-assured. He wears gray shorts, a white T-shirt, and a ball cap. Casual, but normal. I'm guessing she'll assess his outfit at about $120, mostly due to the tennis shoes.

I step back. She'll probably burst in any second to brainstorm a meet-cute.

I wait, watching the man.

No Kelsey.

A half hour passes, so I quickly shower and dress and head downstairs.

She's not there, either.

Has she already met him?

There's a basket of pastries on the table. Coffee is brewed and ready in the pot, but it looks to have been set up automatically. There's no evidence that Kelsey has been down.

I step up to the sink to look out the back window. He's out there, an impressive pile of neatly stacked firewood growing at his feet.

This is too much to deal with before coffee. I find a mug and pour a cup. I take it straight black, needing the jolt.

Maybe I'll text her. She could be sleeping late. It's not like her, but we did a lot of driving yesterday.

I realize the *whack, thunks* have stopped. I return to the window. The man must notice me there, because he waves and points to the back door.

He must want in. I head there and open it.

"You must be the guy staying in the house," he says, stomping his shoes before coming in. "Sorry to bother you, but I wanted to fill up the downstairs wood rack."

"Won't it be a little warm for a fire?"

He chuckles. "It will, I guess. But heck, I don't know what they're going to do at a summer Christmas tea. We have all these traditions, but they're set up for winter." He takes off his cap, runs the back of his hand over his forehead, then sticks it on again. "Mom is running the show."

"Do what you need to do," I tell him. I'll text Kelsey now, so she won't show up downstairs in something she wouldn't want her future husband to see.

"I'm Randy," he says, extending a hand. "You met my brother, Jack, yesterday."

"I see the resemblance. I'm Zachery."

Randy tilts his head. "You look like—"

And here we go. The recognition. I steel myself to be outed as the man who does objectionable things to old women during bingo.

"—this guy I played ball with at UW. A dead ringer. You have family up here?"

I'm momentarily taken aback. "Nope. Just a sister in LA."

"Dead ringer. It's uncanny." He heads for the back door. "I'm going to bring a load through."

"You need a hand?"

"Oh, no. If my mama catches me letting a paying guest haul firewood, she'll skin me alive."

"We don't want to upset Mom."

The screen door slams as he heads back through.

I sit down with my coffee at the round table in the center of the kitchen. I didn't realize our house would be the center of so much activity.

Randy comes through with a stack of firewood in his arms, aiming for the swinging door between the kitchen and the front room.

I forgot to text Kelsey. I better do that or she might come down to investigate all the noise.

But then there's an "Oof" and a crash, and logs start to fall.

"Oh, my gosh! Are you okay?"

I stand up. It's her. She came in through the swinging door at the same moment Randy tried to go out.

He fumbles for a moment to keep from losing the entire stack of wood. Kelsey reaches down to pick up a piece, but the swinging door makes its return and smacks her on the butt.

"Oh!" she cries and stumbles forward into Randy a second time.

More firewood falls.

I rush forward to help.

"I've made a real mess of things!" Kelsey cries, trying again to pick up a log.

But Randy laughs. "It's all right. Careful with your feet."

Kelsey glances down at her bare toes, then realizes how she's dressed. Her hands go up to her hair, all over the place in a messy bun.

This makes the gray sweater she's been wearing slide open, revealing the dancing bears on the front of her pajama top, plus several inches of her belly.

"Oh, my gosh," she says. "I'm . . . Oh, gosh."

I slowly back to the far corner of the kitchen to let this play out. Maybe they'll forget I'm here.

Randy shifts the logs he's still holding to one arm and extends a hand. "I'm Randy, Jack's brother."

Kelsey takes it for a quick shake, then pulls her gray sweater around her. I catch her glancing at his hands. There's no wedding ring. I already looked.

"I'm Kelsey." Her gaze finds me. "I'm here with Zach. Not with-with Zach. We're just traveling together. We work together."

Randy glances back at me. "Interesting. Is it a work trip? Don't see a lot of business travelers in Glass."

"No. Yes. Well, a little of both, I guess." She's flustered.

I sip my coffee, trying not to smile. I'm curious to see how she's going to get out of this one.

"A little of both is a good thing. Will you be here long?"

"Yes. We'll want to check out the event at the tree farm. It looks fun. It's why I came here. To Glass." She fusses with her hair again, this time holding the sweater closed with the other hand.

"That's great. We've never done it before, but the whole town is getting involved."

"Why this year, then?" Kelsey asks.

"We've had a tough couple of years with the family farm," Randy says. "It's no secret. Not as much call for it, especially with the national forest permits to cut down your own. We're trying to pivot."

Kelsey's eyes go round, like cartoon characters when they realize something huge has just gone down. "So you're saying the town is having a festival to save your family's Christmas tree farm? Like, right now? While I'm here?"

Randy chuckles. "That's about the heart of it. I'm going to run this load to the main room. I'll be back in a few." He kneels to gather the fallen logs.

When he passes through the swinging door, Kelsey looks at me and mouths, *Oh, my God.*

She hurries over and takes my coffee cup, grimacing at the lack of cream or sugar. Or caramel drizzle. She passes it back. "I can't even believe this."

"You couldn't put this in a script. Nobody would buy the pitch."

"Hallmark would."

"They've already done it. Five hundred times."

She punches my arm. "Hush. It's obviously meant to be."

I can't argue with that.

Randy comes through the kitchen, giving us a nod before heading out the back door.

Kelsey watches him from the kitchen window. "I mean, his family owning a *Christmas tree farm*, and the festival to save it is enough, but you know what's really got me going here?"

I sip from my cup, not wanting to hear the answer. This introduction is far more painful than the last.

She goes on. "I didn't even have to fake that meet-cute."

I set down my coffee. "Really? That looked like a classic move."

"You think I would have come down here looking like this if I knew my future husband was about to crash into me while lugging firewood he cut with his own hands?" Her voice drops to a whisper as Randy passes through the kitchen again.

"So, it was a genuine meet-cute, then." The coffee sits in my belly as heavy as one of Randy's perfectly cut logs.

She can't take her eyes off the man as he pops through the swinging doors.

"I can feel it, Zachery," she says. "Everything I planned for has led me right here from the moment I sat down across from that fortune teller."

And the worst thing about it is I think she might be right.

Chapter 29

KELSEY HANDLES THE BALLS

I definitely never wanted to meet my future husband in a ten-year-old gray sweater and saggy PJs.

But here we are.

When Randy heads outside again, I race up to my room, taking the stairs two at a time.

I have to shower, dress, and fix whatever first impression he just got!

The water doesn't want to heat, but I'm in a hurry, so I rapidly wash my hair in the bracing cold spray. I can't handle a shave in that, so I do it afterward, managing to nick my shin in a way I haven't done since I was fifteen.

Are these signs? Signs of what? Warning? Humility? To literally take a cold shower and chill the hell out?

I don't even know anymore, and I don't have time to pull a tarot card. I yank a brush through my wet hair hard enough to make myself yelp. *Calm down, Kelsey!*

I choose a soft green dress with a white belt and white tennis shoes. I go for classic with my hair, blow-drying it straight and pulling it back with a white headband.

Barely there makeup. Minimal jewelry.

Randy looks like a no-fuss, no-muss type.

I turn in front of a full-length oval mirror on a stand. For a moment, I wonder which ancestors of Randy's family might have looked at their reflection in this very glass.

I like it. All of it. The history. The land. I'm not even bothered that the tree farm needs saving. I have every confidence that the summer event will be wildly successful, and the family won't have to worry about financial solvency.

If you're going to buy into the romantic storyline, you have to go all in.

I hurry for the stairs, well aware that I took the better part of an hour to get ready and Randy might be gone.

But halfway down, the movie starts rolling like any climactic scene when the heroine descends from an upper floor to capture the hero's heart.

INT. A BRICK WYOMING HOMESTEAD—DAY

KELSEY, 25, in a demure pale-green dress with white accessories, walks down a curved staircase.

Below, RANDY, 28, and his brother, JACK, 30, stand on either side of a fireplace, the metal wood stand filled with freshly cut logs. They have a bin of holiday decorations at their feet, an artificial garland sticking out over the edge.

It's happening. It's happening!

Randy's eyes take me in. I think he might remark upon my change in appearance, but he simply grins.

"We should ask a woman's opinion," he says, lifting the end of a fake garland. "We don't know what we're doing."

"I'm happy to help," I say.

Randy tugs on the greenery, which drops dozens of plastic bits as it unfurls. "I say the fake stuff is garbage, and we should cut a fresh pine bough."

I turn to Jack. "What's the downside?"

"It's summer. A real pine bough will wilt into a sad, brown pile of needles in this heat. In winter, they last a couple of weeks."

"I see." I pick up the other end of the garland. "You don't use fake ones?"

"Not since I can remember," Randy says.

"We can cover it in balls and ribbon and nobody will notice," Jack says. "We have too much to do to cut boughs that might look bad by the time the week is over."

"We don't have fresh pine where I come from," I tell the men. "Fake garland is the only kind I know. We can make this work." I realize I've taken the wrong side when Randy frowns. I quickly add, "And if it fails, then we cut boughs closer to the day."

"All right," Randy says. "But it won't be half as nice."

Now it's on the line. "I can make it nice."

"Give her a chance," Jack says.

I can practically see the script writer congratulating herself on the double meaning of the line. *Yes, Randy, give the girl a chance.* Well played, madam.

I take the garland and tug at the individual wires that hold the molting branches together. "These have to be fluffed or they look terrible." I twist the wiring, and a shower of plastic needles falls to the floor.

"This does not look promising," Randy says.

"Maybe it's like Charlie Brown's Christmas tree," Jack says.

I'm determined to make this work. "It'll be all right. These were good-quality garlands. They just need some love."

"See," Jack says. "All you need is love."

The script writer for this scene is on *fire*.

Randy socks his brother's shoulder. "Fine. We should find the ribbon and balls."

I almost make a joke about balls, but think better of it. It doesn't match my wholesome look. I'll tell it to Zachery later. He'll find it hilarious, even if it is out of context by then.

The garland starts to take shape as I work on the wires holding the plastic branches. Jack takes off for another part of the house, leaving me with Randy.

"That is looking better," he says. "It's nice of you to help. You're a guest."

"I like decorating for the holidays." I come to the halfway point, my fingers already sore from the rough wire. It's a small price to pay. "Does your family go all out?"

"That's putting it mildly," he says, searching through the box. "Between this old homestead that we rent out, our parents' house, Jack and Mindy's place, and Grandmama's cottage, it's a lot of lighting, trees, and pine boughs."

"Plus the tree farm. I guess it's busy at Christmas?"

"Insanely." Randy retrieves a bag of tiny gold packages glued to green wire. "I think these go on that."

"Christmas picks," I say. "I used to shop for those with my mom. She liked adding things like this to the garlands."

"It fills them out," he says. "Doesn't work so well with fresh boughs, though. We just use ribbons on those."

I finish fluffing the end of the garland and hold it out. "Will it do?"

Randy takes the length of plastic pine and stretches it out. "That looks good. By the time we add the rest, it'll be all right."

"It won't ever look like authentic pine, but it'll be pretty. It's probably easier to work with for decorating since you can bend the wire into place."

"Yeah, the boughs are tricky."

We both sit on the floor, twisting the tiny gold boxes into the branches.

"Where does your mom live?" Randy asks.

The question stabs me, but it's a pain I'm used to. "She died when I was twelve."

"Oh, damn. I'm sorry."

"It's all right. It's been thirteen years."

"So you did this with her?"

"I did. She liked to have coordinating decorations on the garland and the tree. And never multicolored lights. White only."

Randy laughs. "Grandmama is a white lighter. Mom likes colors. Dad stays out of the fight."

"Is Grandmama your dad's mother or your mother's?"

"Dad's. Every Christmas, there's a battle between his mom and his wife when it comes to lighting the retail section of the farm."

"I think I'd stay out of that one, too."

We work a few more moments until we get to the last gold gift.

Randy watches me place it. "It looks great."

Jack returns with another plastic bin.

"I found red ribbon and gold ribbon," he says. "But only red balls." He sets a box on the floor by us.

"We put the Christmas picks in the garland," Randy says. "Kelsey fluffed it."

"I knew it would look good," Jack says. "I have to run. You got this?"

"We do," Randy says, and something about the way he says "we" makes my heart speed up.

Jack gives us a nod and heads out the front door.

I take the spools of red and gold ribbon and hold them both up to the bough. "What do you think?"

"You're the expert. We're lucky you checked in."

I set the gold ribbon aside and begin weaving the red into the wired branches. "It's fun."

"Do you have a lot of work to do during your stay?"

Right, this is a work trip. "Our boss is at Cannes, so we aren't too busy."

"Cannes?"

Dang. I don't want to tip him off to our Hollywood connection too soon. "The city in France." Still true.

"And you decided to do your work in Glass because . . ."

"The summer events. I wanted to learn more about them."

"Is that part of your work? Are you a newspaper reporter or something?"

If only. Then I'd be living out the Hallmark dream. "No. I just do a lot of research for my job."

"The first event is Wednesday night. It's a hayride through the tree farm."

"That sounds delightful." *Now invite me!*

"Jack and I have to get the lights strung before then, as that's the whole point of the ride. But we get to go on it. One of us will be on each wagon, telling the history of the farm."

"I definitely can't miss that." I can picture it, the lights weaving through the trees, the night sky, and Randy talking to a group of people about his family history.

It's too perfect.

If he's going to ask me to come.

But he only holds up the garland. "You think it needs balls?"

No, but he does, and to use them to ask me out! Maybe he has a girlfriend. Or he likes men. I start to deflate. "Maybe a few." We pull a half dozen from the bin and tie them into the branches.

"Those look good," he says, standing effortlessly from the floor, holding the garland. "Let's see how it fits." While he stretches it across the wood mantel, I awkwardly pull myself to standing. If he isn't going to ask to see me again, this is not the moment I was hoping for.

"Mom will love it." Randy takes a step back to admire our handiwork. "And she'll appreciate that we have less to do on Saturday. You'll be here for the Christmas tea?"

"I will," I say. "I should study the schedule of events. I want to do as much as I can."

"It's spread out," Randy says. "There's no reason you can't do them all."

Here we go. "Do *you* do them all?"

His eyes take in my face. "I better. It's our tree farm on the line."

I should probably not be forward, but I'm tired of all the failed meet-cutes so far, and this one looks promising if he's available. "Are you planning to take anyone with you?"

"I was thinking about it."

I can practically see the camera angle. His face, slowly growing into a grin.

I see where this is headed, but I play along as if a director and a script supervisor hang on my every word. "Anyone in particular?"

Now the close-up, his eyes sparkling. "There might be a new girl in town."

"Oh, really? You'd take a chance on a stranger?"

"She seems like a good bet. She's got a good eye for decorating. I could use her tomorrow at the retail tent on the farm."

Finally!

"I think she might be able to help out with that," I say.

"Excellent. You think she'll meet me on the porch tomorrow morning around nine?"

"I bet she can make that happen."

His grin somehow gets bigger. It's too soon in this love story for him to lean in for a kiss, but man, it sure feels possible.

This part of my road trip is looking up.

Chapter 30

ZACHERY STAVES OFF THE DEMON

Yeah, I saw the whole thing.

Kelsey didn't make any ball jokes, which was probably a good call. I think she had to rein herself in, though.

When Randy leaves, she races up the stairs, then stops short when she sees me leaning on the rail. "Hey."

"Phase two initiated?" I ask.

"He's coming for me in the morning."

"Good. It's what you wanted."

"It is." She swirls her skirt absentmindedly. She's giving Doris Day vibes.

I back away from the rail. "Well, it's a good thing you didn't make any plans for today, because Desdemona sent a ridiculous amount of work. Jester couldn't get through to you, so he wrote me."

"Oh! I left my phone upstairs." She hurries toward her room.

"Let me know what I can do to help."

She twists the knob. "If she has someone she wants you to take out, will you go back to LA?"

That's a good question. "She hasn't asked. I might tell her I'm in Ibiza." Desdemona knows that is my no-work zone.

"Okay, good." She disappears inside her room.

My phone buzzes.

Jester: Find her?

Me: She's coming.

Jester: How is the trip going?

Me: She met a local. They're going out tomorrow.

Jester: Is he a serial killer?

Me: Unlikely.

Jester: You doing all right?

I hesitate. Am I?

Apparently, I wait too long to reply.

Jester: I'm worried.

Me: Don't be.

Jester: When are you going to stop this nonsense and tell her how you feel?

Me: A half an hour after never.

Jester: It's not right. She should know.

No way. If I can't play this straight, she'll feel guilty, particularly after the night we had.

Me: We're all right. She's happy.

Jester: And you're miserable!

He might be right. I'm going to have to find some way to distract myself with all this going on. I'll lose my mind.

Jester: I knew it!

I hesitated again.

Me: I'll live. Forward any of the work you have that I can take off K's plate. She's got plans.

Jester: All right, honey bear. But I think you should nip this misdirection before you go plumb crazy.

Me: Not my story here. It's hers.

Jester: Can't blame me for worrying.

I hear Kelsey's voice in the other room. She must be talking to Desdemona. It's late afternoon in France. I fully intend to help out if her workload gets in the way of her husband plan.

When my phone buzzes again, it's Kels.

Help!

I hurry to her room. She stands in front of the tapestry she normally hangs on the wall behind her desk to make a pretty video background.

"He's right here," she says.

She wants me on the call?

I'm not dressed for work, which I realize is a grave error. Desdemona will call it out. I've never once worn shorts to the office.

"Hold on," Kelsey says. She sets the phone face down on the desk. "Get a suit jacket on!" She waves me off.

I race to my room, grab a jacket, thankful the collarless shirt look is back. When I return, she says, "He had to finish a call. Oh! He's done."

I take the phone from her, careful to keep it angled above the waist and with the tapestry behind me. "Hello, Desdemona."

She's sitting on a veranda, the Riviera in the background. "What is your availability?"

"I'm heading to Ibiza in about four hours," I say. "What's your timeline?"

She waves a hand. "Nothing pressing. But Catalina Ferrig will be in town at the beginning of June, and I want her to accept the lead role for a *Romeo and Juliet* remake."

"I'm sure she'll be interested in that without my help."

"Luigi Casperra is directing."

"Oh." Catalina made clear on a late-night talk show that she'd rather go blind than take direction from Luigi.

"I want her to be absolutely swooning when we approach her. Give her the full work. Make her want to be someone's Juliet."

I catch Kelsey looking away, her lips tight. "Understood."

"Give me back to Kelsey."

Kelsey slips in close so I can hand off the phone in front of the narrow background. It's tight, and her body brushes against mine.

I quickly step away, but not before everything ignites. Maybe I should go back, return to my old game. Plunder the future Juliet.

But the idea doesn't appeal like it once did.

Instead, I find myself watching Kelsey bend over to take notes on the pretty paper left on the antique side table she's using as a desk.

Desdemona barks out rapid orders. "We'll need to contact our usual BG for a cattle call of three hundred extras under thirty."

"Call the BG for background extras. Got it."

"Contact a few hot models in trashy clothes for close-ups. They can be SAG. It's a big-budget concert scene, and they don't want to CGI the floor, only the mezzanine."

Kelsey scribbles madly on the paper.

It makes me smile, watching her handle the Demon's demands so easily. Kelsey was so green at the beginning, with no idea that BG stood for *background extras* or that SAG meant actors who were part of the professional acting guild. She's good now. She's competent. More than that. She's fantastic.

But she's not *mine*. I have to tear my gaze away.

Desdemona hasn't paused for a breath. "Make sure the BG is fully represented on the set. No rando assistants. I want brass. We're using them for that soccer movie, right?"

"Yes, they gave us the extras for the arena."

"I'm thinking about coming back to watch that one to make sure everything's good for the big one."

Uh-oh.

Kelsey stops writing. "You're going to come in person?"

"That's what I said."

"That's in two weeks."

"I know. I hate it, but I should probably be there."

Kelsey looks up at me. I can see the panic she's trying to tamp down. "I can handle it. I really can. I can take Jester. Zachery, even."

There's silence for a minute, and Kelsey watches me, trying to hold her neutral expression for Desdemona.

"Maybe. Tell me how the conversation goes when you book the concert-scene crowd."

"Okay. I'm on it. We'll handle it beautifully."

Then her phone goes dark. Desdemona isn't one for polite sign-offs.

"Two weeks?" Kelsey wails. "That won't be enough time."

I walk over to her and drape an arm over her shoulder. "You'll totally convince her you've got this. She doesn't want to come. Show her she doesn't need to."

"But I have to be there. Why is this happening? I just got a great new possibility!"

"I can be there. Jester can be there. We're babysitting a company babysitting a herd of extras. It's going to be fine."

"You think it'll be all right?"

"I do."

"Okay." She lets out a long, slow breath. "I guess I better get to work."

I leave her sitting on a vintage chair, furiously tapping on her phone.

I wish I could let Desdemona come, force Kelsey back to LA mid-romance, and take my own shot.

But that's not what I'm here for.

This is about Kelsey.

Chapter 31

KELSEY MEETS THE IN-LAWS

When I step onto the porch the next bright sunshiny morning, Randy is already waiting for me in work boots, jeans, and a T-shirt. I refuse to allow my brain to put a price tag on this outfit.

Too late. $125, dang it.

I'm practical in denim shorts, a white cotton shirt with cap sleeves, and tennis shoes. With a bow on my ponytail, of course.

Only when I hear the neighing sound do I realize we're not alone. Two horses pull a wood box cart with a high seat in front.

"Oh!" I say. "*Two* horsepower!"

He chuckles like that joke is even a tiny bit original. "Your chariot, our master decorator." He bows low and gestures to the step to the seat.

Oh, boy. I look for places to hang on, but there aren't many. I fit my shoe on the narrow step, which is really high for me already, but when I try to rise, I immediately fall back again.

Randy comes up behind me to help, moves his hands as if trying to figure out where to safely grab me, then decides he can best assist me from up top.

He jumps into the seat and leans over to extend a hand. I manage to pull up and plop into the seat with a lot less grace than I imagined.

I've gone Hollywood soft. Maybe this is why everyone in Beverly Hills does Pilates.

"We didn't have a horse cart on the dairy farm," I tell him.

He grins. "I bet not. Ours is mainly for show. It's not the fastest way to get from A to B. But people love it."

And I admit, I do, too. The *clop, clop* of the horses' hooves on the concrete drive is a merry soundtrack as we cross the front of the house. There's a double-grooved path in the yard off to one side that has clearly always been there for this very purpose.

At first, we appear to be headed straight for the trees, but as we get closer, I realize a narrow channel has been cut through the forest.

"We're taking a shortcut," Randy says, and for the first time, I realize I'm going deep into the piney woods with a perfect stranger.

Am I going to end up on a missing persons billboard? Who would buy the billboard? Not my dad. Not the Demon. Could Zachery make the police do it?

What picture would they use? It better not be the one from the *Forty-Seven Dead Men* premiere, where my stupid dress made me look six months pregnant, prompting calls from all my siblings when the designer tagged me in the photo, which wouldn't have happened except in the upper corner, comedian Mitchell Barinski was making a silly face.

He's the reason the photographer bothered to upload it.

To make matters worse, I was experimenting with dramatic eyeliner wings when I should not have been. At least not by my own hand. My shaky, unpracticed hand.

They will totally use that photo on the billboard.

My fingers graze the lump of phone in my pocket. I'm tempted to tell Zachery to make sure they don't use that bad photo, even though it's one of the few up on Getty Images.

But if I do that, he might figure out I have billboard fears. Then he'll show up, and he's already proven he's ready to punch someone, no questions asked.

Sometimes he might benefit from asking a few questions first.

"You all right?" Randy asks. "Penny for your thoughts."

Oh, hell no. These are $10,000 thoughts, minimum, if the tabloids pair them with the right photo of Zachery.

I peer up at the towering forest. "What kind of trees are these?"

"Mostly you're seeing aspens, but we'll go through frasers, grand firs, and blue spruce."

"Which ones are the best for turning into Christmas trees?"

"I'm partial to the firs because they have that holiday pine smell. But a lot of people like blue spruce because the limbs can handle heavy ornaments and pets don't tend to eat the needles."

He's clearly asked this a lot in his line of business. "I think the smell might be important. I don't have any pets."

"Not a pet person?"

Should I be?

"I can't have pets where I live."

He tilts his head. "In Alabama?"

Oh, I'm going to dig myself a hole. "Apartment lease. At the dairy, the animals all had a job. Mousing. Herding. You get it." That's all true.

"I reckon you're pretty handy, growing up on a farm. We have quite a few dogs roaming the grounds, but they all end up in someone's bed come evening time."

"Lucky dogs." Only after I say it do I realize it sounds like a come-on.

Randy grins. "Ol' Blue is my favorite, even though technically she belongs to Jack. She'll sniff me out in a hurry once we hit the retail portion of the tree farm."

It isn't long before the trees become sparse, then orderly, and soon, there are rows of them in varying sizes, from the seedlings in box beds to the towering ones near the forest.

A square, rough-hewn wood building squats near the center of the rows. On either side, red tents are in the process of being erected, the sides flapping in the breeze, not yet tethered to the ground.

"We're here?" I ask.

"We are. The hayride will start at the main building. We'll have a food tent and a Christmas tent." Randy shakes his head. "I'm not sure what we're selling in that one since we don't have new stock in. Mom's in charge of that."

"It's so organized!"

As we ride along a more traveled path between rows, heading for the building, a blue-gray heeler breaks away from a trio of dogs and runs straight for us.

"Is that Ol' Blue?" I ask. The dog is seriously strong and bounds at us like demons are chasing her.

"Sure is." Randy stands. "Come on, baby girl. Get on up here." He slows the horses.

Blue doesn't miss a step, but leaps straight onto the seat and into Randy's lap. She eyes me warily, like I'm encroaching on her man.

I reach over to pet her, but she growls. I pull my hand back.

Randy shifts the reins to one hand and rests his palm on the dog's head. "Now, Blue, don't be jealous. This is Kelsey. She's all right."

Blue drops her head on Randy's thigh, but she keeps her eye on me. That part would never make the love story. The dog has to love me!

We pull up to the tents. A midfifties woman comes out of the building, arms full of light strings. "Oh, good. I wondered where you've been. I need you and Jack to hang these." She glances at me. "Who's your lady friend?"

Lady friend!

I hop off the seat, landing with what I hope is at least a modicum of grace. "I'm happy to help. I love Christmas in July."

"Except it's only going to be June," says a younger woman, frowning as she tries to step around two collies that keep weaving around her legs. "Georgie, Finnegan, please!"

The dogs sit for a moment, as if trying to prove they can behave, but within three steps are back to getting in the woman's way.

Randy rounds the back of the cart. "That's Mom and my sister, Gina. She's not thrilled with our summer endeavor."

"I've barely recovered from Christmas. July makes more sense, but I know, I know. We want to make it an end-of-school thing." Gina sets a pile of heavy wire rings on a long table outside the closest tent. "Am I really making pine wreaths in this heat? They'll wilt in a day."

Their mother looks up at that. "You're right. Don't do natural wreaths. Maybe make some out of ribbon. And maybe not Christmas colors. Summer."

Gina separates the wire circles into piles. "Did we order ribbon for this? And I guess I can google how to make them?"

Their mother places the light strings onto the table. "Isn't the internet full of tutorials?"

"Kelsey here's good at decorating," Randy says, and if he were anybody else, I would have kicked him. I'm not ready to perform in front of future in-laws!

His mother turns to me. "Excellent. You and Gina figure out some sort of wreath that will hold up for seven days. We need a dozen of them to decorate the light poles on the main path." She gestures to the narrow road that extends from the buildings to the forest. Each row has an old-fashioned lamp pole at the end.

"Happy to," I say, even though I'm anything but. I might kick him after all.

"Kelsey grew up on a dairy farm in Alabama," Randy says. "She's staying at the homestead."

"How lovely," his mom says, walking forward to extend a hand. "I'm Carrie Hanover. How long will you be in Glass?"

Her hand is rough and strong, like my mom's once was. It knocks me slightly off center. "We'll be here a week, maybe a little more."

"We?" Carrie's head tilts.

Oh, crap. I quickly add, "My coworker, Zachery, and I."

"I mentioned them the other day after I accepted the reservation," Gina says to her mother. "A man and a woman, separate rooms."

"Is the master bedroom downstairs still getting renovated?" Carrie asks.

Gina nods. "We have to fix the shower."

Carrie turns to Randy. "You should get to that."

"Yes, ma'am."

Gina turns to me. "You're from Hollywood?"

And there it is.

I think fast. "Zach grew up there." Still true while admitting nothing.

But Gina is persistent. "But you two work together?"

"We do."

"Don't grill her, Gina," Randy says.

"The girls can talk about things while they make wreaths," Carrie says. "You and Jack are hanging lights."

Oh, boy. Now I'll not only be trying to impress the future in-laws, but I'll also be separated from the future husband I barely know.

I wish Zachery had come with us. He's so good with people. He could easily deflect questions and put on the charm. Maybe I'll text him an SOS.

"We'll have to go into town to get ribbon," Gina says.

"I'll come, too," Carrie says. "I need to make sure all the apple cider has come in, plus check on the pies."

Gina pulls a set of car keys from her pocket and spins them around her finger. "You're going to get a proper tour of the town."

As we head toward a dark-green truck, I glance back at Randy.

He's getting an elbow to the ribs from his brother as they each sling rolls of lights over their shoulders.

What have I gotten myself into exactly? Is this an accepting bunch, or is this how they recruit free help around here?

As we arrange ourselves in the front seat of the truck, me squished between Randy's mom and sister, I think of *Midsommar*.

If someone puts a wreath of flowers on my hair, I'm jumping out of this damn truck.

Chapter 32

Zachery: 0, Wood: 1

The first SOS from Kelsey arrives midmorning.

Kelsey: I've been forced to shop in town with the future in-laws.

Me: Are you okay?

Kelsey: Forget the rom-coms. What are the early plot points of horror movies?

Me: You mean when they're gathering unsuspecting victims?

Kelsey: YES, THAT!

I chuckle to myself. Drama. Kelsey thrives on it. I'm about to look up some good horror movie setups when another notification comes through. It's a Google pin for where she is.

Kelsey: In case you need to help law enforcement locate the body.

Me: I think in towns like this, the sheriff is always in on it.

Kelsey: ZACH! Oh, gotta go pick out ribbon.

Me: For your wedding?

Kelsey: My funeral wreath.

No more dots appear. She's really gotten herself involved.

I review the proposal and contract terms of the background talent company providing the extras for both the soccer movie and this upcoming biopic with a concert scene.

Everything looks fine with the proposal. I've typed up an email on Kelsey's laptop for her to look over and make sound more peppy, then send to Desdemona.

I'm glad to help. Kelsey's getting what she wants.

When I save the draft, the view switches to a page of all her email drafts. I'm about to click away, but the sheer number of them makes me pause.

Eight hundred.

Who stores eight hundred unsent emails?

They're all addressed to Patti Whitaker.

Kelsey's mother, who died when she was twelve.

The most recent one is dated three nights ago. *That* night.

Subject line: I did something unwise.

I click away. I'm not going to read any of Kelsey's emails to her mother.

I close the laptop, feeling shaken.

Something unwise.

Probably that was me.

Does she regret it? Was she confessing?

I pace the floor, wishing I could read it, knowing I can't.

I want to reach out to her and say something. I need to know that she's real, not some ephemeral spirit that came to me in Colorado and asked me to possess her, like she has me.

I pick up my phone to text her. I can't stop myself.

I will be there for you no matter what.

I wait, willing her to answer. My heart pounds in my throat.

But there's only silence.

More silence.

More silence.

I circle her room, once, twice, three times. I resist picking up her nightclothes and bringing them to my face.

I will not obsess. I will not get weird.

In fact, I need to get out of here.

When the door latches behind me, I'm locked out of her room since we have different keys. The house is set up for separate parties.

I breathe a sigh of relief. Temptation averted.

Kelsey is doing what she set out to do. Find a man worthy of her, not someone from Hollywood, upwardly aspirational, fake, or indifferent.

But the need for her only grows as I wander the house, up and down the stairs, standing before the mantel where she decorated the hearth.

His family's home. The fireplace that witnessed their history.

They'll love her. Of course they will.

He'll love her. How could he not?

I sit on a chair in the kitchen, which feels more neutral than any other space in the house. I call Jester.

"Honey bear!" His voice is a balm. "How goes it with our girl? Did you woo her yet, or is she still seeking a hunk in flannel?"

"She's off with her future mother-in-law," I say, propping my feet up on the kitchen table like I can command their space.

"Oh, dear. You sound like that last man I dumped. You sure you're okay?"

I never said I was okay, but there's no need to point that out to Jester. "How's the home front?" I ask. "We had to stave off a call from Desdemona yesterday. I did Kelsey's work while she rides on a literal horse-drawn cart through a Christmas tree farm."

"Oh, no. It's that serious? You know how this script ends."

"I do."

"Pooh bear." His tone is a lament. "Maybe you should come home to Jester. I'll find you a nice hot starlet to ease your pain."

"Desdemona has already set me up with Catalina Ferrig."

"Oh, she's a firebrand. I'd plow that field if I was into flora and not fauna. You take the flowers. I'll handle the animals."

Right. "She hinted at coming back for the soccer scene. She's worried about the BG we hired since they're doing the concert film."

"She mentioned that. I figured you'd have a wrap by then, at least you. If Kelsey's found her man, maybe she can cut loose."

Would she? Quit her job for a man she barely knew? My neck flushes with heat as my blood pressure rises. Surely not.

I never intended to lose her for good. Not out of the industry, where she's so good at what she does. And certainly not in the middle of nowhere.

Damn fortune teller and her road trip.

I keep my voice level for Jester. "I don't know how it'll go down, but at least one of us will have to return."

"Well, I have your backs. Desdemona is none the wiser, and I don't think we'll hear much from her until it gets closer."

I walk to the back door of the kitchen. "Let me know if anything changes."

"Aye, aye."

I shove my phone in my pocket. The axe sits on the tree stump. There are a few uncut cross-sections of a tree nearby, more wood than would fit in the fireplace stand.

I push through the door and contemplate the axe. I've never cut wood in my life. We sometimes had a fire, but with the year-round warmth of Southern California, a digital flame was far more common.

I lift a block of wood onto the stump. It can't be that hard. I work out. I can bench-press the equivalent of any woman I've carried into a hotel room.

I pick up the axe. It feels good in my hands, hefty and firm.

I lift it over my head and bring it down on the wood with a mighty swing.

The blade bounces off the surface, nearly knocking me sideways.

What the hell?

I examine the wood, wondering if there's more skill to landing the blow.

I shift the piece so that I'll hit it at a different angle, then lift the axe again.

This time the axe sinks deeply into the wood.

Okay, then.

But when I try to lift the axe out, it won't budge.

Shit.

I stand on the trunk, tugging on the axe handle.

It doesn't move.

Great.

No matter how I struggle, strain, or heave, it remains solidly in the wood.

Just like the sword in the stone. I'm clearly not the man to be king here.

The city boy yields to the men of Hanover Tree Farm.

Chapter 33

KELSEY ROUNDS THE RIGHT BASE

Everyone at the various stores watches me curiously as we buy ribbon, taste-test peach pie, and load two crates of bottled apple cider into the bed of the truck.

Carrie answers their questions easily. I'm a guest at the house and helping out. No one digs too deeply, at least not in front of her.

When we get back to the tree farm, I don't see Jack or Randy anywhere. Gina sets me up at a long table in the wood building with the ribbon, wire circles, and some plastic greenery to fill them out.

"Good luck!" she says, and I get the feeling she's pleased as punch to have dumped this task on the poor unsuspecting girl who dared show up with her brother.

When she's gone, I snatch up my phone to text Zach.

Me: Forget the horror movie. I'm free labor.

He writes me instantly, as if he's been waiting.

Zach: What are you doing?

Me: Sitting alone in a building, expected to produce ribbon wreaths. I don't even know how to make them.

I glance around. On the back wall, a long counter holds the cash register and racks of knickknacks, snow globes, ornaments, candy bars, and light-up necklaces.

The two side walls are filled with shelves of decorations, carved statues, and even some taxidermy, including an entire family of squirrels in Santa hats.

I can't seem to avoid that no matter where I go.

Zach: You want me to come?

I do, desperately. I'm not sure what I've gotten myself into. But I can't ask him. Apparently, my fate is to make ribbon wreaths.

Me: It's okay. This is my dystopian nightmare.

Zach: Where's the husband?

Me: I have no idea but he better be ring shopping.

Zach: If it's less than a carat, send it back.

This makes me smile. Zachery is good in every situation.

He sends me a link, then another, all short instructional videos on how to make ribbon wreaths. The last one says, "Impress your mother-in-law!"

I have to laugh. Zachery gets me. All the way to the bone.

The door creaks open, and I quickly snatch up a roll of ribbon.

It's Randy.

"Hey, lady," he says. "Did my sister scare you off? Mom's a softy."

"I'm not easily frightened."

He drops into a chair on the opposite side of the table. "You're a real trouper, that's for sure." He picks up a roll of ribbon. "Making any headway?"

I realize I have no way of cutting the ribbon. "I was about to embark upon a reconnaissance for scissors."

"I got you." He heads for the back counter, and I swiftly mute my phone and play the first video, praying I'll learn enough to start the project in the scant seconds he'll be gone.

But Zach's good, sending me a clip that cuts to the chase, showing how to wrap the ribbon around your fingers and secure it with wire all around the circlet.

"Is there some wire around here?" I ask him, keeping my eyes on the video. "Something low gauge I can use to tie the ribbon on?"

"For sure. It's in the storage room." He heads through a back door.

Great. More time. I pick up the end of the ribbon and practice the wrap a few times. The video speeds up as the woman places all the fat loops around the edge and then secures the final one, covering the end of the wire with a bow. I can make a bow.

I shut the phone off and push it aside as Randy comes back into view. He sits again, sliding a pair of scissors and a roll of silver wire across to me. "Is it hard? If you can teach me, we'll get done faster and I thought I'd take you into town for lunch, if you'd like."

Finally. "Sounds great. And yes, it's easy." And I can assess his finger dexterity. The thought brings a blush to my cheeks, but then it's not Randy's hands I picture, but Zachery's.

Nope, no. Danger zone!

I pull a second spool of ribbon from the bag and roll it to Randy. *Focus, Kelsey.*

It takes a few tries to show him how to wrap the ribbon around his fingers, press it against the circlet, and secure it with wire, but by the time we're halfway around, we're both fairly competent with it.

Rather than teach him the trickier bit with the bow, I set him to making a third while I finish the ribbon off and wire in the greenery.

When I hold it up, I think it looks good.

"Hey!" Randy says. "That's nice."

We keep going.

"I'm guessing that since I'm staying in your family's homestead, your roots go way back in Glass."

"Over a hundred and fifty years. It used to be a logging operation, but my great-great-grandfather realized pretty quick that we better be responsible about the land or we'd be out of trees." Randy's fingers fly around the circle.

"A forward thinker, then."

"Practical, anyway. Tree farms got popular in the fifties, when people from the city would come out to cut their own in the national forest, then realize it's nice to have someone fell it for you and tie it to the car."

"I bet."

"It's not easy, picking a good one in the middle of everything, or felling one if it's surrounded by other trees. A lot of half-felled trees met their tragic end to no good use, and we became the answer."

"Now you grow them specifically for Christmas trees, I take it."

"Indeed. We augment from the forest and bring them to the tents, but we thin the right parts to allow all the trees to grow well."

I set aside the second finished wreath and reach for the one Randy has filled with ribbon. "Does everyone work on the farm, or have some members of your family branched out?"

He laughs, a deep chortle that I feel in my belly. "*Branched out.* I like it. My dad is an only child, so he took it over from Grandpap. When we moved Grandmama into the cottage, we were able to rent out the homestead for weddings and events, and that helps supplement the income. Gina mainly handles all that."

I want to ask what happened to make the business falter enough that they need to fundraise this summer, but I know to shut my mouth. It doesn't matter. Not on the first date.

The silence stretches as we work. I guess he isn't going to ask about me, which I probably prefer right now. I won't have to tap-dance around my history.

Jack comes in, pronounces our work "good enough," and takes the finished ones to hang. By the time he returns, we've completed the last one.

"Lunch, then?" Randy asks.

"Sure."

We take the same green truck back into town, Blue between us, her tongue hanging out. It should be charming with the beautiful town, the dog, and the already-familiar drive.

But Randy and I seem to have run out of things to talk about.

When we sit down at a sandwich shop on the square, Blue lying under the table, I aim to come up with a safe topic. "What's high school like here? Is there a football team? Is another sport bigger?"

It turns out Randy played football, and for the next thirty minutes, through ordering, eating, and paying the check, he finds an endless number of stunning plays, close calls, and big wins to tell me about.

I hold my smile for so long that it feels plastered on.

I'm out of practice talking about small-town things.

But Randy catches himself. "Listen to me," he says. "Bending your ear the whole time about my glory days. What about you? What was high school like for you?"

Okay, then. This is an improvement over the last two.

"I did theater. One-act play."

"You're an actress?" He frowns. "From Hollywood?"

"No, no, I'm not an actress. Not in the least." I have to fix that misperception fast.

And leave out my degree in theater arts, I guess, the one where I started in acting but switched to tech and design skills when I decided I could never handle the reality of being judged for something so personal as my looks and the way I acted a part.

I never auditioned for anything, only did small performances required for my classes.

"I was more behind the scenes," I say quickly. "I can paint a mean garden wall."

I reach for details that skirt the acting stereotype. "I learned how to run a light board. I was too afraid of heights to climb the catwalk to change the bulbs, though."

Randy laughs lightly at that. "I might have been, too."

Then it happens!

INT. SMALL-TOWN SANDWICH SHOP—DAY

KELSEY, 25, in denim shorts and a white shirt, sits across from RANDY, 28, in work jeans and boots.

He reaches for a chip at the same moment she moves toward her glass, and their fingers brush each other.

They look at each other in surprise, as if neither one of them guessed you could tell that someone was "the one" from an accidental touch.

The zip of electricity I feel is bright and sharp.

Hallmark first base! Exactly like it's supposed to happen!

After the accidental brush of our hands, Randy takes my fingers and clasps them in his. "This all right?"

"Yeah," I say, breathless.

I'm breathless! From holding hands!

His thumb moves across my knuckles. "You like to wear a lot of rings."

"I do?" I mean, I know I do, but I'm not wearing any now at all. I didn't want any confusion about my availability, plus that didn't seem very farm-girl.

"I can tell from the tan lines. See?" He lifts my hand, and sure enough, there are the barest blurred rings of paler skin. I can even make out the ghostly circle of my favorite moonstone.

"I guess I'm outdoors a lot." I've never noticed this myself. It must have happened during all the walks from the office to my car. California sunshine at its finest.

I take in his face. He's not as handsome as Zachery, but that's like comparing someone to Brad Pitt. Most men would lose.

His face is tan and well honed with a sharp jaw and broad, sweeping eyebrows. His eyes are hazel, the glittery kind that always make me think of the sparkle batons I loved as a kid. I had one just like his eyes, gold and brown and green and blue.

"You still owe me at least twenty minutes of high school bragging before we're even," he says. "Were you an A student? I bet you were. You look sharp as a tack."

Nobody ever says I look smart. Sunshine, yes. Pretty, sometimes. Bright, often.

"I thought blondes couldn't be smart," I say.

He reaches out to tap my nose. "You're the whole package, I bet. Beautiful and brainy. And crafty, too. And a farm girl, so you know hard work. Girls like you don't come into Glass, Wyoming, very often."

The glow in my gut is warm and good. This is happening.

I glance around the tiny restaurant. "It's all so beautiful here and the shops are quaint, and that homestead of yours is a dream."

"It'll be mine when I want it. Jack took the original cabin when he got married, and Gina prefers to live in town. It's too much house for me right now, although Mom thinks it's set up nicely to be a bed-and-breakfast. All depends on how I settle down."

During this, his fingers keep their easy pressure on mine.

"Is that what you want?" I ask. "A bed-and-breakfast close to the tree farm?"

"I think it sounds all right. This is where I started, and this is where I'll end up."

Unlike me. I shot out of that dairy farm the first chance I got. My father without my mother was unbearable while I was growing up. And it never got any better, no matter how many times I went back between college semesters to try again. He was toxic and mean, and most of us escaped.

Without the glue of our mother's care, we scattered, talking only a few times a year. Twice, we managed to get everyone back at Christmas, but the way it ruined everyone's holiday made most of us quit trying. I haven't gone back in years.

I really don't want to go there, and this is looking good. I want to know more about Randy. The urge to jump as many hurdles as possible is strong. "Do you have other interests? Anything else you ever wanted to do?"

He shrugs. "No point in it. Jack went to college. Got an ag degree. Then he came back and did the same things he was doing before, minus about forty thou in our parents' savings. Didn't seem much point in it, so I skipped."

"That wasn't that long ago. You could still go."

This unsettles him. "I don't see any reason to leave. And if I like somewhere else better, doesn't that mean I never belonged in the first place?"

"I don't think so."

"What about you? You left your parents' farm."

This is hitting close to home.

We've strayed from the formula. The questions are going too deep. Aren't we supposed to be baking something? Cupcakes? A pie?

Where's a bunch of carolers when you need them?

But then I hear it. The strains of "We Wish You a Merry Christmas."

I peer out the window at the sun-drenched landscape. A teen boy in shorts and a tank top saunters by.

The sound grows louder.

"There they are!" The woman who took our order leaves her damp rag on a table and heads to the door.

"It's the school choir," Randy says. "They're doing the same rounds they do at Christmas. It's amazing how the whole town is getting into the spirit of the fundraiser."

"The school lets them wander and sing?"

"It's the last week of school. We timed the dance to be their last day to encourage people to come celebrate. The teachers are tired, so I guess they went out caroling." He grins. "I bet some of them sneak off to Harvey's Sweet Shop to buy candy."

A group of ten children, all aged ten to twelve or so, sing as they walk along the sidewalk of the square. Behind them is a woman with a harmonica, blowing an occasional note to keep them in tune.

They see us watching them and pause on the other side of the window. The woman at the door throws it open so the sound can penetrate.

"And a happy New Year!"

Now it does seem odd, since it's only about to turn into a happy June, and of course the kids are all in shorts and sandals.

But for my purposes, it's perfect.

The script is holding up exactly right.

And when I think about it, I can see myself at the homestead, greeting the latest visitors, baking bread from scratch and sending them off with a jar of my own preserves with a cute checkered bow.

And kids. Two of them, totally into their grandma Carrie.

This is what I was thinking of. Randy described it exactly.

The dairy farm life without the dairy farm work.

Living like my upbringing without the bitterness.

And with a bonus—the opportunity to meet new people all the time even though I live in a tight community.

I think I just found my dream.

Chapter 34

ZACHERY TURNS ON A DIME

I don't have to talk to Kelsey to know she and Randy hit it off.

It's all over her face.

They pull up in a green truck, dust blowing behind it, as I sit on the upstairs deck, using my phone to research a director Jester sent me, work that normally goes to Kelsey.

They shouldn't be able to see me up here. They've been gone all day, and the light is fading.

Randy stops the truck, then rushes around the front and opens the door for Kelsey.

They don't do that in Hollywood, not unless it's a driver or a valet. Even so, I'm hit with a bite of regret that he's more courteous with her than I am.

She steps out with a huge smile, giddy as a schoolgirl.

Randy takes her hand as they head up the steps to the front door.

Thankfully, that's below me and I can't see him kiss her, if he does. That's Hallmark third base, but maybe Kelsey's thrown it out the window again.

The last person who kissed her was me.

I crank the music in my earbuds to ensure I can't hear anything, including if they go up to her room. I close my eyes to the darkening sky. This is what I'm here for. Kelsey. To watch over her.

I'm doing my job.

My job was not what I did a few nights ago. Absolutely not. But that's the vision that comes back to me.

Her dress, falling to the floor.

Her body, trembling in my arms.

My hands, covering every inch of her.

I shouldn't have done it. I'll never get the thought of her out of my head.

I try to switch to some other woman, anyone. Claudia Bonatello, for example. She's an A-list actress now. I see videos of her all the time.

But I can't. I can picture scenes from her last movie, just nothing from real life. My memories are fuzzy on the edges, like a pixelated image from an old video game.

And I can't conjure any emotion for her. Probably because there never was any.

I don't seduce these women with any agenda, despite what Desdemona thinks. If there's no chemistry when I take them out for a premiere or a festival, then I leave them be. But often, it's nice, feeling like I'm a real part of the Hollywood game. The woman in my bed is the bonus, even better if she didn't really need me in the first place.

Hands on my shoulders startle me hard enough that I jump out of my chair. I yank my earbuds out. Dust rises up as the truck drives away.

"You were lost in thought!" Kelsey says.

"I was." I tuck my earbuds in my pocket. "How did it go?"

She sits in a rocking chair next to me, her toe setting the chair in motion. "It got better."

It got more than better. That's plain. "Did you make the wreaths?"

"Yes, and thank you for the videos. They saved my bacon."

"Did they turn out well?"

"Everyone thought they were lovely. Randy helped. Then we had lunch, then we set up the tents for the hayride on Wednesday. Then we had dinner, too."

"That's an auspicious beginning."

"There were rough patches. But in the end, I think he has an idea for his future that sounds pretty nice."

I shift on the chair, suddenly feeling the uncomfortable hardness of the seat. "And what's that?"

"This house." She gestures to the wall behind us. "His brother, Jack, took a different property, and his sister prefers living in town, so this will be his when he's ready to take it over."

"Isn't it generating income as a rental?"

She draws a knee up to her chin and wraps her arms around her shin. "He's hoping to marry and run it as a bed-and-breakfast. He has plans to turn the library downstairs into a children's room, and block off it and the master downstairs so that the upstairs is devoted to holding guests."

That sounds like a nightmare. "So, you would always have strangers tromping through your house?"

"That's what all bed-and-breakfasts do. And even though you live in a small town, you're always meeting new people. It wouldn't get boring."

She's bought into the idea. That's clear. "So that's what you'd do? Marry the local lumberjack and host a B and B?"

She frowns. "Does that sound so terrible?"

"What about your talent, Kelsey? You make movie magic."

"Only when the Demon approves. And gets the credit."

"But it's what you love. I've seen your face light up when you find a perfect pairing."

"Only for them to refuse the script!" She drops her leg, sitting up tall. "I thought you were on my side on this! Why did you come if you're going to trash the good thing I find?"

"You've known this guy, what, twenty-four hours?"

"I'm not marrying him, Zachery. I haven't even kissed him yet."

This makes me feel better. I force my tone to come down. "Why not?"
She rocks the chair. "I'm on Hallmark bases." Her eyes light up.
"We hit first base and it was pure accident, just like the meet-cute. He
reached for a chip, and I reached for my glass, and our fingers touched!"

I have to hold myself back from saying, "And remember when you
fell to pieces when I touched you? How we almost flew into the sun?"

But I swallow it. It has to remain unsaid. She asked for my help that
night, and I gave it, like the work emails I've written on her behalf, like
the wreath videos I sent.

It's all the same. Moments between friends.

"I'm glad," I say. "Maybe whoever wrote the first Hallmark movie
knew what he was talking about, and everyone copied it because it was
true."

Kelsey sighs with a dreamy smile. "Between the free labor and the
way lunch started, I thought I was going to be cutting and running on
this one. But it completely turned around."

"Life can do that."

"It can." She rocks a little longer. "I'm sorry it turned the wrong
way for you."

"It's fine. I wasn't made for movies."

"I think you were totally made for movies. It just went the wrong
direction."

She's really pushing on this. "My life is fine."

"Is it, though? A long stream of women without attachments." She
goes quiet for a minute, and I wonder if she's now counting herself as
one of them.

"By most any standard, I have lived the dream."

"But what are you living now? Do you want to settle down? Your
sister got married. Do your parents ever ask about that?"

They don't, not anymore. "Dad kids me about all the actresses. I
think he might be half-proud."

"And your mom?"

I don't talk about my mother much with Kelsey. She knows the basics, that my mother was a Broadway singer but never felt she reached the pinnacle she hoped for. Her career, by all accounts, was also fine, the kind most people dream of. But she was never the lead in anything huge, never nominated for a Tony. Sometimes I think she was almost relieved to fall in love with Dad and move to LA and have a family. The pressure was off.

Until I started singing lessons. Her joy when I did school plays and performed in choir was one of my driving forces. She sat in on every lesson, every rehearsal, and never missed a single performance. I became her everything.

Now, she looks pained if I sing so much as "Happy Birthday" to her.

I had the dream, too. It's not that she forced something on me I didn't want. But other opportunities came faster, movie roles, stardom. I thought she'd be thrilled that I wasn't leaving California.

But I noticed that her face never lit up the same when she saw me after signing that first movie contract.

I disappointed her. I disappointed myself.

I realize time has passed, but Kelsey doesn't press for an answer. "She wanted me to sing," I say. "She'll never get over that I didn't."

Kelsey sits up. "You still can."

"You think I didn't knock on those doors?" I haven't admitted this to anyone. "Nobody wants an industry joke bringing negative publicity to their theater."

"When was the last time you tried? The reputation fades."

"Not as long as I continue walking the red carpet and keep the tabloids busy with their hilarious headlines."

It doesn't happen all the time, but if a photographer gets just the right shot, they exploit it fully.

Beer Junket Bimbo? Zach Carter's Latest Starlet
Reenacts the Famous Nip Slip

Who Called G-23? Is Zach Carter Dating the Bingo Crowd Now?

Kelsey sinks back against the chair. "Why do you do it, then? You could let it all fade out."

That's just it. I don't want to fade. "That would be giving up."

She nods, her hair glowing from the window light. It's full dark out now. "I get that. I would do a lot of questionable things to avoid going home to Alabama."

"You think my dates are questionable?" It's fine for the tabloids to think that, even for my dad to think it. But not Kelsey.

"No, no. Having been the recipient of the full Zachery treatment, I'm very confident that you are an absolute gentleman other than not realizing the extent of your power."

My heart speeds up. What does she mean by that? "So, I'm absolved?"

"Fully. I was really talking about my own life. Working for Desdemona sometimes feels like being the evil mastermind's apprentice."

"I'm definitely not enjoying it like I used to. She's getting more desperate as she becomes increasingly irrelevant."

"You think so?"

"Kelsey, you're the one making all the good calls. She's skating on your talent to bolster her reputation."

"Then why does she make me so miserable?"

"Fear."

Kelsey rests her chin on her knee. "Maybe we both need a change."

We both say it at the same time.

"Jester."

"We can't leave him," Kelsey says. "Although he's been with Desdemona longer than either of us."

"He does seem immune to her brutality."

"Maybe his colorful clothes are a force field. Her harsh words invert into birdsong and giggles."

This makes me laugh. "He definitely makes it work."

She stands and pats my shoulder. "Speaking of which, I better go see if there are any fires to put out. Thank you for being so much help, Zachery. I don't know how I would be managing on this trip without you."

She kisses the top of my head and goes back inside.

Her day turned on a dime.

And because of that, so did mine. Just the wrong direction.

Chapter 35

Kelsey Is Fine All Fine

The evening of the hayride is warm and breezy. I decide to walk from the homestead to the tree farm, a journey through the forest that no longer makes me nervous, having traversed it several times in the last two days.

I helped sort inventory, put on price stickers, steam tablecloths, and organize displays.

The brothers cleared the path of the hayride, fortified the tents, and borrowed a second cart and a pair of horses from a neighboring farm to double the number of rides they can sell tickets for.

And Randy and I hit Hallmark movie second base: the almost-kiss. We were admiring his grandfather's hand-carved bird ornaments, looked at each other with misty eyes over his being lost too soon, like my mom, and leaned in.

Only to have Gina stomp into the room, upset that the Grinch-themed Christmas mugs she ordered weren't going to make it in time for the tea.

The way Randy grinned at me when we were thwarted made *my* heart grow three sizes.

As I walk along the pine-scented path to the tree farm, I totally understand the urge to burst into song. I've enjoyed Carrie's company as we worked side by side. Even Gina, who seemed abrupt when we first met, has grown on me.

When I step out of the woods, Ol' Blue spots me right off and bounds down the row to greet me. Somewhere along the way, she must have decided I'm all right. It might have been the bits of chicken I've started keeping in a plastic bag to feed her.

I'm not above bribery.

Randy looks up from where he's stringing lights along the edge of the second cart. "Hey, Kelsey! You ready for a wild night in Glass?"

I laugh. "I think so."

He pauses to take me in. "You sure look pretty in that pink dress."

I turn in a circle. "I didn't have anything Christmassy."

"It's perfect."

"Can I help?"

"Sure." He moves to the back of the cart to help me up. I'm better at it now. Hay bales have been placed all along the walls of the cart. "There's some red ribbons to tie on the sides."

I pick one up and sit on the hay to wire it in place.

Carrie comes out of the food tent. "Good to see you, Kelsey. That cart sure did need a woman's touch."

"I've got it!"

Randy's father, Jed, emerges from the building. We met yesterday. He's a slightly larger, somewhat redder-faced version of his sons. "You got power in the food tent?" he asks his wife.

"Yep. The cider's heating," Carrie says.

Jed frowns. "I guess hot cider makes sense."

"It's not good cold."

He nods, then notices me and raises a hand. "Heya there, Kelsey!"

"Hello, Jed."

Randy grins at me. "You fit right in, my lady."

"I kind of do, don't I?" A happy trill goes through me. So what if it's been only a few days? Who says this has to be hard?

And we're still on Hallmark time. Randy hasn't kissed me yet. We haven't been alone. It's been busy since that first day.

But tonight, he's promised me a solo ride after all the others are over. I feel like a young lass from *Little House on the Prairie*, waiting on her beau to make her his girl.

I can't wait.

The preparations are barely in place when the first car parks in the gravel lot. Then more people arrive. Then more. I spot the lady from the sandwich shop, and several kids from caroling. Among them is Jack's wife, who teaches fifth grade.

"You ready for the first round?" Randy asks, pulling me up to sit on the driver's bench with him.

"Totally." I turn to look behind us. All the hay bales are filled with mothers, fathers, kids, and older couples. Jack's cart is filling up, too. The ones who didn't fit wander the tents and the rows of trees, eating peach pie and drinking cider.

"This is a good turnout for a Wednesday night."

"We're just getting started. It'll be packed for the square dance Friday night. School will be out, and everyone will feel like celebrating."

The energy of all the happy people makes the air feel electric. Randy pops the reins and the horses begin their steady *clop, clop* down the path.

He begins his spiel. "The first Hanover moved to Wyoming in 1875."

I stare up into the night. Beyond the lights strung between the poles, the stars shine among the wispy clouds. The day was warm, but evening has a bite to it as the wind picks up.

Randy notices and leans in. "Feel free to sidle up if you need to get warm."

I do.

He calls back over his shoulder, "Grandpap Hanover turned the farm over to my dad, Jed, in 1992, and passed on two years later."

I watch him talk, pointing out the family burial plot off to the left, in a small clearing surrounded by majestic aspens twinkling with white lights. Grandmama won that battle. I understand she's formidable. I try to imagine being widowed for thirty-plus years.

My father is already thirteen years in.

Mom deserved so much more in the thirty-nine years she got. I stare up at the moon and whisper, "I won't let that happen to me."

Randy reaches over to squeeze my hand. I don't think anyone's noticed, but then I catch two of the kids giggling and watching us. It's adorable. All of it.

We do four hayrides until it gets too late for the families. Jack takes the last round of young couples, and his parents shut down the tents.

"You ready for our ride?" Randy asks.

My heart speeds up. It's time to see if we've got anything beyond a few days of congenial labor and a few handholds.

Hallmark bases, I remind myself firmly. *No rolling in the hay on the back of a cart.*

That would be Zach territory. It's true what I said to him on the porch the other night about the actresses he courts. I sometimes field their breathless phone calls the next day, asking if there's any way they could star in something with him. They get big dreams after a night of his attention. Nobody is ever unhappy the morning after. There are zero complaints.

For a moment, I flash to his hands on me, his earnestness, his care. My body heats up. I get it now. Everything they felt. Zachery is a dream.

Wait. No. No no no. This is a hayride with my possible future husband. There's no room for Zach on this cart!

I force myself to give Randy a smile. This is what I came here for. The real deal. No Hollywood fantasy.

Randy flicks the reins, and we take off down the path beneath the lights we passed under many times tonight. The night is even cooler, and I snuggle against him.

We pause by the family graves, and Randy nods at them in respect.

Instead of returning to the tents, we turn off toward the woods and the homestead. It's dark here, and Randy bends down to flip on a powerful flashlight that's aimed at the ground to help the horses find their way.

We're in deep shadow.

"It was a lovely event," I tell him. "I think your farm is the pride of Glass."

"It's a cornerstone of the town." He squeezes my hand. "What do you think of it here?"

"It's lovely. I am a southern girl, though. How cold does it get in winter?"

"It's bitter. I won't lie. But we have our ways of coping."

"Do you?"

He chuckles. "I plan to install floor warmers in the master bedroom of the homestead. That'll help."

"That does sound nice."

"Then there's always other things."

The cart slows, and one of the horses snorts in the dark.

Randy faces me. "Is it all right if I kiss you, Kelsey?"

"It is."

He leans in, his mouth gently finding mine.

Third base. I'm supposed to know by now how I feel. It's the great crescendo of the movie. There should be a soaring soundtrack.

And I like it. I do. His mouth is warm and gentle, like he's got all the time in the world.

I scoot in closer, to see if he'll take it deeper. And he does, his tongue sliding along my lips until I part for him.

It feels right, I keep saying to myself. It's a good kiss. A perfectly wonderful, normal kiss between two companionable people.

We kiss a little longer, slightly jostled by the cart's slow progress, until the lights of the homestead invade the darkness, and he pulls away.

"I'm glad you came to Glass, Kelsey," he says.

"Me too." I fit my head in the space between his neck and shoulder. I'm jolted to another moment, another shoulder, another neck. Zach's arms, around me as I sobbed. He'd touched me so deeply, further in than I let anyone go, other than my mother in the emails I write but cannot send.

Zachery got me there. He reached that inner part of me I never let heal. Have never wanted to heal. I want to miss my mother all my life.

I'll just tuck the memory of Zach in there with her. I have to. He is not for me.

And I like Randy's kiss.

And the cart ride.

Really. I do.

It's all perfectly *fine*.

~

It's not particularly late when I head up the stairs of the homestead.

Zach's door is open. He's sitting against the headboard of his bed in casual shorts and a T-shirt.

"Knock knock?"

He looks up. "How was the hayride?"

"Good. Really nice turnout. Should have made decent money."

He sets his phone aside. "Any progress with the husband?"

I sit on the far corner of his bed. I don't dare get any closer, not after the direction my thoughts took earlier.

"We made out in the woods on the way home."

I watch him carefully for any signs of jealousy or disappointment. His smile seems genuine. "Was it everything a girl could hope for?"

I kick off my shoes. "It was good. I like him. He's good. His family's great. Maybe these sorts of relationships really can happen."

"Sure looks like it."

I run my hand along the dark-green bedspread, unwilling to hold his gaze. "It's only been a few days. I barely know him. But it's promising."

"Not something unwise?"

My head snaps up. That was the subject line of my email about the night with Zachery. He can't know about that.

But he does. His face is frozen, like he didn't mean to say it.

"Did you read my emails?" I want to jump up, shout at him, but I feel paralyzed.

He swings his legs around to move closer to me. "No. Not one. I saved a draft of a work email I wrote for you and saw some subject lines. I shut your computer down immediately."

My chest heaves with fear. I have always kept the emails on my laptop so no one would ever see them. But I handed it right over to Zachery.

"Kelsey, do you want to talk about them?"

I can't quite catch my breath. I try to slow down, but I'm gulping air.

Zach pulls me to him. "Breathe with me. You're okay. I didn't read them. I wouldn't."

He presses my head to his chest, exaggerating his breathing. I work to match him. Long inhale, long exhale.

His hand slides through my hair, making my scalp tingle.

He feels so good. His chest. His arms. His unbelievably good smell.

A pulse beats down low.

I want him. I want him again. I want him always.

I can't.

A sob forms in my throat, and I'm unable to stop it before it escapes.

"Kels?"

He can't know this emotion is about him. I rush out an explanation. "I started writing emails to my mother in high school."

His hands stroke my back and my hair. "Do they help?"

"Always. The farm was so hard after she died. Dad was so terrible. Work, chores, get up early, make no mistakes. You couldn't complain, and you could never cry."

"What would he do?"

"Make you work harder. We all learned quickly to hide our feelings."

"So you wrote the emails."

I nod against his chest. "I don't do it as often now."

"But you did the night we were together."

I nod again.

"Do you want to talk about it? Why it was unwise?" His voice rumbles in his chest. I can feel it in my cheek.

I do. I really do. I want to tell him how it made me feel. How I opened up. How I fell into him and no longer felt afraid of facing anything. That it wasn't unwise at all, other than knowing I couldn't have him. That I might eventually need him like I used to need my mother and lose him, too.

Mom was the one who made farm life fun. Who let us sleep in and pretended we were doing inside chores. Who took us out for our birthdays and did more than buy presents, but gave us her presence.

And now here's Zach, showing me what intimacy can be like. More than touching and chemistry.

Connection. Real, true feelings. I had them. He brought them out.

But he's not for me.

His hand moves down, and his thumb accidentally grazes the side of my breast.

I flinch.

I can't do this. I'll fall right into him.

I'll let him take me to those places again. I won't be able to escape a second time.

I jerk away.

"I have to go, Zach. I'm all right. I really am. I'm sorry you saw the subject line. I'm fine. We're fine. It's all okay."

I slide away from him and pick up my shoes.

I don't look back at him. I know what I'll see. Perfect, handsome, muscled, irresistible Zachery, his shirt rumpled from where I just left it. On his bed.

So close. So tempting.

But absolutely, completely, the worst possible thing I could do.

I lied about being fine.

I'm most definitely not.

I need to write an email about this. Think it through. Sort it all out.

I need my mother.

Chapter 36

ZACHERY THE DANCING CHICKEN

I barely see Kelsey that week. She helps with the tree farm events, decorating, organizing, and fitting in like I've never seen her do in LA. Every evening when she comes in, she looks better, more energized. Happier.

Despite all those parties, premieres, auditions, and work meetings we've attended together, I've never seen her glow this way.

I have to admit that she belongs.

I can't find any fault with Randy, either. Kelsey says she feels safe and secure with him.

Unlike me, who bashed in the faces of *two* men as well as literally seduced her into oblivion instead of talking her through her worries like a proper friend would have done.

I was *something unwise*.

But Friday night brings the big dance, and Kelsey begs me to go as she arranges her hair in a curly golden mass.

She passes me a container of bobby pins to hold. "I only know the family, and they'll be really busy. I'm petrified that this will be the time people come up to talk, and I'll be all alone, and I know I'll say something stupid or out myself as Hollywood."

"You're becoming less Hollywood by the day."

She pulls a pin from the plastic case. "You think so?"

"Look at you. No more glamour makeup, no high heels. You wear nothing but pastels. I bet you're itching to trade that hybrid for an SUV."

She jerks her face toward me. "How did you know that?"

"Because there aren't any charging ports for a hundred miles?"

"You checked?"

"I've been doing everything I can to make your life easier."

She secures another curl, then reaches out to squeeze my arm. "You have been the best friend, Zachery."

Other than that time I plowed into her against the wall.

"I want the best for you, Kelsey."

She turns back to the mirror. "What do you think? Do I look the part of the small-town girlfriend, pretty but not flashy, well dressed but not a show-off?"

"You're perfect."

She turns to me with a smile that washes over me like warm rain. "You always say that."

I don't push the point. "You have your proper small-town icebreakers prepared?"

She sits up straight, then tilts her head with an easy smile. "Don't you love the look of those pies? I'm always looking for a good chocolate recipe." She clears her throat. "Are we behind on rain this year? Sure seems dry."

"Don't mention global warming," I warn.

She relaxes into normal Kelsey mode. "Wouldn't dream of it."

"Good girl." Saying those two words, though, makes me think of her, the dress at her waist. *I'm going to take this dress off you.*

She is not for me.

I'm the one who farts in old ladies' faces on-screen, who pisses in fountains for the cameras, who dates for visibility, for press, for nothing resembling this shining hope I see in Kelsey.

"I'm ready." She looks me up and down. "Is that what you're wearing?"

I glance at my Armani shirt and Luca Faloni trousers. "Too much?"

"It's over a thousand dollars, each. Can you find anything under five hundred?"

"We could stop by Wally World."

"Hush. How about jeans?"

"Mine are—"

"Right. Even more expensive than those pants."

She really is nervous. "Nobody here is going to assess the value of my wardrobe," I tell her.

"But you look different. You stand out."

"Should I stay home then?"

"No! I need you."

"Let me go buy something." I should have known to buy something less audacious before now. This day was always coming.

"No time. It's fine. You're right. It's just me. Let's go."

We take her hybrid rather than my Jag because it looks like a normal car. Mine doesn't fit in at all among the practical Fords and Chevys.

When we pull up, music pours out of the American Legion hall, the doors thrown open.

I pay for our tickets to get in. The room is brightly lit for a dance. I'm expecting a band to be playing, but there's a man onstage with a microphone and a laptop, barreling out commands to the groups of dancers all doing coordinated moves.

"I don't know how to do any of that," Kelsey says, moving closer to me. "I'm about to chicken out."

"Most people aren't dancing," I tell her, steering her toward the bar. "Let's get some wine in you, and it'll be better."

She takes in the room while I get the attention of the man behind the counter.

But he laughs when I ask for a chardonnay. "We got a box of red back here. Will that do?"

I nod and hold up two fingers. "Wine for you, too?" he shouts over the music, doubt all over his face at my decision.

I realize I better fit in or Kelsey will get even more anxious. "No, I meant two drinks. Make mine . . ." I glance over the collection of bottles lined up on a shelf. "Michelob."

He nods and pulls one out of an ice chest, popping the top with the inside of his elbow. Then he drags the box of wine up to the counter and pours an entire red plastic cup full of it. That's like half a bottle. That'll get her relaxed.

I pay for the drinks and head back to Kelsey. "Here you go."

She stares at the cup. "What is that?"

"Your Wyoming chardonnay."

"I better get some pie to slow down that wine," she says.

We head over to the bake sale. Three ladies guard the pastries. I've never seen a spread like it. Brownies, cookies, every kind of cake, at least twenty pies.

"What can we get you?" one asks.

"I'll have some apple pie," Kelsey says, then looks at her red wine. "Actually, make that chocolate cake."

She's trying to pair box wine with dessert. Classic Kelsey.

"Anything for you, handsome?" The grandmotherly woman gives me a wink.

My trainer would throw himself on the pyre of sugar if he saw this table. "I heard there was someone in this fine town who makes a coconut pie so good that I'll want to propose marriage."

All three women start giggling. Kelsey smiles over her cup. I'm pleased to have made her happy.

"Abigail makes the best coconut pie," the grandmother says, elbowing a tall woman with cat-eye glasses, "but she's spoken for. I, however, got three proposals based on my bourbon-pecan pie back in my day."

"I think I must try a slice of this commitment-inspiring pie."

Abigail nods in agreement. "And Eleanor's been single since 2004."

"Oh, hush now, this boy's no older than my Frankie." Eleanor cuts a generous slice of a pecan-topped pie and hands it to me. "Enjoy your pie."

I tuck a handful of bills into the donation jar and toast her with the plate. "I most certainly will."

The three women animatedly chat as Kelsey and I settle at the end of a long table lined with chairs.

"You're going to charm the bloomers off the ladies," Kelsey says.

"And that will make clear that I'm on the lookout, and you're devoted to their favored son Randy."

She sinks her fork into the cake. "Smart. This is why I brought you."

We've made it most of the way through the desserts when Randy shows up. "You're here!" He leans down to kiss her hair.

I avert my eyes, concentrating on a wayward pecan.

"Thank you for bringing her, Zach," he says.

"Of course."

"You sure you don't want me to help out?" Kelsey asks. "I totally can."

"You've done too much already. Enjoy yourself. Zach, you'll dance with her, right? Keep any other prospects off my girl?"

I stuff down fifty dark responses. "Of course."

"Great." He squeezes Kelsey's shoulders. "Save a slow dance for me, all right?"

"Of course." She watches him disappear through a side door.

"What does he have to go do?" I ask, pushing the pie away. I no longer have any appetite for it.

"He and Jack are taking turns patrolling the parking lot for fights."

That gets my attention. "Fights?"

"These events tend to bring out hostility."

"Okay, then."

She shrugs. "It was the same in Alabama. Farmers and cowboys, blowing off steam."

The square dancing comes to an end. "Now for a line dance!" the man onstage announces. A new song begins.

Kelsey groans. "This was a staple at every school dance and wedding where I grew up."

"What is it?"

Her eyes get wide. "The Chicken Dance. You don't know it?"

"Should I?"

She laughs and jumps up, pulling on my arm. "Come on. You have to learn it."

She leads me to the center of the room, where mostly older people and little kids have congregated.

They start making weird motions with their hands, then flap their elbows like a bird.

Oh, I get it. Chickens.

There there's a hip wiggle and four claps.

"That's all there is!" Kelsey calls over the music. "You better not just stand there."

I catch up at the elbow flap and keep going.

Kelsey's face is bright with laughter. "You're doing it!"

The next phase seems to be walking around the room, locking elbows with people. I meander, doing the motions, then it's time to be a chicken again.

"I think I like it now!" Kelsey shouts. "It's more fun with you!"

It *is* pretty silly. We make another round of the floor, and a few people say hello to Kelsey and mention Randy.

This brings on the glow. It's that belonging. She's been looking for it, ever since losing her mom and having her family scatter. She has no living grandmothers. No female family to speak of anywhere.

Here, she's got it. Role models in spades. A community.

I'll flirt with old ladies for her. And I'll dance like a chicken.

But I won't be the person who ever takes it away.

I will be happy for her.

I *will*.

Chapter 37

KELSEY AND THE QUEEN OF GLASS

The final event of the tree farm's summer Christmas is the tea.

I wake up to the downstairs buzzing with voices. Right, we were warned when we checked in that this would be a busy day. We agreed to it.

The bathroom is in the hall, and I wish I'd known what time people would start arriving so I could have been ready ahead of them. I'm deathly afraid of Randy's mom or sister or any of the women I've met spotting me looking like something the cat dragged in.

Once I get across the hall, I better not leave the bathroom until I'm summer fresh.

I gather the nicest dress I brought on the trip, a silvery sheath that is the closest to my Hollywood style. It was one of my very best finds at a sample sale, and is worth several thousand dollars.

But its elegance is in its simplicity. I feel certain that half the women coming to the tea will think they could have sewn something like it themselves.

I pick up my hair supplies and cosmetic bag and ease the door open.

When I peer into the hall, I spot Zachery's shaggy head also leaning out of his room. He sees me, and we both laugh.

"I guess the tea brigade has landed," he says.

"And so early. It's seven a.m. and the tea isn't until lunchtime!"

He shakes his head. "I'll keep myself scarce."

I sneak across the hall, dashing to the bathroom when I hear a voice that might be someone coming up the stairs. I'm literally panting as I lock the door.

This is wild. I've gone to Hollywood parties and walked straight up to famous directors, A-list actors, and all variety of intimidating people.

But this Christmas tea has got me sweating.

Grandmama will be there, for one thing. It'll be the first time we meet. Her approval is apparently essential. Two of the girls Jack dated got the boot based on her opinion.

According to Gina, Randy has never introduced anyone to her. But Grandmama has been giving him hell that she's going to die before he gets a wife, so he asked me last night, during our one slow dance, if I'd be up for meeting her even though we haven't known each other long.

After two cups of wine that probably equaled a bottle, I agreed.

But now I'm questioning everything.

The speed of this courtship.

How much I really know Randy.

The water runs cold. I never got around to asking anyone about the water heater and got used to it. And for some reason, it's at this moment that I realize I've completely dropped the ball on work all week.

Zachery has done all my research, drafted all my emails. Since Thursday, when we got busy for the weekend events, I haven't even read them over. I've just hit send.

Maybe it'll slow down after the summer events are done.

I blow-dry my hair and curl the ends. I allow myself a smidge of sparkle in my makeup. Just enough to be festive, but not so much that I draw attention to it. Last night, I saw the line drawn between the practical women of Glass and the ones who put a lot of time and effort into their appearance.

There weren't a lot of the latter, and they seemed separate somehow, as if worrying about something as useless as looks makes you untrustworthy.

I don't like it, but small towns can be that way. Mine was.

Even with the divide, no one was unpleasant about it, at least not in front of me. This is unlike Hollywood, where getting catty about someone's physical appearance is a cherished pastime.

This is better. Everything here is better, other than the cold showers.

If I stay here much longer, I'll ask Randy to fix it. He and Jack and their dad can manage just about anything, from running electrical to rerouting a drain. The tree farm requires a lot of upkeep, even if there aren't any animals.

And that's the best part. Farm life without all the cows. Just a pair of horses and a passel of dogs.

When I proclaim myself ready to face the ladies downstairs, I move all my products and even my damp towel to my room in case this bathroom needs to be used by guests of the tea.

I'll remind Zachery to do the same, although as I do one more bathroom check before heading down, I bend over to sniff his ungodly wonderful soaps.

Heaven.

I knock on his door. He peeks out, running his hand through his hair. He's visibly relieved that it's me. "Oh, hey, Kelsey."

"I'm thinking the bathroom downstairs might not be enough for the tea. You might want to move your things or else entrance half the county with the siren call of your fancy soaps."

He laughs. "Will do." He opens the door a little wider. "You're looking more California today."

My body heats up as he takes me in. For a moment, I revel in it, letting him fill me with self-confidence. Then his eyes meet mine, and I want to sink into him. Will this feeling never go away?

Focus, Kelsey. Don't let the charmer ensnare you, today of all days.

I give him a silly curtsy. "Do you like it, kind sir? I'm seeking the approval of the queen." There's a waver in my last word. I have to pull it together.

Zachery doesn't seem to notice. His chuckle is low and deep. "The all-powerful grandmama. Good luck."

I straighten, trying to keep my wayward emotions under wraps. "Thank you. Will you come down for the tea?"

"Hell no. My understanding from last night is that no man with a pair of balls in his possession will step foot at the homestead during teatime. Their words, not mine."

"Okay, well, text me if you need me to sneak you a tea cake."

He nods. "Have a good time."

When he disappears into his room, I take a moment to compose myself. *Of course you get mesmerized, Kelsey. He's the most handsome man you've ever met. He can charm the girdle off a grandma. It's okay. You're okay.*

I take the stairs slowly, trying to get a feel for what I'm about to walk into.

Gina is downstairs, and my chest loosens as I see her also wearing a nice skirt and blouse. I made the right call to dress up.

She turns to me. "Good morning, Kelsey. Sorry we barged in so early. The teas have to steep and the deliveries start arriving at nine. Mom wanted all the tablecloths prepped." She lifts the arm of a steamer and puffs out a hot cloud.

"I can help with that."

She shakes her head. "You're wanted in the library."

I freeze. "Grandmama?" I whisper.

She nods. "Break a leg."

I smooth my dress, more or less glad we're getting this over with while I'm fresh. I haven't spilled anything on myself yet.

I can do this. I once walked up to Robert De Niro to ask about a role. Now *that* was intimidating.

How hard can a grandmother be?

The library is a small room compared to the others. The two side walls are filled with bookshelves, although not a single title seems to have been published after 1985. There are framed family photos sprinkled throughout the shelves, along with odds and ends that look to have been picked up on vacations.

There's a window on the back wall and, beneath it, an old-fashioned round-backed red velvet sofa. An oval coffee table holds a silver tea set on a shiny tray, along with a fresh bouquet of red and white flowers.

Grandmama sits tall and stiff in the center of the sofa, holding a cup and saucer in both hands like she's posing for a painting. She wears a shiny green dress with long sleeves and a high neck. Her hair is a puff of silver. Behind her, the woods are thick and lovely through the window.

She watches me enter with eyes dusted lightly with gray shadow. I feel like I've entered a throne room and should curtsy, but instead I take a seat on a high-backed wood chair to the left of the coffee table.

Should I wait to speak until spoken to, or does that make me a ninny?

I cross my feet at the ankles and arrange my hands on my lap. "Hello, Grandmama. I'm Kelsey Whitaker, a friend of Randy's."

She rests her saucer on her knee. "It's about time that boy settled down."

Is it? I realize I know very little about Randy's dating life, or his past at all, other than his football statistics. We've spent most of our hours together for six days, but they've been practical, mostly decorating and organizing and running errands. We've had one lunch, one dinner, and a hayride where we've been alone.

That's not much to go on, even though it already feels like I've been part of the family a long time.

I realize I might ought to be saying something. "He's a nice boy. You all raised him well."

Grandmama's eyes narrow, but she catches herself and takes a sip of tea. "I hear you've been a big help to everyone, even if you did drink excessively last night at the dance."

I guess nothing gets by this woman. "I'm not used to the deep pours of Glass."

She harrumphs a short laugh, and I think this is a good sign, but then she goes on. "I hear you're staying at the homestead with another man."

That probably is a bigger deal. "We've worked together for years."

"Why did you come to Glass for your work? Are you a journalist? Trying to get to know the locals?"

"No. I—well, I like to learn about communities. That's true. But I'm not a writer or a journalist."

"Then what is it exactly that you and this man do?"

I have a feeling my vague explanations from the last few days, that we file reports and do research, won't work on Grandmama.

"We work in the movie business."

This gets her attention. "In what capacity?"

"We help connect the actors with the roles that are best suited for them. We research past projects and keep a database of headshots and résumés. We don't generally put the leads in place, as they're often attached as part of the package that goes to producers to secure funding, but all the supporting roles, the bit parts, and the extras are chosen by us to be approved by the director."

"How interesting. And you can do this from anywhere?"

"Sure. Most auditions are done via self-tape now. When a director asks for a certain type of role to be filled, say a young mother down on her luck, in her thirties, maybe a certain ethnic profile, I find someone who fits the part."

She leans forward. "Are there roles for grumpy old women?"

This is something you can almost never escape. I think most everyone, somewhere deep inside, once had a passing dream of being a movie star. "Sometimes, there are."

She sets down her cup and leans back. "This is the most interesting thing to ever happen in Glass. Hollywood, right here at the homestead!"

This is going far better than I thought. I'm already racking my brain for any projects where I can get her on the set as an extra. I'd have to get her in the system. She'd have to travel. It might be best if I used my home address for her.

"Kelsey, what are your intentions here? Gina tells me that your booking ended yesterday."

"That was because of the tea. This day was blocked off, but we were happy to stay. I'll make sure Gina gets us back in the system so we pay properly."

Grandmama waves her hand at that. "No, I mean when are you leaving? I'm sure a week isn't long enough to leave my grandson with a broken heart, but will that happen? You toy with a young man in that designer dress and then head back to your real life?"

I glance down at the shimmery Givenchy.

"Did you think an old lady from a rural town wouldn't recognize a high-end dress when she saw it?"

"No, I—"

"Is it amusing to be around the simple folk with your high-and-mighty Beverly Hills audacity?"

I recognize a hole when I'm in it. I maintain my upright pose, hands in my lap.

Grandmama doesn't relent. "Can you explain yourself?"

I can only reach for the truth. "I tried dating in the city, and the men are too . . . too everything. I wanted to find someone more authentic."

Grandmama sits back against the sofa. "Oh. I see. And do you think you've found it in Randy?"

"Maybe. It seems good so far. Ask me in a month?"

"And will you be here in a month?"

"I hope so."

She clasps her wrinkled fingers, adorned with several large gemstone rings, in her satiny lap. "All right, then. Do check in with me each Sunday and let me know how things are going. Randy is not used to girls like you. He might be a mite gauche. Allow me to direct him when he goes awry. I have some pull with my boys. And tell him to fix the blasted water heater. It goes out every summer. I'm surprised you haven't complained about the cold. It shows some grit."

She picks up her teacup for a sip, grimaces, and sets it back down. "Go find my daughter-in-law and tell her to make the tea stronger. It's like drinking warm sugar water."

I stand up. "I will. Thank you, Grandmama. Nice meeting you, Grandmama."

She waves me on and I get the heck out of Dodge.

I know to quit when I'm ahead.

Chapter 38

ZACHERY RIDES AWAY

When the Christmas tea is over, I scavenge for leftovers in the over-stuffed fridge downstairs. There's everything my fitness trainer would hate: pie, cake, tiny sandwiches stuffed with mayonnaise mixtures and cheese.

I may have to take up firewood chopping to stay in shape. There isn't a gym for fifty miles.

Speaking of axes, the one I buried in the wood out back is gone. There's no telling if they know I did it, or if they think Kelsey gave it a go.

The kitchen smells of mixed perfumes and herbs. The ladies opted to go classic with hot tea even as temperatures pushed into the nineties. It's officially June, and the kids are out of school. The events were timed to make it a celebration of the start of summer.

But I did some digging as the festivities came to a close. I'm no financial whiz, but I've heard my dad talking about banking my whole life. I understand profit and loss, assets and liabilities.

While the ladies did their tea drinking, I started adding up what I thought this week of fundraising was worth.

Five-dollar hayrides, kids free. Ten-dollar tickets to the dance, minus expenses, plus the baked goods donation jar and bar sales.

Unlike actual Christmas, when the tree sales are the bulk of the gig, the only retail items were ornaments and knickknacks. With my insider knowledge from Kelsey that Gina was the sole cashier and bored out of her mind, they couldn't have taken in very much with that.

Needing to fundraise means they aren't supporting the family, or that supporting the family makes them fall short on the business expenses.

Jack's wife works at the school, which might cover their basics as a young couple. Gina has an apartment in town but no other job. Grandmama requires upkeep in her cottage. I'm not privy to where Randy lives, but his parents have a house.

There's income from this homestead, but judging by the open availability for me to extend a second week, they don't bring in huge amounts with it.

I'm not sure how this tree farm supports them all.

I sit at the table with a platter of sandwiches and pull out my phone. I wonder . . .

I quickly pay for a real estate report on this property.

And there it is. A lien.

A big one.

One so large that it would take fifty weeks of fundraising like they just did to cover it.

I shove the platter aside.

This tree farm is doomed.

But what can I say about it?

Kelsey came upstairs all aglow that their grandmother liked her. They worked out a deal, she said. If Randy acts badly, Grandmama will set him straight.

Now I wonder—why would he act badly?

Footsteps race down the stairs. "Zachery? Zach! Where are you?" She sounds frantic.

I stand up, knocking the chair back. "Kelsey?" I rush through the swinging door.

Kelsey's at the bottom of the stairs, holding her open laptop. "Oh shit oh shit oh shit oh shit!"

"What is it?"

She looks at me, and I realize she isn't upset, but over-the-moon excited. "The two actors Desdemona chose for *Limited Fate* weren't available! The director wrote me back, asking for new leads. And get this! The script caught the attention of Andrew Fontaine—you know the one, right?"

"The Oscar committee. I do."

"It's on their radar in preproduction. I knew this script was special. I told Desdemona we had to put all our energy into it. Actors will be willing to lowball their pay to get Oscar buzz. It doesn't matter that the budget isn't great."

"You still want Jason Venetian and Gayle Sumners?"

"You bet I do. I knew it the minute I met him."

"Even if that action sequel he did tanks?"

"Any publicist worth their salt can spin that into proof that Jason was meant for serious films."

"Does Jason want serious films? A lot of men would rather be Thor than a sensitive sculptor."

"He'll want it. I know it. He got pigeonholed after that tire commercial. The beefy tough guy. But he's not. He's got soulful eyes. Mark my words, one well-lit close-up from when he sees that jaded graffiti artist, and he's America's next heartthrob. Like Leo after *Titanic*."

"I trust you, Kelsey, but Desdemona won't go for it. That agent tweaked her ego, so he's dead to her."

"I could put it in. She doesn't even have to know." Her eyes scan the email as if she still can't believe it.

"What makes you think the agent will change his mind?"

She walks to the kitchen and sets her laptop on the table. "This." She switches tabs. A headline reads, New superhero limited series announces leading cast.

I skim through it. This is the one we were pretty sure was taking Jason away from us.

"He's not on the list," Kelsey says, almost bouncing with excitement. "They passed him over. He and his agent are going to be reeling from that, especially since Jacobs was all over him at that party, promising him the moon. The agent's going to throw him at something to keep him out there."

"Especially if there's Oscar buzz." I sit beside her. "But Desdemona will have told Jester not to take his call."

"I'm handling it myself. *And* I already sent a message directly to Jason."

"Sounds like you have it under control. But how will you handle Desdemona if he takes it?"

She closes her laptop with a snap. "I may simply blow up that bridge when I come to it. Is she confirmed for LA in a week?"

"No. Jester's monitoring her airline bookings. Looks like she trusts us to handle the extras at the soccer match."

Kelsey lets out a long exhale. "This is so perfect. Everything this summer has been so perfect."

But something crosses her mind, making a line appear between her eyebrows.

I'm guessing that's me. Probably if her husband material found out about how recently she and I hooked up, it wouldn't go over so well.

Something in me snaps, ever so gently, like a twig in the woods. But it makes me say, "I did a little digging."

"On what? Jason?"

I unlock my phone and show her the lien on the tree farm.

She sits straight up. "Why would you do that? Why would you spy on the Hanovers?"

"I'm worried. You love your job. It's working out. Are you really going to give it up on a doomed farm? You know this fundraiser doesn't even make a dent in that."

She shoves my phone at me. "I can't believe you! Why can't you be happy for me? Grandmama knows about my job. She thinks it's fabulous! Maybe I can have it all! Just because you failed at everything you ever tried doesn't mean I will."

Well, damn.

She snatches up her laptop and races out of the kitchen.

Kelsey doesn't usually come out swinging. I've touched a nerve.

I put away the sandwiches, giving her some time to cool down. Then I quietly climb the stairs and stand outside her door, forming the words that will smooth this over.

I knock. "Kelsey?"

Her voice is tight. "What?"

"Can I come in?"

I hear her footsteps, then the door swings open. She instantly turns and returns to her spot on the bed, the laptop open.

"I'm sorry I looked. I'm trying to have your back."

"We knew the farm was in trouble before I met anyone. They're not hiding it. The amount doesn't matter."

Maybe it doesn't.

She closes her laptop, and I wonder if she's writing her mother.

"I'm sorry I punched you where it hurt," she says. "I didn't mean it. I think you had the level of success the rest of the world dreams of."

Had. Of course. The joke, the has-been. I know who I am.

"It's all right. I shouldn't have snooped."

Her brows are furrowed hard, her lips pinched in a tight frown. "Zach, it might be time for you to go back to LA. I'm good here. I have people to talk to. Things to do. I belong. I think the workload at the farm will settle down now that the events are over, and I won't need you to cover my research and emails. I appreciate that you did it."

I sit on the edge of her bed. She looks ethereal in a T-shirt and loose gym shorts, her makeup still sparkling and her golden hair in ringlets.

I love her, I realize. I honestly, truly love her.

That's a damn nuisance. More to recover from.

And she wants me gone.

"Here's the thing," she goes on. "I've covered all the Hallmark bases. It's time for regular dating stuff." Her eyes cut to the shared wall of our rooms. "And I think I can't fall into that with you so close. It's different now between us. I didn't want it to be different after what happened, but it is."

I get it. And I'm not exactly interested in hearing what goes down between her and Randy, either.

"It's good timing," I say. "If Desdemona does return to LA, I can run interference. We can switch from Hallmark movies to those sitcoms where someone is trying to be two places at one time."

This sparks a smile from her. "You can say she just missed me, then have Jester in a blond wig pop up across the field."

I manage to laugh. "Exactly. We have you covered. Go ahead and have it all."

She reaches forward to squeeze my arm, and I have the sinking feeling that this might be the last time she ever touches me. She'll fall in love with Randy, make a name for herself by casting the next Oscar-winning film, and that will be that. She won't need me or Desdemona or anybody.

She'll live out her small-town, Hollywood-adjacent happily ever after.

"I'll get out of your hair first thing in the morning," I tell her.

"You've been the best wingman a girl could ask for." She shakes her head at herself. "And I might have asked for more than I should have."

I indulge myself with one last lean toward her and press my lips to her hair. "I was happy to oblige."

Then I leave for my own room, the overstuffed suitcases, and prepare for life without her.

Chapter 39

Kelsey the Big Shot

The homestead is strange without Zachery in it. I watch his Jaguar from the balcony, dust blowing up from the tires as he leaves.

I'm on my own.

I head down to the kitchen to eat leftover sandwiches for breakfast. It's six a.m. in LA, and the time zone will be a struggle to get work done. I'll have to duck out of whatever I'm doing at the farm midmorning to call Jason Venetian and the director, then hopefully Gayle's agent.

I'm making this happen.

I make a mental list of what needs to be done. Choose different scenes from the script, definitely. Send those to Jason and Gayle. Help with their tapes. Harder to do at a distance, but I don't think Gayle lives in California anyway.

There's work to do here at the homestead. The mugs and plates were all washed and dried and put away after the tea, but the enormous percolator and quite a few serving platters were left to drain on the sideboard.

I open all the cabinet doors, looking for the spots where they go.

I find more platters with space for the ones we used, so I slide those in the cabinet.

But there's nothing that will hold the oversize electric pot. It must go into the storage room. A few of the women referred to it while we were preparing yesterday, but I didn't go in there. It's across the hall from the kitchen.

An extra wall was put in when the homestead was first listed as a rental, in order to lock the guests out of the portions that held family heirlooms that didn't fit elsewhere.

It's a good-size area. If I had to guess based on its size and placement, it's a formal dining room and possibly an additional closet. I imagine those spaces are crammed with things wanted safe from guests.

I turn the lever to see if it's locked as usual, thinking that maybe someone from the tea left it open so we could return the percolator.

And I'm right. The handle moves down, and the door pops open.

The first space is exactly as I expected, a formal dining room filled with chairs, a grandfather clock, and a cherrywood antique dining set, including an enormous hutch filled with china.

I walk up to it, admiring the classic pink rose designs on the plates, and the heavy crystal. We never had anything like this at the farm. Mom and Dad eloped away from scattered, dysfunctional families that we kids never met. I doubt many of them are even still alive.

But this set is well preserved, ready for a formal meal. I like that it exists, that normal families hold on to mementos and pass them down.

There's an archway to another area beyond the dining room. Interesting. I wonder what it is.

I skirt chairs and small tables, some filled with old lamps and stacks of black-and-white framed photos. But when I get close enough to see inside, I stop short.

Someone lives in here. There's a mattress on the floor with mussed sheets. Boxes everywhere burst with clothes, books, and mail. It's a mess.

A plate sits on the floor by the bed, a couple of half-eaten leftover sandwiches sitting on it. I recognize them from the tea.

Then I spot a pair of boots. I know those.

They belong to Randy.

He lives in this long, narrow room?

I glance around. There's an oak wood desk shoved in the corner and a brown leather chair covered in coats. This was an office.

I turn to the inside wall. Yes, there's a door that should lead to the library where I met Grandmama. They must have moved a bookshelf in front of this door on the library side to close it off.

I wonder why Randy never told me he was living here. I don't think they disclosed that someone would be in the house at the same time as us. Zachery would have mentioned it. It's no big deal, no different from Livia at her bed-and-breakfast.

But weird to keep it a secret.

My phone buzzes. It's a text from Randy.

Want me to swing by in the truck and pick you up on the way to the farm?

He's specifically pretending he's coming from somewhere else. Or maybe he already ran an errand. I try to think about the other times he's come to fetch me. He gave the impression that he lived elsewhere, but he never lied about it. Just an omission.

I text him back. Sure. I'm ready.

My stomach knots. I picture the lien Zachery showed me. Maybe they really are in financial straits, enough that Randy has to stay here to save money.

That's okay. It's his house anyway. We'll figure this out. Do a social media push, get this homestead full of guests. There's three rooms upstairs plus the main suite downstairs. That's a lot of rooms we can get money for.

But even so, the uneasy feeling won't leave. I haven't been to Randy's parents' house, or Grandmama's cottage, or Gina's apartment. What if none of those exist?

I imagine them all squeezed together in a room like Charlie Bucket's family before he gets the golden ticket.

No, no. Surely not.

But the doubts have crept in.

This is a fine time to be without Zachery. Who can I talk to about this?

I hear the truck rumbling up the drive and practically sprint out of the room, racing past the packed dining table and into the kitchen.

I close the door carefully, trying to make sure I leave it exactly as I found it, firmly closed but unlocked.

Then I barrel out of the kitchen, as if that matters, and slow my breathing to appear calm and pleasant as I head for the porch.

Because I am. Chill. Happy. I've learned nothing that matters.

But I'll pay more attention.

Randy seems the same, other than there's more ease when he leans in for a quick kiss before opening my door. But when I sit in the tall green truck that the whole family seems to share, I look longingly at the spot where Zachery's Jaguar used to sit.

I'm in this on my own.

Everyone's at the tree farm when we arrive. Carrie and Jed. Jack and his wife, Mary, who is done with her teaching duties for the summer. Gina. Even Grandmama sits in a lawn chair, watching them take down the tents.

"Time to undo everything we did," Randy says.

But today, there's no added "And we sure appreciate your help." Not even a hint that maybe a paying customer at the homestead who has a regular job is going out of her way to be here.

It feels expected.

I'm being taken for granted.

Like family, I guess, but it isn't sitting well with all the other discoveries.

Grandmama holds out her hand to me as I pass. "It's Kelsey," she says with a smile, and that warm feeling comes over me again. Of course they're going to treat me like family. I got the matriarch stamp of approval.

"Good to see you, Grandmama," I say.

"Why don't you and Randy come to the cottage later for lunch," she says. "I haven't seen the two of you together, and I would like a chat."

Okay, so the cottage exists.

Carrie rolls a long length of rope across her arm. "We were going to have them over to our house, but I suppose that can be tomorrow." She stacks the coil onto a stack of the others that were holding down the tent flaps. "We have all the time in the world now, right?" She laughs as she shakes her head. "This was a lot!"

So their house exists, too. And she's explained why everything seems topsy-turvy.

I overreacted.

"Of course," I say to Carrie. "I'll have to make a few calls at some point today, but I'm mostly free." It might be time to set some boundaries.

Carrie dusts her hands off. "Grandmama tells us you're a big-shot Hollywood moviemaker."

This makes everyone pause, even Randy. I realize he and I have never talked about my job. Grandmama was the first person I told.

I guess I had secrets, too. Kettle, meet pot.

Jed slings a rolled-up floor tarp over his shoulder. "I thought you were from Alabama."

"I am," I say quickly, feeling the pierce of all the family's gazes on me. "I grew up on a dairy farm outside Birmingham. Then I went to college in theater arts and became an assistant to a casting director."

Gina seems excited by this. "What movies have you worked on? The *Barbie* movie? Did you cast Margot Robbie? Because I loved her in that."

"No, I didn't cast *Barbie*." Heat starts to rise to my face. It's always complicated explaining how our process works.

"What about *Guardians of the Galaxy*?" Gina asks. Then her eyes go wide. "Did you discover Chris Hemsworth? Was he grateful? Who have you met? Who is the biggest star?"

"Let the girl be," Grandmama says. "I get all the gossip first, at my cottage, for lunch today. Now back to work!"

Everyone disperses.

I don't know what to say. I guess I should have expected this would happen at some point.

Randy sniffs. "I didn't realize you were such a big deal." He heads toward the main building.

I have to hurry to keep up with his long, rapid strides. "I'm not. I'm really not. Zachery is a much bigger deal."

"You mean that man who slept in the room next to you? Who ate breakfast with you when you were barely dressed?"

"Wait. What?"

We go inside the building, and I let the door close behind me. The lights are out, and it's dim inside, bins of unsold merchandise scattered across the floor.

Randy whirls around. "That first morning. You came in there with barely a stitch on, ready to have breakfast with that man. You thought I forgot?"

"He's a coworker. You've known that since we met."

He frowns. "I know it. But you just said he's a big deal."

"In the industry. Not to me."

Randy taps his foot a moment. "All right. I get it."

"I was the one who wanted to travel. He came along to make sure I was okay, like a friend would, like a brother."

"But he's not a brother."

Oh, if he only knew.

But I press on. "He did a lot of my work for me so I could be with you. I could never have done so much with the tree farm if he hadn't helped."

"His car was gone this morning."

"Yeah, he left. He's gone back to LA."

"So, you don't need a brother anymore." He seems to be calming down.

I hold on to the back of the chair I sat in the first day, when I made the ribbon wreaths. It already feels like ages ago. "Exactly. Once he saw I was well situated here, he went back."

"You're thinking about staying here in Glass?" He steps close enough to take my hand.

I let out a sigh of relief. We got past this moment. Maybe soon I'll ask him about his living arrangements.

His thumb slides over the back of my hand. "I'd like it if you did."

This is it, I guess. The moment where the script is complete. The intention to follow my happily ever after will be stated. The swoony music will rise. We'll have our biggest, best kiss, and roll the end credits.

INT. HANOVER TREE FARM RETAIL BUILDING—DAY

Randy, 28, leans in—

"I have a meeting in LA," I blurt. "Next week." I don't, but I probably will. If the director wants me, I'll go. Might as well put it out there.

He freezes. "You have to go back already?"

"It's a big movie. The biggest thing I've ever done. It might win an Oscar." It's not even cast yet, but here I am, saying it.

"Oscar, huh?" He drops my hand. "So, you *are* a big shot. I reckon you won't have time for a pissant little town like Glass."

His words cut me. "But I've been here. Helping. I made wreaths. Set up your tents."

"Sure, right till you have to run back to the city. I can't have a wife who takes off for LA every time she has a damn meeting."

I take a step back. I've forgotten my most critical lessons. The men need to feel important. I can't be bigger than they are. They don't function well when they feel small. "I can do most of it from here, but sometimes I have to be there. Or New York."

He grunts. "New York. A girl like you. From Alabama. In New York."

"It's just a city."

"What if we have kids? You gonna leave them to jet off to some Hollywood party?"

"We don't know that it will happen that way." I can argue about how he shouldn't diminish me, but in this, he's right. I haven't thought ahead to how trying to stay relevant in the business would affect having a family.

Maybe I do want more than a small-town bed-and-breakfast.

He scuffs his boot on the rough floor. "I reckon you can't see the problem because you aren't a family type. You don't think about your community. You think about your job."

Why is he pushing me like this? He barely knows me! Is he this thrown off to learn that I have a life outside Glass? That maybe I'm good at something other than ribbon wreaths?

My anger gets ahead of me, a very dangerous place for it to go. And I say it. I don't want to. But my mouth is way out in front. "At least I have a job. A real one. One that pays for me to have a place to sleep that isn't a mattress in a hidden room of an old house!"

He sniffs. "You've been snooping around."

"I was putting away the items from the tea I worked for *your family*."

His expression is dark.

And that's it.

I already know.

There will be no happily ever after in Glass, Wyoming.

The small-town life isn't going to be for me.

Maybe my faith really is going to wither.

Or maybe some random actress pretending to be a fortune teller sent me on a dumb, pointless mission based on fear.

"Tell Grandmama that I will sadly have to turn down her kind offer for lunch," I say. "It's clearly time for me to go."

For a moment, I think he'll relent. He bites his lip and adjusts his ball cap nervously, like he knows he's done the wrong thing.

Maybe this was just the dark moment, the part of every movie where dejection sets in, the sad music plays, and it seems impossible for the couple to be together. The tension before the big finish.

But the script is all garbled, a complicated mess that will have to be edited.

Randy gestures for the door. "Well, go on, then. Back to Hollywood."

I'm tired of this. Tired of people telling me what I can and can't do. Who I am. What I am. Desdemona. G-spot. Simon. Randy. My father.

I want my mother.

I run out of the building, not stopping to say goodbye to anyone.

Down the rows of trees. Through the forest. Bursting out the other side when I get to the homestead lot.

I have to pack. Have to get out of here.

This plan was a mistake.

The real ending is me, back where I belong, casting the most perfect two people in a movie I believe in with all my heart.

Screw love. Screw small towns. I'll be Desdemona, powerful and single, and people will quake when they see me.

It's fine. I'll be fine.

I was not meant for this kind of romance. I tried it in Alabama, in college, in Los Angeles, and on this ill-fated trip.

I've struck out.

It's time to go home. To glitz. To glamour. To the whole business.

I'm so grateful I figured it out in time.

Chapter 40

ZACHERY MAKES ALL THE WRONG MOVES

It's eighteen hours from Glass to Los Angeles. A smart man would do it in three days, a determined one in two.

But I'm an angry, disillusioned one, so I drive straight through.

When I get to my house, I dump my suitcases by the door, take a shower, shave, put on a *ten-thousand-dollar* suit, because I can, and because I know Kelsey would find it over the top.

Then I call up Catalina Ferrig. A dark-haired vixen is exactly what I need. I'll convince her to be Juliet, no matter who is directing. I'll be at the top of my game.

"Zachery Carter," she purrs. "I've been waiting for your call."

"You wouldn't believe where I've been." I pop open my laptop and quickly scan for events far from LA. "But I'm headed to . . ." I pause. "A lovely little film festival in Venice. I understand it's absolutely gorgeous this time of year. Would you accompany me?"

She hesitates. "And what does this getaway involve?"

"I'll call around. Get some premieres lined up. Some photo ops. I have several designers who would love to dress you for it."

"And for undressing?"

I don't even hesitate on this. Despite my reputation or Desdemona's demands, I'm not one to put pressure on anyone. And while Catalina's tone is sultry, I can hear the concern. I can be charismatic without playing the cad. "The lady takes the lead."

"Hmm. What are the strings?"

"We discuss what an enchanting Juliet you would be. Our office is casting it."

"Oh?"

"You in for a discussion about it on a gondola beneath the Bridge of Sighs?"

"Tell me where to be."

"Our office will send the information. I'll pick you up for the airport on Thursday. That'll give us a day to recover before the film events."

"You move fast." Her voice is a purr again. No hesitation this time. She's in.

Time to go for broke, it seems. "But slow where it's important."

"Oh, my."

Yeah, I've got her.

I drop my cell phone on my bed. There. Done. I'm back to my manwhore ways, getting my ass out of town, and it'll be fine. No Kelsey. No regret. Moving on. I have no choice.

She's in good hands. The right hands.

Time for me to head to the office.

When I arrive, Jester is pulling files out of the wall of cabinets, an old system Desdemona insists on keeping.

He looks up as I close the door. "You're back?" He steps off the stool he needs for the top drawers. "Where's our girl?"

"She fell for the lumberjack from Wyoming. Grandmama approves of her, and she's living the small-town dream. That's a wrap."

"Well, damn, Zachery. I thought you two were gonna figure it out." He heads to the coffee bar and pours me a hefty cup.

I sit at Kelsey's desk, fingering the glass unicorns. "Thanks. Yeah, I don't know what she's going to do about Desdemona. She can't work from Wyoming indefinitely."

Jester perches on the corner of Kelsey's desk and sets the cup in front of me. "For sure, for sure."

I take a sip, savoring the jolt of caffeine. "I'm headed to Venice with Catalina Ferrig. I need tickets for me and her for Thursday, plus hotels and cars. I'll handle getting the festival passes."

Jester moves to stand in front of me with his arms crossed like he's Perturbed in Pink. "You can't possibly."

"I can. And it's on Desdemona's orders."

"How will we cover for Kelsey if Desdemona comes for the soccer shoot?"

"Not my problem." I'll keep my distance from now on. Maybe even cut Desdemona loose. If Kelsey's going to be gone soon anyway, I don't have much keeping me here.

"Think it over before you get all rash," Jester says. "Sow your oats with Catalina if you need to, but promise me you'll come back for the shoot. It's next Tuesday. You can be here. I assume you're going to *Festival Cinema?*"

"Yeah."

"Fly back Monday. Be here."

He's really pushing this thing. "I'll think about it." I set the unicorn down. I never did learn from Kelsey what they were for or where they came from.

But after learning more about her, including those hundreds of drafts to her mother, I bet I know. They belonged to her mom, or were gifts from her, or some shared experience.

I did something unwise.

That's what she said in her email.

It was true.

Anything with me is unwise. Even Catalina might be unwise, letting me seduce her into working with a director she hates.

I press the heel of my hand into my face. God, I'm tired.

"Go get some sleep," Jester says. "You look like you've been on a bender. Things will look different with a good meal and some shut-eye."

He's right. I've been awake for twenty hours straight.

I push away from Kelsey's desk, possibly for the last time.

"I'll catch you later," I tell Jester, although it's possibly a lie.

I should go home anyway, work out for the first time since we left, eat something healthy.

And move on with my damn life.

Chapter 41

KELSEY RISKS IT ALL

I take my time getting to LA. I'm not sure I'm ready for Zachery's "I told you so." At least Desdemona is safely away.

I hole up in a cheap hotel in Utah partway through the first day, gathering material to convince the director of *Limited Fate* that Jason is our guy. Jason has already gotten the script I sent him from the homestead and told his agent he better let him read for it.

During the Utah stop, I eat, sleep, and breathe Jason's social media feeds, chasing footage that'll prove he's perfect for the sensitive sculptor. Not just for the director, but for Jason himself to live up to the role as I know he can.

I need him the way I saw him at the party, not his tire commercial or even what I can find from the set of *Darkness Gathers II*. It's in the gestures, the flash of his eyes. I don't want him to attempt a self-tape until I'm there to help.

I finally find what I'm looking for on the feed of a friend of a friend, who films Jason dancing with a young woman on a basketball court in a gritty neighborhood. I sit back, my eyes smarting. That's it. That's how he'll be.

Now to set it all in motion.

It's work I need. I don't want to think about the meet-cutes, the tree farm, or what I set out to do almost two weeks ago.

And I definitely can't think about Zachery Carter. But the farther I get from Wyoming, the more I wonder how I can work with him and not think about what happened in Colorado.

Drake Underwood calls me the next day, while I'm driving through Nevada. I pull over by a ramshackle gas station that reads sixty-seven cents a gallon on a long-dry pump.

"I expected to hear from Desdemona," he says. "Weren't you the one who sent me the other two?"

I don't bother trying to blame that miscast on my boss. I'm not her. "I had misgivings about my previous choices, even though they're both accomplished actors on their own."

"I'm looking at the headshot of a tire boy. You think this Jason Venetian fellow is the right guy?"

"I have a clip for you. Let me send it." I'm praying the clarity of the call means there's a cell tower close enough to patch it through.

I forward the dancing video via text, closing my eyes and crossing my fingers that he'll see what I do. I had hoped I would have a carefully prepared self-tape, but I don't. I'm spending too much time driving across the country to fast-track an audition tape.

There's a pause, then I can hear the background noise of the video. He got it. He's probably in his office and looking at it on a different screen.

The silence is long. Nobody passes me on this stretch of road in the desert. I'm in the literal middle of nowhere, alone, trying to convince a veteran director that a twenty-five-year-old casting assistant with no credits to her name is right about her choice for this film with possible Oscar potential.

I can't think of a less auspicious way to present something that matters so much.

I wish Zachery were here, silently holding my hand. He'd squeeze it at just the right moment, passing comfort and strength from himself to me.

Finally, Drake speaks. "Okay, I see it. So, all we have on him is a commercial and this action sequel that's still in editing?"

"I saw some dailies. I can send them, but it's a very different look."

"I bet."

Another pause.

What would Reese do? Be plucky and positive.

That's good, but maybe I need to think—what would Zachery do? He'd close the deal, make Drake feel like it was all his idea. His brilliant vision.

I grip the steering wheel and pretend it's Zachery's hand. "When you chose *Limited Fate* as a project, I could immediately see its potential. If the central message of the movie is going to come into play as you put your team together, then you have to believe that Caleb and Salena being unavailable was a sign. Fate. I really, truly believe that all the pieces will come together with Jason and Gayle in place."

Another pause, then Drake says, "If this Jason kid can act the way he behaved in that video, I believe you. And I'm very familiar with Gayle. My eight-year-old daughter is huge into horses and has watched that Netflix series from start to finish more times than I can count."

"Do you see how she fits with him? It's in how she gazes up, how she holds herself."

"You like body language."

I laugh. "I think it's everything, and it can't always be taught."

"Can you get them together for a screen test? I'd like to see what they've got in person."

Oh, wow. "Absolutely. What timeline are you looking at?"

"I want the package put together by end of June. Can we do it inside of two weeks?"

"Let me get with the agents and make it happen." And now a page from Desdemona's book. Act like you're the center of everything. "I saw Jason at a party, so he'll be easy to track down. Gayle is likely taking a well-deserved break after six seasons, but I'll get her in."

"Excellent. Shoot to get it done before the nineteenth, before I have to leave LA for a while. Send my assistant the details as soon as you have them."

Then it's over.

I've done it. I've gotten Jason and Gayle their chance.

Fate will determine if they can make it to this reading. It's like I've always known, casting is half talent, half availability.

But this is the biggest, most beautiful opportunity I've ever put together.

Not a mall cop with two lines. Not a random waitress with sass.

And not a leading role under Desdemona's shadow.

This is me.

My legacy.

My perfect pairing of a couple who will light up the screen.

And it's going to have to be enough, because that same magic is simply not happening for me in real life.

~

I reach LA Thursday evening. I'm too tired to even tell Jester I'm back. Tomorrow will be soon enough.

I text Zachery as I fall asleep, letting him know I have Jason back in, but when I wake up the next morning, he hasn't replied.

Maybe he needs more space. That was a brutal last day we had. I'm not over it, either.

But I long to tell him about what happened. That he was right. The whole idea of running a romance on a movie timeline was insane. And things weren't quite right with the Hanover clan. And I know now that I'm too big-city for a small-town love affair.

I'm different. It's something I learned in Wyoming, and that's what the best journeys do.

In addition to finding out that Zachery Carter is the full package.

A really full package.

I put on my favorite Hollywood clothes. High heels (secondhand Louboutins, $125, full price $1,100.) A khaki linen Yves Saint Laurent dress (also secondhand, $250, originally $2,400).

I feel good.

It's warm, and the light sweat that breaks out on the back of my neck is like a welcome home. I choose the Hollywood Boulevard path as I walk from my car to the office.

The foot traffic is light this early, and only a few Barbies and a SpongeBob are out trolling for picture tips among the tourists.

I fairly skip along the stars, considering my plan.

I'll get Jester to call Zachery in, and we can brainstorm how to spin this change in the game plan for *Limited Fate*. Desdemona will have to see she's locked in, that it'll do more damage to disrupt it than to go for the ride.

Drake Underwood is flying in to see this pair. *My* pair. Even Desdemona knows better than to anger a director, and I already have a connection to this one. She isn't the messenger.

I am.

When I walk up to the tiny office lot, I stop short. Zachery's Jag isn't there, but that's not unusual. We can call him in. And Jester doesn't drive.

But Desdemona's black Mercedes is in her spot.

That can't be. She's in Europe. I saw pictures the day I left Glass.

Even if she decided to come to the soccer shoot, that isn't until next week.

I need to prepare myself before going in. She could be back for a lot of reasons, but one of them could possibly be that Drake Underwood's assistant called Desdemona instead of me. Or it could have been Jason's agent. Or Gayle's.

Or someone tipped her off.

I should have known that would happen.

I swiftly walk a block away and sit on a bus bench out of view of the office windows.

First, I text Jester.

Desdemona's back?

Dang it, I should have done that before I left my apartment. Or when I got to LA yesterday, even though it was late.

I should have given him a heads-up about the movie, but no, I only texted Zachery, not that he got the message. He never wrote back.

I thought I would be coordinating everything myself, and I would have time to break it to her.

I steady my breath. *Calm down. She could be here for anything. Play it cool.*

My phone buzzes.

Jester: Oh, darling. I'm not going to be able to help you.

What does that mean?

The next text is from Desdemona.

Get in here.

Okay. It's gone south.

Even though she told me to come right now, I take a moment to text Zachery.

Everything's going down. Desdemona must have found out I recast Limited Fate. Are you coming in?

I watch for the dots that tell me he's replying, but none come. *Where is he?*

In a flash, I realize how much I've leaned on him. At work. In off-hours. He even went along on a trip to find a husband.

There is no better friend than him.

No better lover.

No better anything.

And I need him. I want him. Maybe all I'll ever get is scraps of him between his red-carpet girls, but I think there's something more there. I caught a whiff of it, like the smell of his soap lingering in the bathroom.

I can't wait any longer. I'm desperate, so I put through a call as I stand and slowly head to the office.

It rolls to voicemail instantly. He has it off? Or out of service? Or let the battery die? Where *is* he? He's never been out of touch like this before.

A voice nags at me that maybe he's blocked me. That maybe he doesn't want to know me anymore.

This can't be happening. I can't lose everything. The flannel husband. My job. My best and most important friend.

It's too much. All the losses stacking up. I can't face it. I don't want to go in that office and set my downfall in motion.

I hold my phone up, as if all it needs to get Zachery to respond is open air.

But there's nothing.

The scene comes to me unbidden, like I've done it too many times lately and my mental scriptwriter has a life of its own.

INT. CASTING OFFICE—DAY

KELSEY, 25, looks grim as she walks up to the door of the casting office where she works. She hesitates outside to draw in a deep breath and steel herself.

She enters to greet her coworker, her good friend JESTER, 55, who is wearing a pale-orange-and-white ensemble, like a Creamsicle.

He looks up, his face in a lament. Outside, the thunder cracks, and the rain starts to pour . . .

I'm not far off as I walk inside the office.

Jester looks ready to cry.

And my desk is empty, the entire surface cleared of everything.

A box sits at the foot, my books and mugs and the glass unicorns my mother bought for me tossed inside.

I gasp, rushing forward to check on them. One of the unicorns has a chipped horn. "How could you?" I say to Jester.

"My love, I'm so sorry. Desdemona was in a rage. She did it before I got here."

My anger is white hot. "There is no reason to break my things. These are important!" I pull out the photo of me and my mother. The corner of the glass is cracked.

"Oh, boo-hoo," Desdemona says, standing in the doorway to her office. "The backstabbing bitch is worried about her doodads when she ought to be concerned about who the hell will ever hire her again after this stunt? I've already made all the calls. You sure took your pretty little time coming back here. You needed a couple of days off? Or you only do your dirty work from home?"

She walks into the room like an oversize crow, black pants with a black shawl over a black short-sleeved shirt.

I wish she would fly away, but I'll stand up for myself and *Limited Fate*.

"It was a smart move, Desdemona. You were out of the country." I tug Kleenex from a box to wrap my unicorns before they get any more damaged.

"It was an attack of my status and authority." She advances on my desk, leaning on both hands to peer down at me like a vulture. "You were aware I took Jason Venetian off my roster after his agent was so dismissive, and yet here we are, scheduling a live camera test with him for Drake Underwood."

I gather all my gumption. This is definitely what Reese would do. "He expects me to be there. I chose the scene for the test. I contacted the agents. I spoke to him in person!"

"So did I. And I explained that I had an impertinent know-it-all who got too big for her britches, and she is no longer employed here." She kicks at the box, and I gasp again, trying to keep it from flying across the floor. "Now get out."

Jester kneels beside me to pick up the papers that flew out of the box, real tears flowing. I can practically hear him saying *I'm so sorry*, even though his mouth isn't moving.

There isn't much else to do. I check my drawers, refusing to be pushed out of here without anything that's mine, but they're all empty. Then I take my box and go home.

Chapter 42

Zachery Gets the News

When the plane touches down at LAX after a full week of Italian food and sun, I have to admit that I feel ashamed. I left both of my phones at the house and bought a new one. I'm looking ahead, not back, and only adding contacts as I meet them and decide they're good for me.

Catalina is definitely one. Our trip to Venice ended up being not for two but three, because on the flight to Italy, she admitted that she had a secret wife, one who wanted to avoid the limelight altogether.

I immediately got Sweta a ticket to join us so that the two of them could enjoy the quieter side of Venice, while I escorted Catalina for the very public ones.

The pair was delightful, and I very much appreciated being let in on their secret. Real friendships were made, something I've sorely lacked.

I decide the new phone will be my only phone, since the first two numbers I added were Catalina and Sweta.

I kiss both of their cheeks as we leave the airport, making them promise to join me for dinner soon.

I call for a ride, and only when I'm settled in the back seat do I call the office.

"Desdemona Casting Associates," Jester answers.

"Jester, it's Zachery. I switched phones for the trip."

Silence.

"Jester?"

"I'm not talking to you."

I suspected he might be upset. "I'm sorry I didn't come back for the soccer scene. How did it go? Did you go to observe it or let it ride?"

Silence.

"Jester, I just couldn't come back. I was having the best time in Venice."

"I bet you were, you slathering hunk of hormones."

Jester's never judged me before, but I'm not about to correct him. "I'm in a car to my house, but I can reroute to the office. Catch me up."

He says, "Desdemona fired Kelsey."

And then he hangs up.

I stare at my phone.

How did this happen? Jester obviously blames me for not coming back for the soccer filming.

I don't know how to contact Kelsey. I mean, I know her number by heart, plus her email. But what is the best way? It's midmorning. She's probably at the tree farm.

Randy is probably consoling her over the loss of her job.

I picture him, his arms around her. He'll be happy, I bet. She's his now. They can open their bed-and-breakfast in the homestead sooner rather than later. Kelsey's smart. She'll get it going well enough that even if the tree farm goes down, she can save the house.

Hell, I bet she could single-handedly save the whole farm. Now that's a Hallmark ending. The family will be eternally grateful. They'll throw a parade in her honor. Perfect final scene.

She might not even be upset that Desdemona overreacted. It made the decision easy for her.

But as the car pulls up to my house, doubt creeps in.

If she's happy, why is Jester so upset?

I leave my suitcases inside the front door and head to my bedside table, where my old phones sit on chargers.

I power them both on.

The business one goes bonkers, a beeping, buzzing frenzy.

My private one, less so, although there are a lot of notifications.

I sort through them.

Kelsey wrote me a week ago, two days after I left Wyoming.

Back in LA to prepare for a meeting with Drake Underwood. Jason is doing a live audition with Gayle for Limited Fate!

My body flashes hot. She came back? A week ago? How did it go? She has to be over the moon!

And how did that play into her getting fired?

There's another message the next day, last Friday.

Everything's going down. Desdemona must have found out I recast Limited Fate. Are you coming in?

Then she put through a call. No voicemail.

She needed me, and I didn't even know.

I sink onto the bed.

I wasn't there for her.

I didn't cover for her.

I abandoned her.

I scroll through the rest of my notifications, but she didn't write me again.

By then she must have learned I was in Venice with Catalina.

She would assume what everyone assumed—even Jester, when he called me a slathering hunk of hormones.

I'm sure she's back in Wyoming by now.

Writing her would probably help nothing. She stopped contacting me after talking to Desdemona, which means she doesn't need my help and maybe even doesn't want to hear from me.

Jester acted out because he loves her and blames me for her firing, but the truth is, she was already going to leave us. Her intervention on the movie and raising Desdemona's ire just made it happen sooner rather than later. Maybe that was even her plan—go out in a blaze of glory.

We both know that if Drake Underwood recognizes the brilliance in her pairing, the casting will go through even if Kelsey is gone from the office. Casting directors hold no power to force or prevent a director or producer in making a hiring decision.

I set down my phone.

What's done is done. I hate that she lost getting credit for her movie casting. But she's gotten what she set out for on the trip.

I should be happy for her. And despite what happened between us along the way, I'm trying to do exactly that.

Everything worked out exactly as it should.

Just not for me.

Chapter 43

KELSEY AND THE FOOL

Turns out, Desdemona was good on her *never work in this town* threats.

I called Arista, Jacobs, and Jenny Wolfgang first, knowing they hate the Demon the most, and might be sympathetic to my plight.

Nobody responded.

None of the companies I've interned with, volunteered for, even as a gopher, were interested. I think Desdemona went down my résumé to be sure.

But there are many ways to work in Hollywood. I try catering, delivery, even being a driver.

Nothing. Nobody will even accept my application.

The coffee shop I worked at was willing to take me back, but they had only ten hours a week available. That's not enough for food and gas, much less my East LA apartment.

My choices are few. I can spend the rest of my savings in LA trying to break back in. I have two months or so I could fight this.

Or I can take that money and start again someplace else. Somewhere easier.

I'm not sure what to do.

For the first week, I try to stay up on industry gossip to help my predicament, looking for an in. I was too proud to text Zachery after he ignored my pleas. I checked for his name on social media and instantly regretted it. He's tagged all over the place with that actress Desdemona told him to court. They went to Venice together for an entire week.

I can't even think about that. It's too much.

I search for any information being leaked about *Limited Fate*, but there's nothing. I'm dying to know what happened.

Two weeks after I got fired, I spot a photo of Desdemona in London and know it's safe to go see Jester.

When I come in the door, he stands up to pull me into his emerald arms. He looks like an extra in *The Wizard of Oz*, but I love it. I've missed it.

He pulls out a box of *Peanuts* mugs. "I got these in a few days ago. Zachery ordered them for the office before you two left. I want you to have them."

Hearing Zachery's name physically hurts, a pang in my chest. He never responded to my crisis messages, not ever. Whatever happened between us is clearly over, even the friendship. He ruined it. I ruined it. I don't know. Our relationship became collateral damage.

I hug the box. "How is he?"

Jester shrugs. "He hasn't officially quit, but he's not here, either. Last I heard he was in Ibiza. We're not talking."

I drag my old chair next to Jester's desk. "Why not?"

"He ditched us when we needed him most."

"For the soccer shoot?"

Jester waves that thought away. "That was irrelevant in the end. I'm talking about when Desdemona learned you staged a coup on that movie."

"Did you tell him I got fired?"

"I did."

Is this why he stopped coming in? Or is he washing his hands of this entire part of his life?

I have to know. "How did he take it?"

"I don't know. I hung up on him after I said the foul words."

"Jester!"

The phone rings, but Jester simply punches the button to send it to voicemail.

"I don't have time for anyone who treats my baby girl like dirt. He ran off to Venice like a skank and left me holding the bag when Desdemona showed up. Nobody told me you were handling Drake Underwood. When his assistant called, I assumed the meeting was with Her Highness." His face crumples. "You should have told me it was you. I wouldn't have peeped a word about it."

I should have. I was so focused on driving home. I should have talked to Jester, then talked to Zachery. Maybe even told him how I felt. I could have taken my shot.

No, it was too soon after Randy.

It's a mess. A pile of story pages on the floor. Nothing makes sense. There is no logical flow of events.

And definitely no happy ending anywhere.

"I was probably doomed anyway." I open the mug box to peep at the collection. "Desdemona was going to find out what I did."

"You were always so good at soothing her. Nobody's lasted here two whole years. Nobody."

"You have."

Jester waves me off. "An eccentric old man isn't a threat to nobody."

"You think Desdemona drove off assistants because she was threatened?"

"You know, I think she mainly liked torturing them. You didn't take the bait."

"She's like my dad." As soon as I say the words, I realize it's true. I chose Desdemona to punish myself for leaving the farm. I picked a boss who made demands, who couldn't demonstrate kindness or care. Who felt only work proved loyalty. There was no love. They were both incapable of it.

I doomed myself.

"I see the resemblance," Jester says. "We dumb people sure do torture ourselves."

I pull out the new Charlie Brown. He's so happy with his wide single-line smile. He was tortured, for sure. Lucy and her football. Rocks in his Halloween bag. A lack of Valentines and holiday cards. Snoopy's demands.

Seeing him smile on a mug always inspires me to do the same. I can't help but grin back at him.

Jester's face relaxes. "I sure do miss you around here. You light up a room, Kelsey girl."

"Well, I'm not going to light up anything when they turn off my electricity," I say, snuggling Charlie Brown back into the box. "The Demon did her thing. I can't get anyone to take my call."

"You're not going back to that man in Wyoming?"

"No. We couldn't work it out."

Jester's jaw drops. "He let you go? How could he possibly let you out of his sight?"

I trace the characters on the outside of the mug box. "He learned I worked in Hollywood. He couldn't get past it."

"But you're not working now."

"But I want that option. He was looking for a more devoted wife than I could ever be. Barefoot and pregnant, I guess. Babies and Hollywood don't mix in his mind."

"It wasn't true love, then."

"Not even close." My traitorous thoughts shift to Zachery. No, not him, either.

"I'm sorry, honeypot."

I work up to the final hard question. "Did they recast *Limited Fate*? I wanted those two to get their breakout roles."

"Oh, baby girl, I'm so sorry. Desdemona told the director that Gayle was typecast and Jason wasn't available. She insisted you were too green to understand how the biz works."

So I lost my job for nothing. "Who did she bring in?"

"Nobody. We're no longer casting that project."

"But we had the contract."

"Desdemona canceled it. Drake Underwood is artsy and low budget, so she felt it was no great loss."

"But the Oscar buzz."

"That and a buck will get you a dollar-store medal."

He's right. I got caught up in it. I lost my head. I could see that script on-screen, and Jason and Gayle playing the roles.

But that's not how Hollywood works.

Now, Desdemona blackballing me, *that's* how this town operates.

Zachery's behavior, too, for that matter. Whatever gets things done.

"I think it's time for me to go home," I say.

"Where you currently have electricity, I hope," Jester says.

"No, I mean to Alabama. This is no town for the banished, not when I'm borderline destitute. Maybe I'll be like Dorothy and find out there's no place like the farm."

Jester frowns. "Don't let that daddy of yours crush your dreams."

"I won't let him."

"You're tough. You can stand up to him."

"I will." I hope.

Jester taps the desk. "You could still do it, you know."

"Do what?"

"The fortune teller plan. You're heading home. Summer's not over. Go get your meet-cute. Maybe something magical will happen."

I shake my head. "I think that ship has sailed."

His hand covers mine. "Just keep your options open. Eyes on the prize. Not that you need a man. Nobody needs a man. We're pretty useless."

My memory flashes to Zachery pressing me against the floral wallpaper. "You boys have your good points."

One of his fuzzy white eyebrows lifts. "Oh, to know what flashed through Baby Girl's head."

This makes me smile. "If only."

"If you go the south route, stop at Cara's Caramel Coffee Shop outside of Fort Worth, Texas. It's right off the interstate. They make an iced espresso with caramel drizzle that you'll simply die for. That shop was made for you."

"Send me the Google pin, and I'll be sure to stop. Who knows. Maybe I'll meet my caramel-drizzle counterpart, and we can waltz across Texas." I don't believe it for a minute, but I want to leave Jester happy.

"That's the spirit." He opens his drawer. "You should know you had an influence on this old man." He pulls out a tin. Gummy Bear Tarot!

"You have a deck!"

"This old dog learned a new trick. It's tons of fun. Shall we pull a card for your luck?"

"We should."

Jester shuffles the deck and spreads it in a fan across his desk. "Should you take it or me?"

"Let's both pull one. For our futures."

"For our futures."

I slide one out from the middle, and he takes one from the end.

"On three?" I ask.

He nods.

I give the countdown. "One, two, *three*."

We both flip over our cards.

Jester gets the Fool. "Oh, that's certainly my card," he says.

"It means originality and spontaneity."

"A better definition than I figured on!"

I have the Chariot.

"What's yours mean?" Jester asks.

"It stands for a journey, one where I'll overcome all obstacles."

"That's good, right?"

I nod.

It's very, very good.

There's my sign.

Time to leave the lights of Hollywood behind.

Chapter 44

Zachery Returns to the Whale's Belly

I don't plan to ever step foot in Desdemona Lovechild's world again, but during a dinner with Catalina and Sweta in late June, Catalina admits she might pull out of *Romeo and Juliet.* Her agent can't get through to the director, which is exactly why she was reluctant to work with him again, and the accent coach he insisted on hasn't gotten back to her with only a month until shooting.

I tell her I'll handle it, but I don't have Luigi Casperra's contact information.

So I call Jester.

He doesn't answer. He always knows when someone he doesn't want to talk to is calling, even if caller ID is blocked. It's a weird skill of his, Desdemona's favorite trait.

I'll have to go in. I can't count on a call back, even if I leave a voicemail. And Desdemona's in London. She's kept me in the loop even though I have no intention of doing anything she asks.

But for Catalina, I will return to the belly of the whale.

I stop by the office on a Friday morning, hoping to catch Jester in a jovial mood. I bring his favorite coffee and an entire box of Voodoo Doughnuts.

When I arrive, he's arranging pencils in the original broken Charlie Brown mug that he repaired so many weeks ago, before everything went downhill.

"I see you found a second life for it," I say, kicking the door closed behind me.

He narrows his eyes. "You've got a lot of nerve, showing up here."

"I come bearing gifts." I set down the coffee and doughnuts.

He sniffs the cup and opens the lid of the box. "You've bought yourself five minutes of my good graces." He sips the coffee and sighs. "Just like Kelsey used to bring."

My gut tightens at the mention of her name. He knows somehow, because he sits back in his office chair, palms rubbing together like he's got something good to say. "You miss her, don't you?"

"Who?"

"Who? You're asking who?" He shakes his head. "Both of you are out of your minds."

"Have you talked to her?"

Jester peers at the selection. "Did you think these doughnuts would buy you the price of information about Kelsey?"

I stand there, trying not to lose my cool. "Did you get a wedding invitation?"

He looks up at that. "What are you talking about?"

"She was on a total fast track. Family approval. Planning on turning their old homestead into a bed-and-breakfast."

He looks genuinely perplexed. "At her dad's farm?"

Wait. What is *he* talking about?

"Did she take him to meet her dad?" I was joking, but now I wonder.

"It's too early in the morning for this conversation," Jester says. "Who do you think Kelsey is marrying a scant ten days after she came here to say goodbye?"

This is the most frustrating conversation I've ever had with Jester. "That's what I'm talking about. She's moving to that Wyoming homestead with her tree farm lumberjack."

"You haven't talked to her, have you?" Jester counts on his fingers. "For, well, practically the entire month!"

"Of course not. She found what she wanted. She doesn't work here. Why would I?"

Jester slams the lid down on his box. "Because you two were friends, you ol' fool. You damn yokel. Take back your bribes, mister. I'm not telling you a thing."

I sigh. It doesn't matter. Kelsey is gone. I can't do anything about it. "I'm not here about Kelsey. It's about *Romeo and Juliet*. I need to get in touch with Luigi Casperra's team. Catalina is about to walk on this project."

He stares at me with angry eyes, but finally turns to his computer. "Next time, an email will do." He fires off a message to me. "There. It's in your inbox. Good day."

But he picks up the box of doughnuts and slides them into his drawer, as if he's afraid I'll take them away.

I glance over at Kelsey's desk. It's still empty. I guess they haven't found a replacement for her. I'm not surprised. Desdemona had trouble hiring someone before Kelsey, and the word is bound to have gotten around that she fired this one abruptly.

Something glitters on the corner, small and sparkly. It's in arm's reach, so I pick it up.

It's the tiny tip of one of her unicorns' horns. It must have broken when she packed.

"Was this Kelsey's?"

Jester relents, his mouth drooping. "Everything breaks after Desdemona gets hold of it. Kelsey was devastated about those unicorns. Desdemona slammed them in a box when I wasn't here."

"Did you ever know where they came from?"

His angry face returns, but I can tell he's having to force it. I've known him a long time. "Why should I tell you anything?"

I sit in her chair, fingering the tiny horn.

Jester watches me awhile, but his urge to talk is stronger than his upset. "Her mother took her to a glassblower every year on her birthday. It was literally the only day her father let them out of chores."

"Peach of a man."

"Kelsey's not too thrilled to be going back."

Now his words penetrate. "Why is she going back?"

"Desdemona froze her out. She can't get a job."

"But she was going to stay in Wyoming."

Jester leans back in his chair. "All right. I'll spill. She ditched the lumberjack. He told her she couldn't have both Hollywood *and* his babies."

"He said *what*?"

Jester raises his palms. "That's all I know. She came home, learned she was fired, and has spent the last few weeks trying to find anything else. But Desdemona's got her blackballed in Hollywood, so she's going back to Alabama."

Everything in my body vibrates at once. "When?"

"I'm not telling you."

"When did you last talk to her?"

"Your five minutes are up."

"Jester!"

"Zachery, neither one of you has been worth the tit on a mayfly since you left. Unless you tell me what went down, I'm not saying another word."

I lose my head for a moment, and out comes what I was trying to never admit to anyone. "I fell in love with her. That's what went down."

He sits up, his face going pink. "About time you figured that out. And you still ran off with that woman to Italy?"

"She's . . . otherwise engaged." I'm not about to spill Catalina's secret. "It was strictly for show."

"You know Kelsey saw it. You know she follows all your socials. You know what she thought."

"What do I do now?"

"Go to her!" He leaps from his chair. "Fix this mess! Declare your love!"

"How? Where?" I'm not sure she'll take a text from me, but I can try.

I pull out my phone, but Jester snatches it. "In what Hollywood happily ever after does the hero declare his love via a damn text message?"

He's right. "So what do you suggest? Should I go to her apartment with roses?"

He crosses his arms over his pink pinstriped suit. "She left yesterday. But I know one place she's going to be. Better use that fast car of yours."

Chapter 45

KELSEY'S TRIPLE MEET-CUTE

Cara's Caramel Coffee Shop is adorable from the outside.

It's painted white with light-blue trim, a pink door, and yellow shutters. It makes me think of Jester. I see why he loves it.

It sits in the middle of a huge lot shared with a strip mall that lines up behind it. There's a drive-through, and I consider using it to make better time.

But my legs need stretching. Despite Jester's insistence that I go for more meet-cutes on the way to Alabama, I haven't.

I've taken my time, that's for sure, driving only a few hours a day. I'm in no hurry to return to life on the farm.

It's been a quiet, solitary week on the road. I haven't tried to make any connections. It's been lonely and pensive, nothing like the ride to Wyoming with Zachery in his Jaguar behind me. I may no longer believe in meet-cutes.

I came very close to taking the northern route and staying in Livia's bed-and-breakfast for the memories. But I'm not sure I could have recovered from seeing that bed, the wallpapered wall. I've never felt anything like I did with Zachery.

I'm scared I never will again. And I never even told him.

He knows everything important. All my secrets. The emails to my mother. The way my father treated us.

Zachery would be so angry to know I'm going back there, even if we're nothing to each other now, not even coworkers. But I don't know what else to do. I have to regroup.

And, it seems, I'm going to have to get over him. I never thought I'd lose everything. Even our friendship.

I let myself imagine for a moment that when I get to the farm, he's there. He'll tell my father off, scoop me up, and carry me off into the sunset. Cue the closing theme music.

I laugh, pulling off my sunglasses and shoving them in the center console. I've got to get my head out of Hollywood. Time for the best coffee I've ever had, if Jester is right.

I lock the car. I'm a sweaty mess. Texas is stupidly hot midsummer. The back of my T-shirt sticks to my skin, and I pull it away as I open the door.

The air is thick with the smell of roasting beans and sugar. It's heaven.

I've been worried about money, so I haven't bought much fancy coffee on this trip, but today I'm going to splurge. Then I'll take a photo of my treat and send it to Jester.

He wrote me last week, asking if I'd left yet. I've more or less kept him updated on my packing, selling as much of my stuff as I could, storing the rest, and finally getting on the road.

He doesn't know I've made it to his favorite shop, or Texas, even. I last updated him somewhere in Arizona. He'll be excited, I bet.

There's a mom with a little girl ahead of me, ordering hot chocolate with caramel, even though it's over a hundred degrees out. They have an entire collection of fancy decorated sugar cookies in coffee-cup shapes. One of them says "Bad to the bean." That'll be nice in the picture with the coffee.

The woman in her pink apron couldn't be any more different from the one I encountered in that tumbleweed town on my last journey.

1

"We do caramel every way you can think of, and a lot more you've never dreamed! What can I get you?"

"I have a favorite drink, but I don't want to waste an opportunity to get one of your specialties."

"What's your usual?"

"Iced espresso with almond milk and a drizzle of caramel, shaken rather than stirred."

"Hey! That's our double-oh-seven drizzle, just with a different milk. It's a featured drink." She gestures to a small sign by the register.

She's right! "I better get it, then!"

"What size?"

I'm about to say "grande" when I spot their cup sizes. Here, the choices are "modest," "bold," and "outrageous."

"Let's go with bold."

"You got it."

"Oh, and a 'Bad to the bean' cookie. The pink one."

"Absolutely. Anything else?"

"That's it."

I tap my credit card and take the cookie from her, tucking it in my bag. Now that I've been standing a few minutes, my bladder is screaming.

I hurry to the bathroom. When I wash my hands in front of the mirror, I realize that I'm a seriously hot mess. No makeup. My blond hair is falling out of its messy updo. Nobody would call me Hollywood.

"You're plain ol' Kelsey," I tell my reflection.

It's fine. It'll be fine.

I haven't told anyone in my family I'm coming. I'm not sure I'm staying. That'll depend on how bad things are when I get there. I put most of my stuff in storage so I don't have to show up with my entire life in a U-Haul. Not yet.

I spoke to my dad two nights ago, planning to tell him I was headed his way. He said he only had a second because he had to finish the evening chores.

Always the chores. Always more to do.

"I wanted to see how you were," I told him.

"Be a mite better if my kids hadn't run off all over creation and bailed on the family farm."

"Cal's still there, right?"

"I got left with the laziest of the lot."

Oh. Gosh. "Well," I said, "those chores aren't going to do themselves!"

And that was a long conversation compared to our usual.

When I get to the farm, I'll reserve the right to escape right on out of there if it's too awful. I have little hope I won't eventually be labeled the lazy one as well. Nobody works at the level Dad expects. He should team up with Desdemona. They could be angry and miserable together.

As I head back into the main room of the shop, the barista calls out, "Bold double-oh-seven drizzle with almond milk!" She sets it on the end of the counter.

I head for it right as someone else stands from a chair, slightly behind me. Did we order the same thing?

I walk up, about to ask if this one is mine, when the person behind me trips, bumping into me. I lurch to the side with a grunt. Geez.

A muscled arm reaches for my latte, or maybe it's his, then whips around so quick that the lid pops off, spilling iced espresso all across my shirt.

"Hey!" I cry, finally turning to look at the guy. "What's your . . ."

The words die on my lips.

It's Zachery. Zachery Carter, actor of gross-out comedies from the last decade, walker of red carpets, wearing a gorgeous silk T-shirt (Loro Piana, $575) and mohair shorts (Prada, $1,700).

He's here in Cara's Caramel Coffee Shop in a coincidence every editor would strike from the script as not believable.

He sets the cup on a nearby table, his hand dripping. "Sorry, miss. I'm pretty clumsy." He pulls a handful of napkins from the metal container on the table and starts wiping my shirt. "I thought that was my order."

The room has gone quiet. We're the most interesting thing happening in the shop.

"I'll make another," the barista says, but she doesn't move.

"What are you doing here?" I ask.

His Adam's apple bobs as he swallows, but he doesn't seem to have words. And that's odd. Zachery is never short on things to say. His brown eyes lock on mine.

"Jester told you where I'd be?" I ask.

Now the barista jumps in. "He's been waiting to do that for three days." She calls out over her shoulder, "He finally got her, y'all!"

The other employees let out a cheer.

I turn back to him. "You planned this?"

His hand drips onto the floor. "I figured all those meet-cutes can't be wrong."

"So you did them all at once?"

"I didn't switch our luggage." He glances around. "No elevator."

"He tried to convince us to get in an argument with him, but we weren't Oscar contenders," the barista says. "We've been dealing with him since Sunday. Are you going to get him out of our hair? He already signed his autograph on everything we own."

I watch Zachery as I say, "I don't know. I'm not sure why he's here."

"For you, double-oh-seven with almond milk." She shakes her head. "He made us change our featured drink."

This makes me laugh. "You went to a lot of trouble."

He doesn't meet my gaze, busy wiping his hand over and over.

"Hey," I say. "Since when is Zachery Montgomery Carter anything short of a charmer, tamer of women, slayer of hearts?"

He finally looks up, his expression pained. "Since I wasn't there when you needed me. Since I left you with that tree farmer. Since you got fired and I didn't even know it until it was long over."

The rapt audience lets out a long "Oooo."

Heads swivel to me for my response.

"Are you here to apologize? To say goodbye?"

They all look back to Zachery.

"No. I don't want to say goodbye."

He doesn't? Something can be salvaged after all? A gentle glow starts to warm my belly. "I had to leave LA. There was nothing left for me there."

The crowd shifts, on the edge of their seats.

"I'm there. But I don't have to be there. I can be anywhere." He swallows again, and this time, I see that spark of the Zachery I know. He's waited three days to say these things to me.

"Anywhere?" I ask. "I'm headed to a dairy farm in Alabama."

He steps closer. "Then maybe I want to be on a dairy farm in Alabama, too."

The room murmurs and sighs.

"But what about your red-carpet women? And the others? Livia. Catalina. The ones Desdemona will set you up with?"

He nods, his brows furrowed. "I know it looked like I was with those two. But I wasn't. Not once, not anyone, not since you. I don't want anyone else but you. And I quit Desdemona. I don't work for her, either."

"You did?"

"That office is pointless without you. LA is nothing." He glances around. "Does this count as a small town?"

"We got twenty Starbucks," someone calls.

"Don't say that name in here!" the barista hisses.

"Sorry."

I shake my head. "Doesn't sound like a small town to me. Not with twenty—" I almost said it. "You-know-whats."

"It's not exactly a small-town romance," the barista calls. "But everyone can see y'all's starry eyes. Kiss her already!" She motions to the barista behind her, who hurriedly pulls two cups to make coffees.

"Kiss her!" someone else cries. It becomes a chorus.

Zachery steps in close. "It's got the good tropes. Friends to lovers. Country to city. Reformed playboy." He leans in next to my ear. "All the good sex scenes."

"Shhh." I grip his arm, but I'm laughing. "So, I have to settle for a big-city movie star instead?"

"It's a step down, I know." He lifts my chin.

Zachery. Everything in me says he's right.

It's him. It was always him.

From the champagne to the Charlie Brown mug, across the country, in my noisy apartment. From movie premieres to pizza at home, it's always been Zachery.

"I love you," he says.

"I think I might love you, too," I say.

"We've got all the time we want to figure it out."

I don't need to see the script or read the words to know what will happen.

Because the moment is here.

Zachery Carter kisses me in a colorful coffee shop in Fort Worth, Texas.

And it's way more than a meet-cute.

It's a genuine *happily ever after.*

Chapter 46

Zachery in the Stars

One year later

All three of my phones buzz simultaneously. I need to get rid of one. Or two.

I choose the one that reads "Kelsey" on the notification and pick up the voice call.

"Where are you?" she asks.

I glance up at the street signs. "Crossing Broadway. Two blocks away."

"Allison Firenze doesn't like to be kept waiting. Do you have the roses? She insisted on roses."

I shift the bouquet to the inside of my elbow. "Thirteen yellow ones. Not twelve. Not red. Thirteen yellow."

Kelsey sighs in relief. "Good. Make it look good."

"Nobody buys it anymore. They all know you're my one true love."

She laughs. "Then take more acting classes. This is important. We need good pictures!"

And she hangs up.

I shake my head and check the other two phones. One of them is a reminder to meet Allison at the Edgemont Theater. The other is a text from Jester, also reminding me to go.

Nobody trusts me anymore.

I've had my head in the clouds since we all moved to New York and opened our own casting office, this time for live performing arts. We have everything on our roster from opera singers to dancers to, well, clowns. It's wild how often a production needs a good clown.

I arrive at the theater as Allison Firenze pulls up in a limo.

The driver opens the door, and I slip through the crowd and nod at the security guard, who lets me through the satin rope.

Allison steps out to a wild pop of flashes, smiling and waving in a red gown with elbow-length gloves. That's why she wanted yellow. Red roses would get lost against the dress. She's good. She thinks of the photo op.

I step in and pass her the roses, kissing her cheek. I whisper, "Apparently, I'm supposed to look like I'm madly in love with you. It might be true."

When I step back, her smile is girlish and happy. Snap, snap, snap. *Nailed it, Kelsey. Where's my Tony Award?*

I take her arm, and we walk slowly up the carpeted stairs to the front of the theater. Then we turn, smiling. After a few seconds, I step away and out of the frame so she can get solo shots. Behind her is a sign featuring her face along with the name of the production that will open tonight, *Blinding Red.*

I wait exactly the right amount of time, then step forward to open the door for her. I take her arm again as we pass inside.

It's quiet and dark in the lobby. She lets out a sigh of relief. "Thank you, Zachery. I did not want to do that alone."

Allison's boyfriend of eight years broke up with her two weeks ago, leaving her without an escort to her own opening night. I lift her gloved hand to kiss it. "It was an honor."

We pass the closed-up box office for a hallway that leads to the dressing rooms. The noise levels rise as we approach, the cast and crew already deep in preparations for the night.

Once we're out of sight of any wayward reporters who might be peering in, I give her a bow. "Have an amazing first night."

She kisses my cheek. "Thank you."

We part ways, and I head for a side door.

Doing these deeds for Kelsey feels very different from how they went down for Desdemona. I realize now how much of my self-worth was tied up in those paparazzi moments on red carpets with actresses. It was me proving I was still worthy of the Hollywood game, not a has-been, not a joke. The attention of those women proved it.

Desdemona knew me too well, and she used my need to be seen to ensure those actresses considered her projects first.

I don't need that crutch anymore. And our agency doesn't need to act that way to get projects to cast or find talent eager to work with us.

I'm stopped by a young man I met a couple of months ago. "Zachery?"

"Ahmed, hello!" I shake his hand. "How were rehearsals?"

"So great. I can't thank you enough for getting me cast. It's been a dream come true." He brushes his hair nervously to one side of his forehead.

"You're very talented. Let's see how long this run goes, and we'll talk again. Break a leg!"

I head for the door. I've just burst out of the dim corridor and into the bright light of afternoon when Kelsey calls.

"Jester passed me something interesting. Meet me at the pie shop on Fifty-Fourth. I'll get there before you can walk it."

"We can't talk about it by phone?" I change directions to head for the shop.

"I want to see your face when I say it."

"Are you going to propose marriage?"

She laughs. "You wish." She hangs up.

A small spattering of rain starts to fall, so I pop into a drugstore and pick up a funny clear smiley-face umbrella. Between me and Kelsey, we lose approximately five umbrellas a week. I've stopped buying expensive ones.

As I walk up, I spot her in the window facing the street, and I love the way she bursts into laughter at my umbrella. I do a quick Fred Astaire spin on the light pole before closing it and stepping into the warm crush of the overfilled pie shop.

She's already bought my favorite lemon meringue as well as her chocolate mousse, plus two plain coffees.

I sit on a stool next to her. "Hey! You took a bite of mine."

She reaches over with her fork and steals another. "And I'll take what I want from you anytime I want."

I kiss her for her impertinence, savoring the moment. I love New York in the summer. It's almost worth surviving the winter.

The energy here is different. And live-show casting feels right. There's less pretense. Everyone is talented. Just as many divas, that's for sure, but they're usually worth it.

We've started small, calling in my old playwright friend and then his friends. We didn't need to make money right away. I was able to cover the startup, get Jester moved here, and find a place, about a tenth of the size of my LA house but in the center of everything.

It's been good.

Kelsey jumped right in, and she's been the one to spot the talent who put us on the map. We stick to the scrappy startups, the new productions barely getting by on a shoestring. And we build careers from nothing.

It's glorious.

When I finally release her, I snatch up a fork and attack her chocolate mousse. She easily parries me and pins my fork to the plate. "Women steal men's pie; men don't steal women's. I don't make the rules."

"Fine," I grumble and attack my lemon meringue. "So, what came across your desk?"

She opens a folder and slides a casting call toward me. *Monday by Moonlight.* I scan the call.

"A musical? Okay. They need a male lead. Late thirties, early forties. Baritone. Who are you thinking? Brassworth? That guy who did the revival of *The Music Man*?"

She shakes her head. "I'm thinking of *you*."

Her eyes never leave mine.

My throat tightens. "I haven't seen a singing coach in years. I'm out of practice. I—"

"You can." She lays a card on the printout. It's the vocal coach we've sent some of our roster to, the ones who can afford it. "He has a spot. He's ready to prep your audition material."

I stare at the piano keys on the card. My mouth is dry.

I can't possibly audition for something at this stage. I'm not an off-Broadway singer. I'm a joke who does terrible things in bad movies. I'm an expensively dressed arm for the real talent to walk in on.

"Get out of your head, Zachery," Kelsey says. "Not all thoughts are worth listening to. Listen to me."

She sets down her fork and holds both sides of my head so I can't look away. "Repeat after me."

"After me."

She laughs. "Oh, Zach. Seriously. Say, 'I am the son of a great talent.'"

That's easy. "I am the son of a great talent."

"I am worthy of this role."

That one sticks in my throat.

"Say it!"

"I am worthy of this role."

"I can do this."

"I can do this."

"My beautiful girlfriend will withhold sexual favors if I don't audition."

"Hey!"

She leans forward and kisses me. Then her next words brush my lips. "You are worthy of this role. I'll arrange a private audition. See where you stand."

I stare into her eyes. She knows me, all the way to the bone. My insecurities, always so well hidden behind a smile and a camera flash.

"Is this the first role you've wanted for me?" I ask.

She picks up bits of pie from the plate with the back of her fork. "I've been thinking about it since the headshot for Beatrice Good came across my desk."

"Who's Beatrice Good?"

She pulls out her phone. After a quick search, she shows me the picture. Midthirties. Dark hair. Where have I seen her?

Wait. *It's the fortune teller from the party.*

"You found her?"

"She found us. She remembered us stopping by her table at the Hollywood party."

I might be busted. "And?"

"She told me you paid her to give me a fortune to go find love."

"How long have you known?"

"A couple of weeks." She licks the back of her fork, clearly not upset in the least.

"But you waited to bring it up."

She grins. "I gave it a good think. I figured you were trying to push me in the direction that was best for me. So I'm bringing it up now because—"

"You want to push me in this direction."

Her smile widens. "I love how we finish each other's—"

"Syllables."

She laughs. "That's perfect."

I look back down at the page. "And if I fail?"

"Then I can sigh in relief that I've saved thousands of unsuspecting women from pining over you after hearing you sing. It's hard to share you, you know. But I can do it."

"You won't be disappointed in me?" I won't bring my mother up at this moment. Kelsey already knows.

"You're amazing, Zach, no matter what role you play, center stage or behind the curtain." She presses her palm to my cheek.

I slide my face to kiss the inside of her hand. "All right. Let's see what happens."

"Good." She uses her free hand to stab my pie again. "Too slow!"

I love this woman. Her eyes are like stars as she steals my pie, then pulls out the songs from the audition packet, telling me which ones best fit the impression I should give.

And when Kelsey Whitaker tells you that you're the star she pictures in a role—whether it's a movie, a play, or the one who shares her bed and her dreams—there's only one thing to do.

Exactly what she says.

Epilogue

ZACHERY IN *MOONLIGHT*

Six months later

The tiny bar is packed from wall to wall. I move through the crowd, accepting handshakes and thumps on the back.

"Zachery!" Jester cries. He's sitting on the bar. Not at it. On it. His pale-yellow suit against all the dark wood makes him look like a baby chick in a nest. He presses a hand to his chest and sings the first line of my opening number. *"The moon in the night has been shining down right on my heart!"*

He's drunk. Totally drunk.

I give him a little salute, not sure I can make it all the way to the counter, which is three deep with people trying to shout their orders.

I look for Kelsey. I finally spot her talking to Mike McKenzie, the producer of *Monday by Moonlight*, no doubt already working on our next casting contract. She bowed out of this one when I got cast to avoid a conflict of interest.

She plays by the rules, that's for sure.

We've developed one of the deepest, most thorough rosters in the business. The new agency moved into the black right after the end of its first year, and it's all due to her.

She's a marvel.

We even broke in my dressing room earlier today, a few hours before the opening-night events began. It was a killer way to start my comeback—Kelsey bent over the makeup counter, facing the mirror. I got to take in every inch of her as I slid inside. I love watching the rosy blush spread across her chest.

It will never get old.

She notices me and waves me over. When I'm closer, I realize my mother is with them, all five feet of her almost disappearing in the crowd despite her stilettos.

"Mom!" I pick her up with a hug.

My dad and sister approach from the bar side, trying not to spill drinks as they make their way toward us.

"My beautiful Zachery," Mom says, pressing her hands to my face as I set her down. "I was talking to your producer. They're thrilled to have you in their musical."

Mike grins at Mom. "What I wouldn't give to see the two of you in a mother-son role. We just have to find the right story!"

Mom can't fight back her smile. "Wouldn't that be something?"

"It sure would." Dad hands a drink to her. "You were terrific, son. Just amazing."

Anya shrugs in her usual sisterly way. "You were decent."

Mom elbows her. "Coming from the woman who more than decently took over a Fortune 500 company at age thirty-seven, while pregnant!"

"And popped out the cutest nephew I could have imagined four hours after staving off a media storm," I add, accepting a glass of champagne from Kelsey, half-empty of course. She's been sipping from both of them.

I don't mind.

"She's brilliant!" Mom says. "My beautiful, perfect children!"

"I'll let your family celebrate," Mike says, lifting his empty glass. "Epic opening night, Zachery. Everyone is pleased." He heads into the fray near the bar.

Kelsey wraps an arm around my waist. "Best match of role to actor I've ever done."

"Unlike that disastrous sculptor movie," Mom says. "What was it called, darling?" She turns to Dad. "*Terrible Fate?*"

"*Limited Fate*," Dad says. "What a shame. It had such potential. The couple had no chemistry."

I glance over at Kelsey. She sighs but says nothing. Drake Underwood hired someone else to cast it in the end. Jason went on to make another action movie. Gayle hasn't appeared in any projects since Netflix.

Desdemona still does her thing, torturing her new staff. But the crossover between Hollywood and Broadway is minimal. We got a new start.

From the back corner, a chorus of singing begins. My stomach tightens. It's time.

It's not that I doubt the outcome of what's about to happen, but I did invite some unexpected people, and I don't know how that will play out.

The singing gets louder and louder.

Jester stands up on the bar, moving his arms as if he's conducting them. I didn't count on that, either.

The bartender nearest to him tugs at his pant leg, but he is undeterred. More people start to realize a song is starting, and the room quiets.

The rest of the cast of *Monday by Moonlight* filters in, stuffing the room even more tightly. The crowd parts as best they can as they make their way to me.

"What's this?" Kelsey asks, but then she goes still.

I follow her gaze. And there they are. The missing siblings. Sid, Vanessa, Alana, and Cal. Cal's wife, Katie, stayed behind with Kelsey's father, who said he didn't have time for a foolish trip to New York when there were cows to tend.

I hope she doesn't feel disappointed that he didn't make it.

Her arm on my waist tightens. "You brought them here?"

I squeeze her back. "This is your success as much as mine."

Her eyes fill up; then that's it, she's gone, rushing to embrace her youngest sister first, then gathering in the others. The oldest, Cal, seems a little abashed at the emotion but allows himself to be brought into their group hug.

The photographer I hired for tonight joins Jester on the bar so he can get shots. The bartender lifts his arms in a "what gives" gesture, but mainly he and the other workers are swamped, so he lets it go.

The sound grows louder as the singers find their way to the center of the room. They've started with the opening number, but when it's time for me to come in, they transition into a song from the middle of the musical that doesn't require my participation.

It's a slower, more thoughtful number about nighttime being when the shadows come, bringing doubt about what is true.

The siblings walk Kelsey back to me.

"This is such a surprise," she whispers in my ear. "Why didn't you tell me?"

"Your dad wouldn't come."

She shrugs. "He probably would have ruined it anyway. Thank you."

She kisses my cheek.

Then the song shifts to the finale. Kelsey's siblings help part the group at the bar so I can lead Kelsey toward it. I climb up on the wood chair, then onto the counter, exasperating the bartender even more.

Cal helps Kelsey follow me up, and when she arrives, I get down on one knee.

The singers shift to a low hum, a buzz of song in the background.

Kelsey's hands go to her cheeks. "Zachery?"

"Kelsey Whitaker, you hold the supreme gift of pairing a person with their destiny. Sometimes it's in movies, other times onstage. But on a summer night in Colorado a long time ago, you asked me a question that made me realize there was something more to me and you than coworkers."

Several whoops come from the crowd.

Her cheeks pink up. "I know you're not about to talk about that night."

I chuckle. "Thankfully, the tabloids aren't nearly so interested in stories about Broadway singers."

Now she laughs. "True."

"You have shown me who I can be. Not the joke I thought I had become. But the real me. The person who cares. Who can love."

Kelsey brushes her hand across my cheek. "You always could."

"But I chose not to, until you."

I turn to Jester, who's making his way along the bar. "Excuse me, hey now, oooh, I like you." He's working the whole crowd. He arrives, tugging a black velvet box from his pocket. "I believe you need this."

Kelsey shakes her head at him and leans down to kiss his cheek. "Somebody help our dear friend down."

Cal and my father take Jester's arms and lift him off the bar and to the ground.

"But I was going to do a little dance," he says to a smattering of laughter.

The singers get louder, the happy lilt of the final number coming around a second time.

I open the box to reveal a ring that would be ostentatious in Hollywood, but I know Kelsey will melt over.

And she does, her jaw dropping. "Zachery!"

"Kelsey Whitaker, will you do me the honor of becoming my wife, to love and cherish as long as I live?"

She holds my gaze a moment. "Yes. Yes, I will."

Another cheer goes up, and the singers break out in full belting chorus. *"The moonlight at night gives way to the bright sun of morning!"*

I slip the ring on her finger, then stand up to gather her in my arms.

When I kiss her, it's familiar and new all at the same time. I never intended to get here, never thought anyone would see past my facade.

But this golden girl from Tinseltown is the one who knew me all along.

And we may have written the script in all the wrong ways, but it didn't matter.

Because every love story is different.

And this is the next page in ours.

AUTHOR'S NOTE

Oh, all the wonderful movies I watched as inspiration for this book! Here were some of my absolute favorites:

- *Sweet Home Alabama* and *Legally Blonde* (gotta channel that inner Reese Witherspoon!)
- *Single All the Way* (Is there a more perfect holiday rom-com? I don't think so.)
- *Notting Hill* (Did you catch Zachery's new version of the famous "I'm just a girl" quote?)
- *Serendipity* (And they both reached for the gloves!)
- *The Wedding Planner* (She got her heel stuck and he saved her!)
- And we can't forget the classic *When Harry Met Sally* (That carpooling road trip banter!)

I stood on the shoulder of giants as I crafted this story.

I also got my hands held by some amazing people:

Bart Baker: Man, am I glad I met you. We've known each other for years now, but when it came time to figure out a Hollywood love story that was just a hair off the beaten track, you came through for all my Hallmark, screenwriting, and Tinseltown questions. With a bonus of being a great friend. I owe you.

To my Montlake Team: Maria Gomez, Lindsey Faber—you make this so easy. I am in such good hands, and you're so delightful to work with. It's a dream job.

To my agent, Jess Regel: We did it again. Thank you for sorting my wheat ideas from the chaff. I'm mostly chaff.

I had some real cheerleaders on this one. Julia Kent, Olivia Rigal, Blair Babylon, Pippa Grant, Tricia O'Malley, Danika Bloom, Lainey Davis, Erika Kelly, Cat Johnson, Jami Albright. Times got tough for me during the writing, and there you all were, in DMs and Zoom calls and texts. *Thank you.*

And my Sweet Dills. You know who you are. Dillfest is for you.

ABOUT THE AUTHOR

JJ Knight is the *USA Today* bestselling author of romantic comedy and sports romance. She's a fierce mama bear for all the humans under her care: biological, adopted, and those in need of mom hugs. Her books portray characters who learn to push through hardship to find love and belly laughs. For more information, visit www.jjknight.com.